Operation G-spot

Operation G-spot

Jodi Lynn Copeland

APHRODISIA
KENSINGTON PUBLISHING CORP.
http://www.kensingtonbooks.com

APHRODISIA BOOKS are published by

Kensington Publishing Corp.
850 Third Avenue
New York, NY 10022

All Kensington titles, imprints and distributed lines are available at special quantity discounts for bulk purchases for sales promotion, premiums, fund-raising, educational or institutional use.

Special book excerpts or customized printings can also be created to fit specific needs. For details, write or phone the office of the Kensington Special Sales Manager: Kensington Publishing Corp., 850 Third Avenue, New York, NY, 10022. Attn. Special Sales Department. Phone: 1-800-221-2647.

ISBN: 0-7582-1481-2

First Printing: December 2006

10 9 8 7 6 5 4 3 2 1

Printed in the United States of America

CONTENTS

TERMS OF ENTICEMENT

1

"Oh my gosh, yes! Right there, Colin!"

They were doing it again, screwing like rabbits on speed.

In an attempt to shut out the sound of her brother and his girlfriend, Joyce, going at it in the neighboring bedroom, Liz Hart covered her ears and hummed into the darkness. The non-stop thump, thump, thump of a headboard slamming against a wall and the unmistakable moans and groans of hot, heavy sex refused to be blocked.

Liz uncovered her ears and let free a moan of her own, this one all about misery.

Karma had a real fucking funny sense of humor. The last year she'd gotten her daily laugh by sharing every screaming, quaking detail of her sex life with Colin. He had a major hang-up when it came to hearing about his little sister's exploits. Liz might understand that if she was actually little, or rather young.

She was twenty-four, old enough to be knocked up a half dozen times and divorced just as many. She didn't have kids, a husband—ex or otherwise—or even a potential lover. And that was the reason karma was so funny.

For all she teased Colin by bragging about her many sexual conquests, 95 percent of what she told him was make-believe. Ninety-five percent of her life was a lie. Ninety-five percent of the time she didn't care. Listening to the ceaseless heavy panting and encroaching sounds of orgasm, the residual 5 percent reared its head. And damn was it ugly. Make that jealous.

Just once Liz wanted to move past the fear she carried her mother's promiscuous genes, which made the woman put physical pleasure before anything else, including her daughter, and enjoy sex for the gratifying experience it should be. Just once she wanted to be the bold, sexually confident woman she pretended at. Just once she wanted to be the one screaming, moaning, and soaking the bed with a bona fide orgasm and not one she faked in order to end yet another unsatisfying encounter.

As if on cue, Joyce's emphatic cry rang out from the next room. "Ooh . . . don't st—op. I'm going to . . . come!"

Rolling her eyes, Liz sat up in bed and switched on the nightstand lamp. She couldn't handle playing the part of eavesdropping voyeur a second longer. Since it was after one A.M., she couldn't pick up the phone and call someone either. Not that there was anyone she would call on this particular matter. Imagine the response she would get if she phoned Diane, her friend and co-waitress, and whined she was envious of Joyce's orgasm because Liz had never had one of her own. Like almost everyone else, Diane knew her as the flamboyant, brash sex maniac she impersonated to avoid the psychoanalysis (aka bullshit) that would accompany the truth.

The phone wasn't an option for venting her orgasm envy. Thank God for the Internet.

Six weeks ago, following what should have been an assured climax with a man reputed for his bedroom skills—a night that once again ended orgasmless—Liz had become desperate and searched for support on-line. It turned out that she wasn't the only healthy, twentysomething woman whose mind overruled her body's desire. There were at least two other women who suffered similar ailments.

Fiona lived states away in Michigan but was still in the same time zone. The headstrong lawyer would either be asleep or have her legs wrapped around her latest attempt at orgasm. In Seattle, Kristi was three hours behind Atlanta time. The sex-toy designer could be home . . . and more than likely testing out her latest pleasure gadget.

Unlike Liz, neither Fiona nor Kristi had a problem getting off with the aid of battery-operated plastic. It was when a man entered the equation that their G-spots performed a disappearing act. Liz clearly had no G-spot, period. She'd tried over a dozen of Kristi's guaranteed-to-get-you-off products, and not one managed to do the job.

Sighing, Liz climbed from bed and pulled a T-shirt over her nude body. She ran a hand through her straight, cropped black hair as she padded barefoot to the desk in the corner of her bedroom, fired up her laptop, and connected to the Internet.

A fresh series of moans came from the bedroom next door, and she grimaced.

Oh gawd. Not again.

A year ago, she'd moved into her brother's place to keep him from feeling alone following his messy divorce from Satan in a deceptively sugary-sweet package. Now that Colin had Joyce—a genuinely sugary-sweet package—in his life and, subsequently, someone to share his large house with, Liz seriously needed to think about getting back into a place of her own. Until then . . . *Please let Kristi be on-line.*

Opening up the instant messenger program, she logged into Operation G-Spot, the group the women had created for private chats, and buzzed Kristi.

Liz: Tell me you're there.

Kristi: No can do. I'm in the South Pacific, bare-assed and bent over a lounge chair, while the local orgasm gods fight over who gets to tongue me to climax next.

Liz: As long as you're fantasizing, mind if I join you on that chair? Sure as hell would be better than being here. Yet again, I have the pleasure of falling asleep to the sounds of huffing and puffing and my brother getting his rocks off.

Kristi: Colin's having another sex marathon overnighter?

Liz: Yes! And I'm sooo jealous.

Kristi: Ditto. Have you considered Fi's advice to give the sure thing another try? You said he had you wet before your brother walked in on the two of you.

Liz: Pull-eaze tell me you're joking. Dusty had me wet for a few seconds, but he couldn't finish the job. Besides, as I've told you a gazillion times, the guy's a conceited asshole. If he were the last man alive, I wouldn't spread my legs for him again.

Kristi: Mmm . . . Maybe I should come to Atlanta and give him a try. Way you described him a few weeks ago, he sounds deserving of that conceit—totally dee-lish and hung like an elephant. Not that I have a prob with a teeny weenie, but a big one on a man who knows how to use it sounds damned promising.

Liz: Yeah, promising in a "never going to accomplish the impossible" sort of way. Hey, I gotta go. I just remembered I'm working the breakfast shift. TTYL.

Kristi: Bye. GLGS.

Liz snorted at the acronym as she closed the messenger program. She didn't need "good luck getting some." She needed good luck getting off. And not with Dusty either.

Damn Kristi for bringing up Colin's longtime friend Dusty Marr. The woman could generally be counted on for encouragement and a bad joke or two, just enough to improve Liz's mood. Tonight Kristi hadn't improved her mood a bit but had forced her to lie about working the breakfast shift so she could end the conversation about a guy she would just as soon dropped off the planet.

On top of having a cock that even Liz had to admit was impressive, Dusty was tall, built, blond, and a month and a half ago had managed the improbable. Unlike any man or machine before him, his smooth moves had vanquished Liz's fear of turning into her mother long enough to have her wet and eager to fuck. Before they could move past oral gratification, Colin had come home, found them getting nasty on the living room floor, and burst the hedonistic bubble. After taking things to her bedroom, Liz had tried to clear her mind and get back into the heat of the moment, but to no avail.

And she couldn't be happier for that.

She'd decided to sleep with Dusty because his reputation claimed him a sure thing. The moment she'd stopped thinking with her hormones, she remembered that he was a lot more than a sure thing. He was an arrogant, shallow dickhead who put sex above all else, screwing a different woman every night of the week without caring who his actions might hurt. In other words, he was the male equivalent of her mother.

She wasn't doing Dusty again. No way. Nohow. No matter if thinking of his talented tongue pushing into her nether lips had her sex shockingly moist.

Suppressing the urge to rub her hand between her tingling thighs, Liz stood and returned to the bed. She tugged the T-shirt over her head to reveal tented nipples. Her wetness and the aroused state of her nipples were side effects of the rain-cooled, September night air snaking into the slightly ajar bedroom window. The cold could make a person wet. Tonight it could, because she refused to believe thoughts of Dusty and his sexual prowess were behind her stimulated body.

"What do you say I rub your balls for luck?"

Dusty Marr halted the slide of his pool stick middraw to quirk an appreciative eyebrow at the leggy blonde reclining against the pool table. Decked out in a snug black catsuit with a daring scoop-necked bodice and matching stilettos, the carnal tilt of her smile and the heat in her emerald eyes told him exactly which balls she had in mind. Not the ones on the table, but those stirring to life along with his dick.

He hadn't had sex in weeks, since the night Liz Hart, his best friend's younger sister, had shocked the hell out of him by challenging him to a game of pool where oral sex was the stake. A decade his junior, he'd first met her as a loudmouthed sixteen-year-old. Jailbait personified, she'd already been endowed with all the right assets to have his testosterone spiking, as well as an overt loathing of him that said he would never get his hands on her. Despite the fact that her dislike of him remained intact, eight years later he'd gotten his hands, and his mouth, on her. Her moans of pleasure said she'd loved every minute of it, too. That is, right up until the moment she'd started trembling with the first signs of climax, only to stop short, tell him he sucked in the sack, and order him out of her brother's house.

Despite the recent hiatus, Dusty was no stranger to sex. He loved every aspect of it—from the feel of a woman's soft curves and the breathy gasps and sighs of her coming undone to the knowledge it was the one thing in life he was truly good at. No one he'd ever slept with could believe otherwise.

No one but Liz.

He wasn't about to let his ego or his dick suffer from the accusations of one questionably sane woman.

Dusty signaled to his pool opponent to continue without him. With a wicked smile, he turned to the blonde. He opened his mouth to tell her she was welcome to rub far more than his balls; however, the slender woman with olive skin and closely cropped ebony hair sitting at the bar fifty feet away stopped him from saying a word.

The place was fairly dark and equally smoky. Still, there was no mistaking her identity. Liz. Shit.

What was she doing here?

Outside of that night several weeks ago, she never came to his bar. Not only was Dusty's Backroom located in a small town nearly a half hour from her Atlanta home, but it was also a country bar. Liz was as rock and roll as a person could get.

Stranger than her presence was her attire. She was a jeans and T-shirt kind of gal, a woman who didn't bother with make-up and who didn't need to. Only, tonight she had bothered with make-up, and the jeans and T-shirt were nowhere to be found. A dress the same shade of electric blue as her eyes molded to her curves, managing to cover her from throat to elbow to knee and somehow still look sinful as hell—maybe because he remembered exactly how she looked out of that dress. Tall, toned, and slippery when wet.

His cock hardened further, pressing against the fly of his jeans. She hadn't climaxed for him, but that she'd been dripping wet right up until she'd ended things was no exaggeration.

"Dusty?" a husky feminine voice questioned.

He turned back, realizing it was the blonde who'd spoken. Had they slept together? How did she know his name?

Movement from the corner of his eye had him looking back at Liz. His gut tightened. She had company. Dusty knew those who frequented his bar. Between his gauzy pink shirt and painted nails, which lent serious question to his sexuality, and spiked black with blond-streaked hair, the guy didn't look like a local or someone Liz's brother would approve of. For Colin's sake, he would get rid of the jerk.

"Give me a few minutes," he told the blonde. "I need to take care of something." For an instant she looked agitated, but then her smile returned. Leaning in so that her plentiful tits couldn't help but press against him, she rubbed her knuckles along his whiskered cheek. "As I recall, you're well worth the wait."

Obviously they had slept together, Dusty thought as he started toward the bar. That the blonde was not only back for more, but was also willing to wait for him without asking why proved how inaccurate Liz was in calling him a bad lover. If there was a bad lover between them, it was her. . . . And so it seemed her frilly new friend was trying to find out firsthand.

In a move as old as dirt, the guy slid his arm around her shoulders, then coasted his hand down her side to caress the outer swell of a breast. The hand continued to rub, inching slowly inward. Disgust swept through Dusty, mirroring the look in Liz's eyes. He expected her temper to take flight and for her to punch the unsuspecting schmuck. She didn't move a muscle, but plastered on a smile any idiot could tell was fake.

She might be okay with getting felt up by a creep in front of dozens of prying eyes, but Colin sure as hell wouldn't approve. For her brother, Dusty would save her ass.

Reaching her, he took her free hand and tugged her from the bar stool, dislodging the other man's arm. She was a tall woman, inches beneath his six-foot-one frame. In three-inch spiked heels, her mouth was nearly even with his. She must have done some thickening trick with her ruby-red lipstick because, as he pulled her into his side, he noticed her lips were plumper than ever. Plump and glistening, they brought to mind the way her mouth had looked wrapped around his dick.

The woman might be a nutcase, to kick him out the way she had, but he remembered now that she wasn't bad at sex. At least the oral variety. Those full, gifted lips gave head like no other before her.

He rubbed his thumb in the valley of her palm. "Elizabeth." Dressed the way she was, her full, more feminine name sounded appropriate. "I was wondering when you'd get here."

The feigned smile left her lips and icy blue eyes bored into his. She yanked at her hand. "What the fuck do you want, Marr?"

Dusty smirked. Now there was the Liz he knew. He freed her hand to give her ass a gentle swat. "Such a bitchy tease. You know what that does to me, babe."

"No, *babe*," she retorted, drawing out the bogus endearment. "I'm afraid I don't."

"That's my Elizabeth, always fishing for a reminder."

Kissing her was bound to lose him a night of carnal bliss with the blonde. Dusty glanced back to the pool table where the woman waited in all her leggy glory. She looked like the type who could get her legs behind her ears without any trouble at all. Liz would owe him for the loss, big time.

He looked back at Liz. His attention returned to her lush mouth, and his cock jerked. Though he hadn't planned on getting naked with her again, several excellent ways she might repay him—each of which had to do with leaving a ruby-red ring around his shaft—popped into his head.

"Open up," he ordered, giving her ass another swat.

Her mouth opened, likely to tell him off. Before she could speak, he pulled her snug to him and sank his tongue past her lips. Her gasp pushed into his mouth as a blast of hot air, a sultry puff at odds with the biting pinch of her short nails into his arms.

Call him a masochist, but he loved that bite and the way she brought her knee up, attempting to leave a permanent mark on the family jewels. Loved even more the way she couldn't stop her hot little sigh as he sucked at the softness of her inner cheeks. He brought his tongue over her teeth, across her gums, and twined it with her own stubbornly still one, consuming her taste—a mixture of dark imported beer and white-hot fiery female.

The nip of Liz's nails gentled as he tilted his hips into hers and rubbed his erection against her mound. A second, far breathier sigh slid between their joined mouths, and she shifted her pelvis in a restless way that applied pressure to his constrained dick so forcefully it bordered on pain. Her tongue shot to life, no longer denying her passionate nature, but stroking against his with wild urgency. Meeting that urgency head on, by stripping her naked and banging her on the hardwood dance floor, held real appeal. Any other place and time he might have done it. Here, in his bar, he didn't dare.

He might talk sex here, might even regularly meet a lover at the bar, but he would never risk his authority with his employees by doing a woman while on the job. Hell, he'd already risked too much with his current behavior.

Dusty lifted his mouth from Liz's to find her looking at him, nostrils flaring and breath coming in warm, sexy, shallow pants. The points of her aroused nipples stabbed at her dress, taunting his mouth to pull them inside and suck.

"Bastard." She hissed the word, bringing his attention from her tits to the narrowed set of her eyes and making him question his decision not to screw her here and now.

Had ticked-off women always had this rampant effect on his libido, or did the mad urge to plow into her despite their surroundings have to do with her ordering him out when she'd been on the verge of orgasm? Was her behavior that night the real reason he'd gone so long without sex?

He'd told himself the recent dry spell had to do with a hectic work schedule and not lack of desire. Maybe that wasn't the case. Maybe her accusation of him as a bad lover had messed with his ego and, in turn, his head.

"Looks like you're busy, so I guess I'll see you around," Frilly Guy said from somewhere to Dusty's left.

Liz glanced over and mumbled a good-bye. Leveling her gaze on Dusty, she swiped the back of her hand across her mouth. "Do you want to die?"

Only if they were talking about the little death, and then, yeah, for better or worse, he was rock hard and more than ready. "Man like that only has one thing on his mind."

She went wide-eyed. "Ohmigawd! You think he was trying to get in my pants? And here I thought he wanted to hook up some afternoon for tea and cookies." Dismissing the innocent act, she grabbed her beer bottle from the bar and pushed past him. "I came here to find a guy to fuck, so if you don't mind—"

Grabbing hold of her arm, he spun her back. "Does Colin know why you're here?"

She looked incredulous. "Maybe you've suddenly decided to care if my brother approves of my behavior around men, but I could give a crap less."

It wasn't her behavior around men in general, Dusty told himself, but that around strangers who could be after her for God only knew what reasons. Right. As if his own intentions hadn't taken a far from noble turn. "He worries about you."

"Yeah, well, he shouldn't. I'm a big girl."

She sure as hell was.

He should let her remark slide and her arm go before he made himself look like a complete hypocrite. Blame it on the celibacy streak, but temptation was too great to resist. He sent his gaze the length of her, lingering on her small but firm breasts and then lower to her crotch.

Was she wet for him after that kiss?

Dusty inhaled, half-expecting the musky scent of her arousal to cut through the mixed aroma of cigarettes, perfume, and greasy food. Returning to her eyes, he let the lust reflect in his voice. "As if I could forget."

For a fleeting moment, desire kindled in Liz's eyes, deepening the already-intense shade of blue. Then she pulled her arm free of his hold and planted a hand at her hip. "Let me clear something up for you, Marr. When I said I came here to find a guy to fuck, I didn't mean you. I'm looking for someone who doesn't need a ten-step program to find a woman's G-spot."

The barb pricked deeper than he cared to acknowledge. He pushed out a laugh. "Babe, I had your G-spot pegged in seconds. Or did you forget you were about to come before you pulled the Jekyll and Hyde routine and tossed me out on my ass?"

"I'm not your *babe*, and you're damned lucky you got as far as you did. Now, unless you came over here for some reason other than to piss me off, I suggest you get back to your flavor-of-the-night. As good as you think you are, I seriously doubt Blondie's going to wait forever."

Dusty glanced at the pool tables and found the blonde standing where he'd left her. He should be thrilled the woman had stuck around after witnessing him doing the tongue-mambo with Liz. Another night he would have been. Tonight he could only see the desperation in the move. The blonde would be no challenge for his sexual confidence. Whether or not his recent dry spell had to do with Liz's cutting accusation, he suddenly found he needed that challenge.

Smirking at Liz, he teased, "Watching, were you? Getting jealous?"

She snorted and turned on her heel, flashing a tight ass he knew she owed to daily jogs. An ass, he also knew, that felt more than a little fine filling his hands. "Good-bye, Marr. Be careful not to trip over your ego on the way back to the pool table. An obstacle that big's liable to cause serious damage."

2

Goddamn Dusty.

Liz had come to Dusty's Backroom to prove a point. Despite the fact that she hadn't been able to stop thinking of him and his bedroom techniques, she didn't want to sleep with him again. The plan had been to find another man capable of getting her juicy wet while Dusty was in viewing range. Thanks to the big, arrogant dickhead, the plan had backfired in a major way.

Dusty hadn't stopped at chasing off the metrosexual in filmy pink, who seemed more infatuated with his hair and nails than her body. Dusty had to kiss her, had to remind her exactly how good he was at getting her hot.

And wet.

Damn her messed-up hormones and even more messed-up head, but she'd been dripping from the first touch of his tongue to the last brush of his hard cock. No other guy in the place had looked to be of screwable quality after that. She'd spent the better part of the night sitting at the bar, chatting with Jen, the head bartender. Now that the place was closing, Liz had the pleasure of going home alone and orgasmless yet again.

"No luck?"

Jen had disappeared into the back to help with cleanup, and Liz was taking a last pull from her beer when the amused masculine voice with a slight drawl reached her. She set the bottle on the bar and swiveled on her stool to find Dusty smiling down at her. She growled in the back of her throat.

Could the man not get it through his thick skull that she didn't like him? Didn't even want to see his too-damned-sexy face?

The lights had been turned on high, exposing every lean, lickable angle.

She shivered as she imagined the sandy-blond whiskers that darkened his square jawline and edged into his goatee scraping over her aroused flesh. Rumor had it some women came from nipple stimulation alone. She'd never believed she could be among that highly orgasmic group, but maybe the chafe of Dusty's coarse facial hair over her breasts would be enough to empty her mind of thought and send her body spiraling toward climax.

Yeah, and that idea could go the hell back to wherever it came from. "Not that it's any of your business, but I'm hooking up with someone in the parking lot in a few minutes."

The right side of his mouth twitched. A devilish twinkle lit his dark brown eyes. He propped an elbow on the bar and leaned against it, the collar of his partially unbuttoned black dress shirt gaping open to reveal curling chest hair the same dirty-blond shade as his goatee. "Fucking in the parking lot—sounds like a classy guy."

Pulling her attention back to his face, Liz struggled not to recall how delectable his body was beneath his shirt. Struggled and failed. Every inch of ripped abdominal and pectoral muscle encased in sun-bronzed skin materialized in her mind and sent a shiver through her belly. "Oh, pull-eaze, like you'd know anything about class."

"In case you've forgotten, I didn't always spend my life in a bar."

Reflecting on his high-society roots was far better than reflecting on his body. Thinking about his roots left her cold; thinking about his body left her eager to touch. There would be no more touching between them. Not one single brush.

Dusty had moved from Texas to Georgia seven and a half years ago. From what she'd overheard him tell Colin, he hadn't spoken with his parents since. Why, Liz didn't know. What she did know was that his parents were happily married, wealthy as Croesus, and regularly touted for their contributions to family-oriented organizations. It was hard to like anyone who would cut themselves off from an upbringing so ideal.

"You'd never be able to tell." Snarkiness over her own, all-but-motherless rearing reflected in her voice. Not that she hadn't enjoyed learning about her menstrual period from her red-faced, babbling father. That moment was right up there with their outing to buy a training bra—apparently he'd thought her breasts wouldn't figure out what to do without preparation. They'd figured it out, all right. The little bastards were practically standing at attention and begging to be let out for some playtime in Dusty's hands.

"You've mastered the art of seediness perfectly," she continued. "Speaking of seedy, what happened to Blondie? Have to run home for a quick collagen fix?"

"Wasn't my type."

"Doesn't put out on the first date. My sympathies."

His smile gone, Dusty straightened. "You're acting like an even bigger bitch than usual. Panties still in a twist over that kiss, or is the problem about wetness?"

Hah! As if he'd affected her panties with that puny kiss.

Okay, so maybe he had the tiniest little bit.

Ah, shit, she could lie to the rest of the world but not to herself. Their earlier tango had been about a whole lot more than a kiss, puny or otherwise. Her already damp sex moistened further as she recalled the thrust of his stiff dick.

Was he still hard?

Not that she cared. Really, she couldn't give a rat's ass. Ignoring the urge to rub her thighs together, Liz stood. "Get real, Marr. You know I don't wear panties."

The devilish gleam returned to his eyes. "That's a yes to the wetness."

Rolling her eyes, she started for the exit. "The day your kiss gets me wet will be the same one I start respecting you."

"If you didn't come to see me, what are you doing in my bar? You never come here. You hate country music."

A rasp had settled into Dusty's voice—his voice that sounded far too near. Liz stopped her trek for the door and turned back, barely stifling her gasp. He stood inches away, and the look in his eyes was both challenging and predatory. She took an involuntary step to the side. Her butt brushed against a pool table and she scowled. He could corner her all he wanted; she wouldn't be intimidated.

She narrowed her eyes. "Obviously you suck at remembering as much as you do at fucking. I told you earlier, I came here looking for someone to screw. I wanted a change of pace from the metro scene."

He nodded at the bar's exit. The last of the patrons had disappeared into the night. "Looks like you're shit outta luck." With a cocky grin, he brought his hand to her face and brushed his thumb over her lower lip. "Unless you were planning on the guy being an employee, in which case I'm sure we can work something out."

Heat shot through her, jetting from her lips to her nipples to her core. For a second time, Liz just managed to catch her stunned gasp before it could leave her mouth.

What was it about him? Not only could he get her wet when she was fully clothed, but his simple touch had her sizzling.

She jerked her face away. "Yeah, your memory obviously sucks, or what part of 'I'm hooking up in the parking lot' did you miss?" Placing a hand on his chest, she attempted to push him out of her path. "He should be out there now. In other words, get the hell out of my way."

He glanced at her hand but stood firm. "Does this mystery guy have a name?"

No, but she could pull one out of her ass as easily as the next woman—anything not to re-dredge thoughts of the hard wall of pure masculinity beneath her palm. She dropped her hand away. "Aiden."

The look in his eye turned to something dangerous, at least to her common sense. He moved closer, until he was seriously messing with her personal space. His gaze on her mouth, he brought his hand back to her lips and rubbed the lower one with the pad of his thumb. "Tell me, Liz," he said quietly, huskily, in a way that had her heart hammering, "does Aiden's kiss make you wet?"

"One brush and I'm ready to come." Oh gawd! Nice breathy voice. She sounded ready to throw herself at him.

"Just a brush." Dusty's warm breath whispered along her cheeks and, it seemed, every nerve in her body. He slid forward, barely a movement at all, but enough to have their bodies touching, his chest rubbing teasingly against her breasts, his erection pressing against her sex.

So much for not touching.

If nothing else, she had the answer to her earlier question of if he was still hard. He was, in a really big way.

His mouth came over hers, splintering further thought. One slow, soft, sensual caress and it lifted away. "A brush like that?" he asked roughly. "Or is this more what you were thinking of?" His mouth returned. No softness this time, but his teeth nipping at her lips with stinging little bites that had her nipples aching.

"Or maybe it wasn't a mouth kiss you had in mind." The breath rushed between Liz's lips as he grasped her around the waist and lifted her onto the pool table. Flashing a taunting grin, he went to his knees. He inched her dress up and palmed her naked thighs. "Maybe this is more what you were thinking of."

She gave her head a shake. What was wrong with her? She was sitting here, letting him have his way with her. It was the absolute last thing she wanted. . . . But, oh wow, who knew the cool felt of the pool table could feel so good on bare skin?

Talk about feeling good . . .

Dusty's fingers moved along her inner thighs, easing her dress farther up as they brushed in slow, thought-fogging circles. His fingers stilled when they reached the soft curls at her apex. She hadn't been joking when she'd told him she was pantyless—it was an action meant to bolster her sexual assurance. Now she paid the price. Now he could undoubtedly feel the juices sliding down her thighs, smell her arousal thick on the air. Now was the time to tell him what an asshole he was and get the fuck out of Dodge.

One lone, long finger threaded through her damp curls, and the breath snagged in her throat. Lovely. How was she supposed to tell him to stop now? She couldn't speak a word without risking a sigh, or worse, demanding he screw her immediately.

A second finger joined the first. Together they stroked the lips of her sex, splayed them wide.

His gaze returned to hers, lust thick in its depth. "Nothing quite like sucking on a slick, pink pussy to end a long, hard day at the office."

Liz's belly tightened. No way. He wasn't tonguing her.

She attempted to close her thighs, but the damned things had a mind of their own. Her legs spread wider, welcoming him inside while her breath panted out as if she were a bitch in heat. His fingers stretched her swollen pussy lips, exposing her inflamed clit. Cream dripped onto his fingers and the green felt table beneath her as he lowered his head.

Looking up at her face, he opened his mouth. His tongue came out, over his lips, easing toward her cunt, and then slicing right down its center.

"Ohmigawd!" Her nails dug into the soft, sweaty flesh of her palms. He was every bit as good at oral sex as she remembered. Every bit as good at making her want in a rash, crazy, mindless way she'd never wanted before.

From between his fingers, her clit stood at attention, puffy and red, silently begging to be sucked. As if he could hear that begging, his lips closed over the overly sensitized pearl and tugged. Erotic sensation crashed through her in a tumultuous wave. She swallowed her desperate moan for more.

Dusty's lips lifted. In the next instant, his tongue pushed deeply inside her, and she knew she couldn't silence further moans. And why should she? The pulsing in her pussy said that this was it.

The night. The time. The end of her orgasm virginity. Amen.

Liz hadn't wanted to share this momentous occasion with Dusty, but she'd already come to terms with karma's warped sense of humor. She might as well come to terms with the fact that he could tell how eager she was to do him and voice the need cruising through her body.

"You owe me an orgasm." She spoke matter-of-factly, as if her entire body and the majority of her sanity didn't hinge on the words. "Give it to me now. Fuck me."

He pulled from her body and laughed. "Only 'cause you asked so nicely."

"What can I say, I'm a regular Ms. Manners," she bit out, and then dove her fingers into his hair, clinging, gripping, pushing his face back between her thighs.

His tongue plunged into her juicy center. Deep. Deeper. In. Out. Back in. His goatee scraped over her clit with each stab of his tongue. Warmth spread over her like wildfire, coiling in her belly, licking at her pussy, blistering from head to toe. Tremors sliced through her, slowly at first, then growing in speed, spreading tension from limb to limb, sending her heart into a chaotic thundering tempo.

Oh yes! Oh yes! She wanted to laugh, cry, scream. Thank the orgasm gods for gifting her with this moment. Closing her eyes, she went with the latter.

Dusty had found it. He had to have found her missing G-spot because she was so close . . . so damned close. . . climax. The big O. Finally.

Fiona and Kristi were going to be sooo jealous come the next chat session. Sure they had orgasms, but never with a man. Not even Simon, Fi's king-sized vibrator of a lover, could possibly top this all-consuming feeling of needing to go off like a bottle rocket on the Fourth of July. But enough about Fiona and Kristi. Coming was all that should be on her mind. Nothing else. Not her vow to never sleep with Dusty again. Not feeling like a slut because—

"Yo, Dusty. Everything's cleaned up in the back. Can I take—oh, shit. Sorry, man. I didn't realize you weren't alone."

The masculine voice washed over Liz's heated body like ice water on a sultry summer night. Time and place returned to her in a heartbeat. She snapped her eyes open. Heat burned her cheeks, and disgust roiled through her belly at the sight of Dusty pulling his blond head from between her naked thighs; his head that she held on to so firmly it was as if she planned to keep him nestled there forever.

With shaking hands, she let free his hair and digested the last several minutes.

Jesus H. Christ! What the hell had she been thinking?

She was half-naked on a pool table, being eaten out where

anyone could see her, and why, but for pleasure's sake. For the lone reason of going off like a cream-filled atomic bomb, she'd lowered herself to her mother's standards, forgotten every one of her ethics and acted like a sex-driven whore with a man she couldn't stand.

Dusty stood and looked over his shoulder. "No problem. Go ahead and take off."

"Have a good one," the guy said, amusement in his voice.

"I'll do my best."

The kitchen door banged shut, announcing the man's departure. Dusty hesitated a few seconds, then turned to her. Lust blazed over his face, consuming his features as he lowered back between her thighs.

Liz's repulsion over their behavior shifted from herself to him. He was every bit as into the moment as he'd been before they'd been interrupted, and that just proved he didn't have a single moral in his body. Knowing his track record, he'd probably forgotten who he was with long ago. More likely, he'd never cared in the first place.

Admittedly, for a short while there, she hadn't cared either, but she for damned sure should have. She sure as shit cared now, when she'd reclaimed enough sense to remember she was as close to an atomic orgasm bomb as he was to a saint.

Grabbing a handful of his hair, she yanked. "Unless you want a pool stick shoved up your ass, get the hell off me."

His attention shifted from her crotch to her face. His eyebrows came together, and his hot look faded to disbelief. "You're fucking with me. You don't want me to stop."

She leaned to the side and grabbed the pool stick resting against the end of the table. She waved it at him. "Touch me again and you'll see how much I'm fucking with you. You had your chance, Marr. You blew it."

Dusty straightened and took a step back. "I didn't blow a damned thing. You were about to come before Matt came out of the back." He glanced back at her crotch and smirked. "Way you're dripping, it's clear you still want to."

With a raucous laugh, she snapped her thighs together and pushed off the table, smoothing the dress down unsteady legs. "Get over yourself. The only reason I'm wet is because I have a real man waiting for me outside. One who knows how to get the job done."

He stared at her a moment, then said, "You honestly have a guy outside while you're in here letting me go down on you?" She nodded, and he shook his head. "You're an even bigger nutcase than I thought."

Self-loathing slid through Liz. She hated the way he was looking at her—as if she was deplorable for getting with two men in one night. She held little doubt he'd done the same with women many times. For the sake of her reputation, bogus though it might be, she cast aside her unease. "Maybe so, but at least I won't be relying on my own hand to get me off tonight."

3

Fiona: Hell-o, ladies. Guess who just had one of the best orgasms of her life? God bless you, Kristi. I don't know what I'd do if you hadn't hooked me up with Simon.

Kristi: Singing King Simon's praises again. I take it that means Saturday night's blind date was a bomb?

Fiona: You could say that. The guy was three inches shorter than me (you know about my height hang-up) and had a serious foot fetish. He spent the whole night staring at my feet, talking about licking my toes. Halfway through dinner I couldn't handle it anymore and told him I had an oozing blister. Worked like a charm.

Liz: Lovely imagery.

Fiona: Hey, woman. Long time, no talk. So, did you take my advice and give the sure thing another go? Please tell me you did. Kristi isn't putting any effort into finding Mr. G, and frankly it's making me feel alone in the quest.

Kristi: Like you have room to talk, Ms. I Love My Dildo Better Than Any Man.

Liz: She's got you there, Fi. For the record, I'm glad to hear Simon's still doing the job. Ah, fuck it, I am not glad. I'm jealous as hell.

Fiona: Is it just me, or did you notice Liz ignored my question, Kristi? You aren't holding out on us, are you, Liz? You know I have Old World connections, ways of making people talk. Spill, or swim with the fishes.

Liz: You have me shaking here. Probably wet myself from the fear.

Kristi: C'mon, Liz. Stop being gross and tell. Did you hook up with Dusty again?

Liz: It wasn't exactly a hookup, and it also wasn't worth it. No O . . . the story of my life.

Kristi: Oh, honey, that blows. Did he at least get you wet again?

Liz: No. Yes. A little. Okay, so a lot. But he couldn't finish the job.

Fiona: Why? The lawyer in me detects there's more to it.

Liz: The lawyer in you can stick it up your derriere.

Fiona: Ah-ha, gotcha. Can we say guilty with a capital G? So, what happened?

Liz: Another damned interruption.

Kristi: Oy. Colin walked in on you guys again?

Liz: No. It was, um, one of Dusty's employees. We were kinda getting down and dirty on the pool table at his bar and . . . And the point is I was close, sooo incredibly close, and the idiot guy comes out of the back and pulls this "I didn't know you weren't alone" crap.

Kristi: Pool table, huh? Lots of ball handling going on.

Liz: Ha-ha, and no. Dusty was fully clothed, and his hands were hardly involved.

Fiona: I'll take that to mean he was doing you with his mouth. You know they say, it's harder for most women to come that way. If he had you that close with just a few licks, imagine what'll happen if you give him another chance when you're both naked. Don't give up on this guy. He's got your number.

Kristi: Ooh . . . is it 69?

Kristi: Okay, so I can hear the groans all the way to Seattle. 'Nough with the bad jokes. Seriously, Liz, Fi is right. Either give him another try or hand him over. I wasn't joking when I said I should come to Atlanta and meet him. If you aren't going to go for the big O with stud man, I will.

Liz sat back in her chair and stuck her tongue out at her laptop monitor. Dusty had accused her of being a nutcase last night, but the true nutsos were Kristi and Fiona. Had they forgotten every bad word she'd ever typed about Dusty, or why were they encouraging her to give him yet another try? Maybe there was a chance of him making her come if they could get together without any interruptions, but all that would accomplish was her hating herself after the fact.

He wasn't just a player—that she could handle—he was an unscrupulous man-whore. One who was not, under any circumstances, getting his hands or his tongue back on her body.

As for Kristi's desire to do him . . . The thought of Dusty sleeping with her friend tightened her belly into knots. It was sympathy for Kristi to blame. The woman came across as the type to fall hard once she found a guy who could do her right. If she hooked up with Dusty, bad things would surely happen. Liz's duty as a friend was to tell Kristi to stay away from Dusty.

Unfortunately, her duty as a woman who'd vowed to help the others locate a man capable of finding their G-spot and providing them with the big O outweighed that. Aching belly or not, she had only one option. . . .

Liz: You want him, you got him, Kristi. Just let me know when you can come to town and you're as good as fucked.

Dusty stepped out of his truck and hustled from the parking lot to the community center. Thanks to having to break up an argument at the bar before it could escalate into a physical fight, he was five minutes late. He would be damned if he would be any later. Tonight was all about impressions, and every second counted.

Three days had passed since Liz walked out on him, orgasmless yet again. He should have spent that time worrying over how getting caught messing around at work would affect his relationship with his employees; he'd never intended for things to move beyond a little kissing and groping. Instead the idea that Liz might have had another man waiting for her in the parking lot had goaded him day and night. If she'd had another man lined up and still allowed Dusty to stick his tongue in her, then she'd expected him to fail to make her climax the whole time.

He'd failed at a number of things in life, hundreds of things depending on who you asked. When it came to sex, he wouldn't be a failure in anyone's eyes, damnit.

Sex was his forte. The one area his ego had every reason to soar. He sure as hell knew how to find a woman's G-spot, knew exactly what buttons to push to have her creaming in his hands. And he would prove it to Liz. He had to prove it to her. He now knew for a fact that she was to blame for his recent celibacy streak. She was the first person to threaten his self-confidence on any level since he'd moved to Georgia, and that threat would linger until it was quashed.

Reaching the community center, Dusty pulled open the door and headed into the room across from the entrance. The cooking class was a mix of women and men, young and old; it was also the perfect way to get closer to Liz and convince her to give him another chance at pleasuring her, this time the right way.

Guilt edged up with the idea that what he was about to do bordered on deceitful—he didn't believe in luring a woman into his arms. Then again, you could hardly lure the willing. Even if she'd had another man waiting for her three nights ago (hell, he didn't want to buy that claim), Dusty didn't believe that man had been the cause of her wetness. Liz had been hot for Dusty and Dusty alone. How he treated her over the next hour and a half might sway the evening's outcome in his favor; but if it ended with her inviting him back between her legs for some prime shag time, it would be because she wanted him there 100 percent.

Dusty spotted Liz in the back of the open room, pulling bowls from a floor cupboard. She wasn't facing him, and she didn't need to be. He'd know that tight ass, hugged to testosterone-tormenting perfection in a pair of faded black jeans, anywhere.

His dick stirred to life with the memory of filling his hands with her supple backside. That a mere thought could have such a strong effect on his libido made one thing clear: It had been far too long since he'd gotten laid. If this night didn't end with him screwing Liz, then it would end with him screwing some other woman, regardless if she was a challenge to get into bed and a bolster to his ego, or just another easy, feel-good lay.

Pulling his thoughts from his boxers, Dusty caught the instructor's eye and nodded a hello. A middle-aged man with close-cut, thinning brown hair and a black apron emblazoned with red and green jalapenos, the guy worked his way around the room, answering questions and assisting students at their work stations. Each station consisted of a stove, refrigerator, sink, and several cupboards.

Liz went to the refrigerator in her station, opened the door, and fished around inside. Dusty quickly crossed the room to stand on the other side of the refrigerator door. Several seconds passed and the door closed. He knew the instant she spotted him—her face registered shock, and the eggs in her right hand exploded in her fist, sending shell flying and thick yellow and white liquid dripping onto the floor.

Checking his amusement, he grabbed a washcloth from next to the sink and bent down to clean up the mess. He glanced up at her as he worked. "Nervous?"

Her eyes narrowed, shock fading to revulsion. "No. It's an anxious tic I get whenever I'm about to kick someone's ass. What are you doing here, Marr?"

Standing, he dropped the egg mess into the sink and washed his hands. He reached into the refrigerator for two fresh eggs, then set them on the counter next to the bowls she'd set out. "Cooking. Isn't that what people do in cooking class?"

Liz's gaze narrowed further, suspicion alive in every line of her body. "This class has been going on for almost two months. It's also full. I have a hard time believing even you could sweet-talk your way past those factors."

Dusty grinned. She would be surprised how much a little sweet-talking could accomplish. Since he didn't come here to talk sex, at least not yet, he shrugged. "It wasn't a big deal. I know the instructor's sister."

With a knowing look, she grabbed a container of flour from the cupboard and set it on the counter. "Yeah. I bet you do."

"Her husband was an acquaintance of mine before I moved here."

She whirled to face him. Incredulity shot through her eyes. "Ohmigawd! You slept with a married woman!"

Dusty felt a dozen sets of eyes land on him with the blurted words. He could pretend he wanted to set Liz straight for the sake of getting closer to her and then getting back in her pants. The truth was he had a real problem with her or anyone else thinking so lowly of him. Yeah, he loved sex and women's bodies in general—be they thin, chunky, or somewhere in between—but he would never mess with a married woman. "Amazingly, I don't sleep with every woman I meet," he said rigidly, and then nodded at the ingredients she'd laid out. "What are we making?"

Liz continued to look at him for a few seconds, as if she wasn't sure if she should believe him, but then dismissed the subject. Turning back to the counter, she unwrapped a stick of softened butter and tossed it into a bowl. "*I'm* making pecan pumpkin pie. Thanks to you, I'm already behind the rest of the class on getting the crust together."

He'd learned enough about the class to know each student worked at their own pace. Since her lie worked in his favor, he let it slide. "In that case, let me help you get caught up." He grabbed the two eggs in one hand. Tapping them against the edge of the bowl, he broke them cleanly down the center. The yolks and whites emptied into the bowl, and he tossed the shells into the sink.

"You've done that before." Accusation rang in Liz's voice.

Before Liz's brother had met his girlfriend, Colin had shown up at Dusty's Backroom several nights a week in an attempt to escape what he called Liz's god-awful cooking. While Dusty wasn't ready to win any cook-offs, teaching her what he did know was as good a way as any to get on her good side. "I do some of the cooking at Dusty's."

"Right," she said dryly, "the extra crispy char burgers."

"What can I say, they're my specialty."

Without responding, she returned to the refrigerator and pulled out the egg carton. She set it on the counter and grabbed two eggs. The recipe didn't call for any more, so obviously she was cracking them to prove a point, namely that she could do anything he could and, likely in her obstinate mind, far better.

Fisting the eggs, Liz struck them against the side of a clean bowl. Shell splintered into a dozen pieces, most of which landed in the bowl along with whatever yolk and whites didn't splatter onto her hand and apron.

Curling her egg-slicked hand into a fist, she scowled. "They obviously had defective shells."

With an inward laugh, Dusty grabbed two more eggs from the carton. "I'll show you."

"I don't want your—"

"Like you said, this classroom's equipped for a dozen students. I make thirteen. To get in, I had to agree to hook up with someone already assigned. That would be you." Hearing her sharp intake of breath, he hurried to change the subject. "As for the eggs. . ." He moved behind her, enjoying the sensual slide of her bottom against his groin as he slid his arms under hers.

A low growl rolled from her lips. Before she could follow the feral sound up with words, he took her right hand in his, turned it palm-side up, and uncurled the fist. "Watch and learn." He placed two eggs onto her palm, purposefully stroking the tips of his fingers along her skin, sending waves of heat dancing up his arm and, no doubt, into hers. He folded his hand over hers and brought his mouth inches from her ear. Gently, he used their joined hands to strike the eggs against the lip of the bowl. The shells broke down the center, emptying their contents into the bowl. "It's all in the wrist."

Liz cocked her head to the side, assuring the warm whisper of his breath against the delicate flesh of her earlobe hadn't gone unnoticed. She tugged at the hand he held and pushed against him, attempting to move away. When he refused to budge, she turned and glared. "You honestly said I would be your partner?"

Dusty's attention fell to her mouth. She hadn't worn the ruby-red lipstick tonight or the three-inch heels, but her lips were still damned full and dangerously close to his. His vision from three nights ago surfaced: The erotic image of Liz on her knees, swallowing his cock to the hilt while her tongue licked from base to pre-cum oozing tip. The stirring he'd felt in his boxers upon first entering the classroom and spotting her shapely rear end returned, sending his dick into an almost instant state of hardness.

Resisting the urge to adjust his cramped erection, he forced himself to focus on her tone. It held irritation, but not the usual in-your-face bluntness. Obviously this class meant something to her. Good. For some perverse reason, he generally enjoyed Liz's bitchy behavior, but it would be far easier to get on her good side without it.

Dusty shifted far enough back that she wouldn't feel his hard-on and placed two more eggs in her hand. "Your turn." He folded his hand over hers. "I'll guide you, but the breaking's all up to you."

The inside of his arm rubbed against the outer swell of her breast and she tensed. "I don't—" she started, sounding like she wanted to break something, all right.

"Know how?" he finished, purposely misunderstanding her. "Then I suggest you watch closer this time."

Once more he broke the eggs cleanly into the dish. "Like I said," he breathed centimeters from her neck, "all about the wrist."

This time, a helpless little sigh accompanied the cocking of her neck. Not about to push things so early on, he released her hand and stepped back. "As much as I enjoy breaking eggs, we should probably get back to the pie." He glanced toward the front of the room, where the pie crust recipe was written on a blackboard, and reached for a measuring cup.

Using her hip, Liz butted him out of the way and grabbed the measuring cup from his hand. After filling the cup with water, she poured the water into the bowl, then grabbed a wooden spoon and started mixing. In a hushed voice, she said, "If you're taking this class just to get in my pants, allow me to assure you, the only thing that's going to get blown is your time."

Dusty raised an eyebrow. "Who has the ego problem now? I own a bar with a full lunch and dinner menu. Since I didn't have a chance to learn how to cook growing up the way I did, doing so now makes good business sense."

She continued to add the last of the ingredients, stirring them into a sticky dough and then pressing the dough into a pie pan. Setting the pan aside, she returned to the cupboard and retrieved a bowl for the pie filling. "I don't care."

He lifted his gaze from the curve of her ass. "Don't care about what?"

"How you grew up." She set the bowl on the counter and looked at him. "You think I want to know, but I don't."

"My upbringing's the last thing I want to talk about." And it for damned sure was.

Liz was to blame for his making a comment on his past. Ever since she'd taken that shot at his ability to please a woman, he'd been reliving moments from his youth, all the many ways he'd managed to fail in his parents' eyes. "I was making small talk."

"Yeah, well, don't bother. We're here to cook, not socialize."

For once Dusty was glad for her brusque attitude toward him. Allowing silence to reign, they worked together until the pie filling and the whipped cream that would top the finished product were done. Liz poured the filling into the crust, topped it with a handful of pecan shavings, and placed it in the oven.

Arms crossed, she turned around and leaned back against the oven door. "You want to make small talk. Fine. We have to pass the time somehow until the pie's done. How'd you grow up that you were never exposed to cooking? Wait, let me guess. Your father's a throwback to the olden days and thinks that kinda thing's woman's work, so you were never allowed in the kitchen with your mother."

Dusty's gut tightened. Fuck. He thought he'd sidestepped this conversation. He could hardly ignore it now, when, despite her blasé tone, genuine interest shone in her eyes. The more he thought about what a disappointment he was to his parents, the more his need to get close enough to Liz to prove himself a sexual success grew. The secret was to keep his words light, share just enough to placate her, and then focus on pleasuring her.

He assumed a carefree tone. "Before I answer that, tell me one thing."

She eyed him warily. "What?"

"You aren't being nice to me just to get in my pants, are you? 'Cause I gotta tell you, babe, the only thing I'm letting you blow is my time."

Her upper lip twitched, making it clear she fought a smile. Turning her back on him, she busied herself with switching on the oven light and bending down to look through the oven's glass front. "Bite me, Marr."

Dusty moved up behind her. He brushed the front of his right thigh against the back of her left as he bent down and peered in the oven next to her. She jolted, and he taunted in a low voice, "Exactly as I'd feared—you can't handle just talking around me. You want to move straight to the biting. Next thing you know, we'll be licking each other, then sucking, blowing, fondling . . ." Hearing her breathing quicken, he came to his feet. "My mother doesn't know the difference between vegetable oil and olive oil."

Liz stood. "There is one?" She looked quizzical but sounded slightly breathless.

Another time he would have laughed at both the naïveté (there was a word he would never have thought to associate with her) of the question and her stimulated response to his remark. Now he focused on speaking without emotion coming into play. "Yes, there is. The point is my mother's never cooked, or for that matter worked a real job, a day in her life. She was born into a wealthy family and married into the same. A hired chef does the cooking."

"That had to be nice when you were young, having her around to take care of you and your siblings instead of staying with a sitter."

He snorted. Nice, right. They'd been a regular fucking Partridge Family. "I have two brothers, and I said my mother never worked a real job, not that she stayed home. Mom spent all her time volunteering for my father's company and with anyone else who needed help, so long as it kept her out of the house. Staying away from us kids was one of the few things my parents agreed on." Disgust bled into his words. He gentled his tone as he added, "A live-in assistant took care of us."

A frown flirted with Liz's lips. "Well, I'm sure he or she was nice."

"Yeah, by the time I was nine, I knew more than I ever cared to about being a gentleman in polite society."

Her frown appeared full force. "What about being a kid?"

She looked almost sorry for him; it was the last thing he wanted or would have expected. Time to get things back on track and remember his mission here.

Grinning, Dusty looked at her breasts hugged alluringly by the stretch of her white apron and the pale blue T-shirt beneath.

He waggled his eyebrows. "I'm working on that part now. Whaddya say I come over there and show you what a naughty little boy I can be?"

Though he could tell she fought it, a smile curved her lips, lightening the deep blue of her eyes and softening her tough-girl edge. "I'd say you'd be wise to stop fantasizing and focus on the pie."

His grin kicked higher. She gave that genuine smile to Colin with regularity, but never had it been aimed Dusty's way. It felt damned good. "And your excuse is?"

"My excuse?" Her voice took on a defensive note.

"For acting the way you do," he clarified, regretting the way the question diminished her smile.

She planted a hand at her hip, and the last traces of her smile disappeared. "Just how the hell do you think I act?"

Most of the students had already left. Obviously, Liz wasn't concerned about making a good impression on the remaining few. Still, he kept his voice lowered as he responded with a shrug. "Bitchy around me, cynical around most everyone else."

The instructor's voice resonated from the front of the room. "We have a couple more minutes before class is over. If you need more time, you're welcome to stay after and finish; just leave the final product in the refrigerator, and I'll pick them up for grading in the morning."

The last of the students took their pies up to the instructor and then left. After asking Liz and Dusty to turn off the lights when they were finished and informing them the door would lock automatically behind them, the instructor left as well.

Tension filled the room the instant the door closed behind the man. Liz jammed her hands in the back pockets of her jeans and looked toward the oven. Even turned away from him, Dusty could hear her every breath, coming too fast, too loud. A glance at the floor revealed her shifting foot to foot. His first observation of her tonight was that she'd seemed nervous to see him. As uncharacteristic as the mood was for her, she was definitely nervous now.

Was she afraid to be alone with him? Afraid she would give in and let him finish the job he'd started twice now? Afraid he would show her exactly where her G-spot was and that it wanted his touch so badly, it was ready to stand up and beg?

What would it matter if she did give in? She made no secret of her reputation for getting around. This had to be about ego. She'd told him that he'd blown his chance of sleeping with her again, and she was determined to see the words through. He would make her ecstatic to see that determination falter.

"I can finish this alone," she said tightly. "I'm sure you have plans."

"This is my only obligation for the night. I can handle things, though, if you're in a rush to see Aiden."

Liz glanced back to send him a confused look. "Aiden?"

Relief shot through Dusty. She either had a truly shitty memory, the way she'd accused him of having three nights ago, or there hadn't been a man waiting outside for her that night. The wet, hot state of her body had been exactly as Dusty had believed, all because of him, all for him. That level of excitement was nothing a man who was a failure at sex could accomplish.

He took a step toward her. "Your new boy toy."

Wariness flashed over her face with his next step. "Oh. Right. Aiden." Her gaze shifted from his eyes to his mouth, and she swallowed audibly. "The things that man can do with his tongue." Huskiness peppered her words.

If she was thinking about any man's tongue, it was Dusty's. His blood warmed with the knowledge she wanted his kiss, his tongue pushing between her lush lips and thoroughly loving her mouth. He took a last step forward. The way she had her hands stuffed in her pockets accentuated the already snug play of the apron across her tits. The soft mounds rose and fell rapidly. His dick throbbed.

He reached out. She gasped and jerked her hands from her pockets to splay them in front of her. Clearly, she thought her body was his hand's destination. Soon. Very soon, he would touch her. But only when she was ready for it. Only when she was admitting that she wanted his hands on her.

Grasping the refrigerator door handle, he pulled the door open and took out the whipped cream they'd made earlier in the night. He fingered a dollop out of the bowl and licked the cool cream from his finger. "Mmm . . . We do great things together. This is the second best cream I've ever tasted."

Liz's throat worked visibly. He could almost hear her heart slamming against her rib cage, mimicking the mad beat of his own. He stuck his finger back in the bowl, trailed it through the whipped cream, and brought the digit to an inch from his mouth.

Concentrating on her plump naked lips, parted slightly and issuing the sexiest little gasps he'd ever heard, Dusty murmured, "Do you want to know what the first is?"

"Tonight was okay. Don't ruin it by telling me." The words held no bite. No sarcasm. Just a breathy edge that grabbed him by the throat and made him want to do so much more than just *tell* her about his favorite cream. And he would, and the only things that might get ruined in the process were her clothes when he ripped them from her body.

"I got a better idea, babe. How 'bout I show you?"

4

"Dusty . . ." The one-word warning was all Liz could get out, and she was amazed it even came out sounding relatively calm. She didn't feel calm. She felt like her heart and her pussy were having a contest to see which would explode first.

He extended his hand toward her mouth, until his whipped-cream-covered finger hovered inches from her desert-dry lips. "Try it," he urged in a rough whisper.

She wanted to, wanted to lick his finger off slowly, sensuously. Suck every last bit of cream away. The memory of sucking the salty-sweet cum from his dick as he'd climaxed in her mouth pushed through her mind and further heated the molten liquid burning in her sex.

He obviously ate his Brussels sprouts. They were rumored to enhance the flavor of a man's cum, and his had tasted like her favorite new snack.

"Scared?" Dusty questioned when she remained motionless, silent.

To death.

It was ridiculous to fear him, but the damn man had thrown her for a loop. First by seeing past her bigmouthed and carefree charade to her cynicism. Then with the reality of his upbringing.

She'd imagined his childhood ideal, something to dislike him for all the more. In reality, it sounded like it had been less desirable than her own. Her mother might be an absentee flake whose greatest concern was what man she would do next, but at least Liz had had her father and Colin, misguided though their good intentions were at times. Outside of the letters Colin had exchanged with Dusty following a chance meeting when Colin had spent several weeks at a Texas ranch camp, Dusty had had only his brothers to share his youth with. Who knew if they'd even gotten along?

Damnit, she would not feel sorry for him. What he'd endured as a kid didn't change the arrogant dickhead he'd turned into as a man.

"You know me so well," she managed sarcastically.

He smiled in the way that drew out the sharp angles of his jawline beneath the day's growth of sandy-blond stubble, and her heart stuttered. "Maybe not everything, but I'd like to think I know a thing or two. Like how wet you are right now, wondering what my next move will be. I want to show you my favorite cream, Elizabeth. I want to show you exactly how much I enjoy tonguing you, making you squirm in my hands, making you come so hard, you can't help but scream. Just say the words. Tell me you want it."

Jesus. Liz trembled with the thought of how incredible his tongue felt pushing inside her body, licking at her with slow, firm, masterful strokes. How close he'd brought her to climax twice now.

Only a woman with the IQ of a stick of Juicy Fruit would be stupid enough to break her vow not to give in to him. After all, they were in a public place again. A place where anyone could walk in on them. Then there was the fact that she'd already given him to Kristi. Of course, in the name of orgasm and the *Operation G-Spot* creed, Kristi would forgive her. And, really, it was too late for anyone to be coming around. Even if someone did pass by, the door was locked. It seemed Dusty knew who he was with, too, since he was calling her by her ridiculously sweet full name.

Only her name didn't sound sweet rolling off his tongue. It sounded sexy. Sensual. It made her feel feminine in a way she'd never imagined possible.

Fiona and Kristi might be nutso for telling her to give Dusty another try, but maybe they were also right. So long as she was maybeing, maybe her intelligence level wasn't so far off from that stick of gum because she was seriously considering this.

A little lick couldn't hurt anything, right?

Denying further thought, Liz brought her tongue out slowly, wetting her dry lips before flicking the tip of her tongue across his finger. "Oooh . . ." He was sooo right. They did do great things together. The whipped cream was heavenly. She lapped at his finger, eagerly savoring the sweet, light, velvety taste. She moaned her delight.

"More?"

Hearing the strained sound of his voice, she met his eyes. They burned dark with lust, hunger, and, most importantly, stark reality. He wanted her. She wanted him. One night would be okay. One quick screw to get her off and get him out of her life.

He could pretend he'd come here for cooking lessons, but the truth was clear. He'd come here because he'd yet to give her an orgasm, and his ego couldn't handle that fact; it wouldn't be able to let go and move on until he proved he knew where her G-spot lived and exactly how it wanted to be stroked. He'd come here because the cooking class was one of the few places she wouldn't make a scene, where she would be forced to listen to him, be forced to wiggle her way around his finger and want every little thing he hinted at. His finger that she could go on licking for days . . .

The whipped cream was gone, and it was skin she tasted. Hot, potent, virile male skin.

"It's good." Liz licked her tongue across the tip of his finger and sighed. "Damned good." She traveled her tongue up his finger, knuckle to knuckle, and then turned her mouth on his hand, nibbling along the soft web of flesh between finger and thumb.

Warm. Salty. So incredibly masculine.

Dusty grunted and she released his hand to again meet his eyes. Heat rolled through her with the raw desire burning there, turning his eyes to the darkest of chocolates and cascading a rush of wet warmth from her pussy.

If she hadn't worn panties tonight, she would be dripping all over the classroom floor. Instead she would be dripping all over his hard cock, in approximately three seconds.

Christ, the way this man affected her. The other night he'd had her totally forgetting time and place. And now, now he had her so impatient to get them both naked and panting, for the first time in her life she wished she hadn't made a hobby out of snacking on her fingernails—long ones would seriously come in handy when it came to shredding the clothes from his fine-ass body.

Speaking of fine asses . . .

"You were right—as good as that cream is, it's still only second best. I'd rather have the first." Liz flung herself at Dusty, ready to grab hold of his buttocks while she attacked his mouth, devoured his kiss, stripped away his clothes until only sun-bronzed skin kept her from all that first-class muscle and sinew.

Her hands skimmed the worn cotton of his black T-shirt en route to his delectable behind. Before they could go any farther, she found her hands pushed away from him and pressed up against the refrigerator door along with the rest of her overheated body.

Holding her wrists above her head in one hand, Dusty brought his free hand to her face. He tilted her chin up and teased a warm, damp kiss at the corner of her lips. "You don't say," he taunted, rocking up against her, pressing his dick against her swollen sex, making her ache in a way that couldn't be legal.

"Never second-guess me, Marr. Especially when you're getting what you want. I'm liable to take it away, and we both know how you naughty little boys cry when that happens."

His cocky smirk said what they were both thinking: She could never escape his viselike grip. However twisted it might be, she found herself glad for that fact in a way she would never admit to him. Her happiness shot up a level as he tugged the apron from her body with a quick jerk. That happiness flowed over into the serious jubilant range as his hand fisted in the waist of her T-shirt and yanked.

The sound of ripping cotton filled Liz's ears and spiked her heart rate. Her pussy thrummed as the torn shirt fell to the ground. Dusty's attention dropped to her breasts, half-concealed by a black bra. He had the bra off in the instant it took to pop the front clasp, and he sent the lacy garment sailing. For all she knew, her bra had landed on the range top. If the range was hot from the oven beneath, the lace could catch fire. And wouldn't burning down the building impress the cooking class's instructor? And wasn't her messed-up mind totally attempting to take over?

Cool whipped cream fingered onto her erect nipples had Liz gasping back into the moment. Dusty's mouth came down, latching onto her swollen tit and sucking at the aching crown. The heat of his mouth quickly replaced the chill of the cream. The grip on her wrists intensified. His sucking turned to tender bites that had liquid longing pumping through her veins and jetting to her core. That longing only grew as the coarse hair of his goatee abraded a nipple.

Her hips shot forward, connecting her weeping sex with the hard ridge of his cock. Brushing her nipple with his goatee a second time, he pumped his hips back toward her, pushing his shaft harder against her pussy, applying pressure at just the right angle to bring her clit to hot, hungry life.

Holy shit! Her clit was hungry.

Now there was something she'd never experienced before. Another brush of his goatee. Another pump of his hips. Her clit went from hungry to famished, tingling with its urgent want. Her sex grew heavy, unbearably moist. So damned needy. She whimpered against the erotic thrill of the foreign sensations and knew beyond a fact that, even though he had yet to move beneath her jeans and panties, he not only knew where her G-spot was, but he also had complete control over it.

"Enough of the nipple action. Get the fuck in me!"

Popping the button and easing the zipper down on her jeans, he lifted his mouth from her breast to eye her. "Aren't much one for patience, are you, babe?"

Not tonight. Going fast and keeping her mind from straying was the only way to achieve the orgasm slowly building inside her. Not even that was a guarantee. More like a chance in hell. "Now or never. Your choice."

Dusty's fingers uncoiled from her wrists. The hand at the open fly of her jeans fell away. He took a step back.

Air wheezed in between Liz's lips and died ice cold in her

throat. No way was he stopping. No way would he take her up on that "never" option. He wasn't even supposed to have an option; they were just stupid words she'd spoken to keep in line with the brash-talking woman she made herself out to be.

"In that case, see ya around."

"Don't you dare leave me like this, you dickhead!" Liz clamped her mouth shut the second the words left her mouth. It wasn't fast enough. The knowing smile that curved his lips said he'd heard the desperation in her voice loud and clear.

She opened her mouth to say something more, anything to knock the arrogant smile off his face. His fingers returned to her body before she could get a word out.

Coated with a fresh layer of whipped cream, they traveled over her breasts, across her nipples, and down the slope of her belly. She sucked in a breath as two fingers moved farther south, disappearing beneath the fly of her jeans and then the lace of her panties.

She forgot to breathe altogether when cool cream met with the heated flesh of her pussy lips. One finger speared between the slick folds, caressing the ravenous pearl of her clit, and her breathing returned as a ragged sigh.

"Now, Marr. I said now!" Liz grabbed hold of the hem of his T-shirt and tugged upward. Her mouth watered as his defined musculature came into view.

Goddamn, she could run her tongue all over him.

Then again, no she couldn't. They had to keep things moving along. They had to get to the main event. Get her off and him out of her life. He might be her brother's friend, but she'd already vowed to move out of Colin's house. Once she had her own place, she'd be sure to call ahead and check for unwanted company before dropping by Colin's.

"Like you thought I'd leave you." Dusty's drawl was strengthened with lust, and the rich, husky words stroked over her senses as effectively as his fingers stroked her labia. His fingers pushed into her cunt then, pumping with unhurried thrusts. "You know me better than that, Elizabeth. I'd never leave a woman wanting."

Gritting her teeth at his continual slow pace, she yanked at the button on the fly of his jeans. "At least not more than twice."

For an instant, his fingers stilled and he winced. His fingers started to move again, only slower than before, as if he was punishing her for bringing up his past failures—failures that she knew were all her fault.

"Those times were your own damned fault," he said as if reading her mind.

Admitting the truth to herself was one thing; she would never do so to Dusty. Instead she concentrated on his jeans. She tugged down the tab of his zipper and pushed her hand inside the snug denim. Fisting his erection, she challenged, "Prove it. Stick this infamous, monstrous cock in me and make me come."

He laughed. "I'd hardly call it infamous. Nice to see you're finally acknowledging the monstrous part, though."

Any comment she might have made in return died on her tongue as he pulled his hand from her panties and shucked the jeans down his thighs along with his boxers. His dick pushed free, standing at full, gloriously long and thick attention from a swath of dark blond pubic hair. *Monstrous* might be pushing it just a little, but only just a little.

His cock bobbed toward her, and she practically drooled with the memory of the last time she'd had his hard length buried between her lips.

How would he taste with her second favorite cream mingling with her first?

Though it took time she shouldn't be risking, Liz grabbed the bowl of whipped cream from the counter and went down on her knees. Scooping up a fingerful of cream, she took his cock in one hand and trailed a line of velvety white along the bulging vein that traveled the underside of his shaft. She followed her finger with her tongue, licking the sweet, rich substance until her tongue reached the deep purple head of his cock. Another sweet, totally male substance enlivened her taste buds.

Ah, sooo good . . . exactly the way she'd remembered.

Humming her elation, she lapped at the silky fluid and then sank her mouth onto his dick as far as she could take him. Dusty's fingers threaded through her short hair, gripping none too gently. She applied pressure, pumping his erection with her lips while her tongue caressed the highly sensitive skin in slow circles. His full-bodied groan echoed off the classroom walls and sent a fresh wave of juices trickling into her panties.

"What happened to not blowing anything but my time?"

The words sliced through Liz. Damnit, he was right. As much as she thrived on going down on him and tasting his cum, it couldn't be happening tonight, or ever.

She jerked her mouth from his shaft and stood. Without ceremony, she toed off her sneakers and socks, then removed her jeans and panties and left them in a pile next to her bare feet.

She cast him an assessing look, doing her best to camouflage the excitement that filled her as her gaze slid over his big cock made shiny wet by her mouth. "I was making sure you had enough staying power to actually finish the job for once. Since you planned this, I'm assuming you have a condom?"

"What makes you so sure I planned this?"

Hearing his defensive tone, she met his eyes. They held . . . what? Anger over her accusation? Or was it disappointment that she'd caught on to his ruse? "Don't tell me you think you're so suave I'd miss the setup. Lucky for you, I'm in the mood to get laid and am nice enough to give you another try at locating my G-spot."

Whatever emotion had been in Dusty's eyes gave way to blistering challenge as he grabbed hold of her wrist and yanked her back against the refrigerator door. One of the fingers from his free hand was between her thighs and pushing past her pussy lips before she could get out a breath.

"As I recall"—he plunged deep into the slick valley of her sex and stroked with vigor—"it was right about here."

Liz swallowed her gasp as the violent need to explode clawed at her from deep within. She couldn't help the breathless quality of her voice. "That's not it," she lied.

He pulled out of her, only to plunge back in, this time adding a second finger and quickening his pace. Her eyes widened with the exquisite pressure rippling through her body and soul.

Dusty let out a deep, rolling chuckle. "Lying little bitch."

"So what?" she bit out, struggling not to chase his fingers with her body each time he withdrew. "Anyone can find it with their fingers. It takes a real man to do it with his dick."

A gorgeously cocky grin claimed his mouth. "Real man this, babe."

As quickly as he'd pushed into her with his fingers, he lifted a condom from his jeans pocket and sheathed himself, then grabbed her around the waist, lifted her up his body, and plunged into her slick heat. For an instant, as her legs automatically wound around his waist and his monstrous member filled her, Liz could only gasp and blink. Then all she could do was stare, openmouthed and panting, as her pussy gobbled up his cock, again and again, and raw desire unfurled thick as honey in her belly.

Oh gawd! The man had to-die-for positioning. Each thrust had his shaft rubbing over her clit, the back and forth slide of his pubis adding delicious friction.

Thick, white cream coated both of their sexes and tangled in their pubic hair. Some of it might be whipped cream, but sure as hell not all. Make that not even close to most of it. No, most of it was the juices gushing from her cunt.

From the sweltering heat stealing over her body to the quaking that started in her toes and ended in her nipples, orgasm was building, ready to erupt, to tear through her limb from limb and have her crying out her rapture.

Only a truly experienced man could accomplish such a seemingly impossible task so quickly. Only a man-whore. Which was what Dusty was. But Liz wasn't going to think about that. No way. No how. She was going to be one with that stick of Juicy Fruit and stop thinking altogether. Stop focusing. Give herself over to the moment, to her lust, to the rich, musky scent of sex and something else infiltrating her senses.

What else? It didn't smell good. It smelled, sort of . . . not good. "Wait."

The thrust of his hips ceased. He looked up from the vicinity of her breasts to ask incredulously, "Wait?"

She dragged in a long breath. Burning. It smelled like something was burning. Not like the burning lace of her bra, but . . . Jesus H. Christ! The pie. The pie was burning.

"What am I waiting for?"

She had to block the smell out. The big one was seconds away. The long-awaited O. The climax that would assuage Dusty's wounded ego and stop him from wanting her ever again. The big dickhead would be all but out of her life. Yes, she wanted that. Wanted orgasm even more.

"Nothing. Keep going." Tangling her arms around his neck, Liz brought them breasts-to-chest. She buried her tongue in his mouth and pumped her hips.

Cupping her naked ass in his large palms, he gave in to her silent encouragement. He resumed the pace, thrusting into her with long, hard, well-practiced strokes as his warm, silky tongue lapped at hers.

Seconds ago those strokes had had her ready to spiral into the great beyond of Orgasm Land. Those strokes still felt decent, but they weren't pushing her higher anymore. His kiss was good, but wasn't evoking the magical warmth and wetness she felt every other time he'd stuck his tongue in her mouth. The wild tattoo of her heart and the hasty speed of her breathing had slowed considerably.

Lust was taking a fast boat to Not-Gonna-Climax Land.

Shit. Shit. And shit.

Her and her goddamned ever-thinking mind. She couldn't block out the smell. Couldn't block out the visual of burned pie. Couldn't stop the thought that she wasn't her slut of a mother. If she were her mother, or even the sex-crazed version of Liz she'd led most everyone to buy into, she would be coming up a storm and basking in the glow of climax. Instead she was Liz the never-gonna-come farce.

At least that Liz had values. That Liz had a good reason for not being able to dismiss the burning smell. Because unlike her mother, she was incapable of shutting out the things that mattered most. This class mattered more than an orgasm ever could. It was a step on the way to becoming something more than an easily replaceable waitress. Warped as it sounded, given her penchant for destroying nearly every recipe she attempted, she had dreams of owning a pastry shop. And, warped as it sounded, she would make that dream come true, starting with passing this class.

Burnt pie didn't equate to a passing grade.

She had to make Dusty stop with the damned thrusting and tongue-play already. But she couldn't just end things the way she had the last two times. She couldn't because he would keep coming back until he made her climax and his pathetic big-ass ego could be put to rest.

Fake it.

Yes, she could do that. Had done it dozens of times in the past, when she'd either grown tired of the act or she'd been doing a guy she cared about enough to not tarnish his ego over her deficiencies. Those guys had been too caught up in their own orgasm to notice if hers wasn't exactly bona fide. Dusty might be a man-whore with a reputation of providing more female orgasms than there were women in the state of Georgia, but no way would he catch on.

She had to fake it, for the sake of burned desserts and wannabe pastry chefs, who could barely handle breaking an egg, everywhere.

Forcing her thoughts back into the moment, she grabbed hold of his shoulders and lifted from his mouth. Tossing back her head, she ground her hips against his and rode him hard and fast.

One-one-thousand. Two-one-thousand. Three-one-thousand.

The burning smell sneaked up and invaded her thoughts once more. If she allowed any more buildup time, the pie would be toast and not the kind that was edible.

Nipping her short nails into the soft cotton of his T-shirt, Liz sang out, "Ohmigawd!" She snapped her eyes shut and whimpered long and loud. "Yes. Yes. Yes. Right there. Oh yes! I can feel you all the way to my throat. So deep. So good. Oh wow. This is it. This is . . . I'm com-ing!"

Dusty buried his face in the crook of her neck. His warm, hasty breaths caressed her ear. His grip on her ass strengthened. The push of his dick into her body turned erratic. "Right there with you, babe," he growled. "Oh fuck, am I ever."

The last of the words barely left his mouth when she felt the hot push of cum filling up the condom. Thank God, it was finally over.

Tossing in one last pump, grind, and moan for good show, Liz released his shoulders and glanced past him. "What great timing! The pie's done."

"The pie's done?"

His voice was still thick with lust, but he didn't sound happy. Apparently, he and his enormous ego had been expecting a round of applause.

Looking back at his far-from-elated expression, she smiled. "Sorry. You were awesome. One of the best I've ever had." She forgot about the smile then and swatted his arm. "Now, let me the fuck down. If that pie's burned, your ass is dead."

5

She'd faked it. Son of a bitch, she'd faked it.

Dusty pushed through the galley door of the bar's kitchen. He poured himself a draft from the Budweiser tap and settled onto a stool at the end of the bar. Early afternoon on a Thursday, the place was dead aside from a handful of retired locals and those patrons who worked nights. Damned good thing, too, because the last thing he felt like doing was entertaining customers.

Tossing back a long drink of ale, he replayed the previous night in his head. He hadn't planned on opening up about his childhood even remotely, but doing so had accomplished the goal he'd set out to attain. The revelation had been enough to get Liz talking to him without malice burning in her eyes. And that had been enough to give him the inside track straight to her panties.

He'd had her good and wet for him, breathing hard and anxious to fuck. Up until the moment the remnants of his own climax washed away, he hadn't realized anything was off. The moment the blood returned to his brain, he'd known, though.

Liz had been neither gasping for breath nor basking in post-climax glow, but speaking as calmly as if he'd just served her up an extra crispy char burger instead of a mind-blowing orgasm.

She'd claimed that she'd been on to his game from the moment he'd arrived at the cooking class. She'd also claimed that he was as lousy a lay as a man could be. He'd told himself she was wrong, a true whack-job to believe such a thing. But what if she wasn't? What if he was nowhere near the sexual marvel the women in his past had led him to believe? What if Liz really had known his MO last night and had only given in to him in the hopes he would leave her alone from that point onward? She could easily have faked her excited expression and words. That didn't explain her wetness.

Shit, he shouldn't care why she'd faked it.

He should do what he'd told himself he would do earlier this week and forget Liz's accusation by moving on to a woman eager to remind him that his reputation as an expert lover was a tried-and-true fact. He should, but one word refused to stop niggling at him. One word that had haunted him until the day he'd left his hometown behind.

Failure.

"Did hell freeze over, or since when is drowning your sorrows in an early afternoon beer your style?"

Dusty pulled free of his thoughts at the sound of Colin's voice. A glance at his nearly empty beer mug proved his friend almost accurate. Sorrows might not be the right word, but it appeared he'd been drowning his thoughts anyway.

Setting the mug on the bar, he nodded at Colin. Colin had gotten his light brown hair and green eyes from his and Liz's father's first wife, while Liz's ebony hair and olive-skinned complexion came from their father's second wife—neither woman was any longer in the picture. Aside from sharing a tall, toned build, the two siblings looked nothing alike. That didn't stop thoughts of Liz from resurfacing.

If anyone could explain Liz, it was her brother. And if there was one thing Dusty would never ask Colin, it was about his sister. Ever since Colin had walked in on Liz giving Dusty a blow job, Liz was an off-limits topic. Dusty couldn't blame Colin for that. Hypocritical as it might be, Dusty would be pissed to find his own sister screwing a guy she claimed to hate for the mere sake of pleasure.

He remembered the creep in pink then. Even the idea of Liz acting that way with some random guy disturbed Dusty. Because she was his friend's sister and he felt a sense of obligation to watch out for her. Any other reason was implausible.

Dusty signaled to Jen to get Colin a beer. He shot Colin a teasing grin as his friend settled onto a bar stool. "You are still alive, man. I was starting to think married life had gotten the best of ya."

Colin snorted. "Married life, hell. Do I look shackled and drawn to you? All right, so I'm guilty of the shackled thing from time to time, but there's nothing quite as sexy as Joyce on a power trip with a pair of handcuffs."

"I should have swept her up when I had the chance." The petite blonde had turned out to be on the softer side, rather than the she-devil in the tit-popping top she'd first presented herself as, and, therefore, nowhere near to Dusty's type. Still, he would rather be sleeping with a woman who wasn't his norm than trying to figure out the inner workings of Liz's warped mind.

"We might not be headed to the altar yet, but Joyce is a relationship person." Accusation laced Colin's words.

Had Liz let on to her brother about sleeping with Dusty again? Though she made it clear she wasn't the relationship type, Colin wanted to see her with a steady guy. Raising an eyebrow at his friend, Dusty tested the waters. "That s'posed to be your way of saying I'm not?"

Colin laughed. "Shit no, you're not. I've never seen you

with the same woman more than a couple nights in a row. The point was, you two never would've cut it."

"People change."

Colin eyed him as if he'd sprouted two heads. "Did I miss something?"

If he had, then Dusty had missed it, too. People did change, but he wasn't one of those people. He loved women and had no plans to spread himself thin with any one in particular. As soon as he gave Liz a real orgasm and erased that nasty niggling *failure* word from his mind, he would be back to working the playing field.

Dusty shrugged. "Nothing major. I made the mistake of hooking up with a flake one too many times. You know, the kind of chick that messes with your head?"

Jen set a cocktail napkin down on the bar in front of Colin and placed a bottle of his regular beer on top. Colin thanked the bartender, then, eyeing Dusty speculatively, took a long drink. He set the bottle down, hesitating a few seconds before asking, "This flake have a name?"

The look in his eyes made it clear that "Is the flake's name Liz?" was the question Colin really wanted to ask. Dusty guessed he hedged to not ruin the conversation should he be wrong. For the sake of keeping things light, he lied. "No one you'd know. She's not from around here."

"Then why let her get to you? She'll be gone soon enough."

"Yeah. I doubt she'll ever pass by this way again. Hardly my fault if she's frigid anyway."

Warmth returned to Colin's expression. Slapping a hand on the bar, he let out a boisterous laugh. "No fucking way. You mean to tell me there's a woman out there who isn't interested in sleeping with you?"

Colin and he had tossed barbs at each other from the day they'd met. Obviously Liz's accusations and behavior were working overtime on his ego, because his friend's question pricked damned deep. "She's slept with me a couple times," he said humorlessly. "It's the orgasm part she can't handle."

Colin's look went from amused to stunned. "You can't make her come?"

Once more the question pricked. If anyone had been sitting near enough to hear their conversation, they might well have been fighting words. As it was, Dusty chose to ignore the sting. "She faked it."

"Ouch. Talk about the mighty falling. Did you ask her about it?"

About faking an orgasm? The only thing that would have accomplished was Liz decking him. "Like I said, she's from outta town. Probably just a nutcase."

"Maybe. Or maybe she's the type who needs more than the physical, or a slow hand, to get off for real." Colin reached for his beer, pausing with the bottle inches from his mouth to utter a sarcastic, "Way I hear it, not every woman falls into bed on the first date."

"She's not looking for love. Or shy when it comes to sex."

Colin set his beer back down without taking a drink. He narrowed his gaze assessingly. "For someone just passing through, you know her damned well."

Dusty shrugged, wishing he'd played his friend's comment off as the joke it was intended. "You know I won't sleep with a woman who's after more than a night or two. She made it clear she's not in the market for anything lasting."

Colin continued to eye him, his gaze shrewd. Finally, he looked away and lifted his beer for a drink. He turned his attention to the NCAA football game playing on one of the two ceiling-mounted TVs behind the bar. A full minute had passed when he looked back. Dusty assumed it would be to comment on the game. Instead Colin said, "I never planned to have another relationship after the way Marlene screwed around on me."

Mention of Colin's cheating ex-wife had always bothered Dusty. Before it had been the kind of bother that had to do with sympathy for his friend. This time it was the kind of bother that felt aimed directly at Dusty and ate at his gut. "What's your point?"

"Sometimes we're the last to know what we want. Maybe there's a commitment man in you after all. Maybe the reason you can't shake thoughts of this so-called flake and your inability to please her is because you, God forbid, care about her. Maybe she's the one you want to be committed with."

Dusty didn't bother to hold back his snort of laughter. Liz had him wanting to be committed, all right. Straight to the loony bin.

Whipped cream.

The food-prep area of the restaurant faded away as Liz stared at the sundae in her hand, waiting to be delivered to her family of four.

How could she be expected to serve something so overtly sexual to a kid?

A layer of fluffy cream had never looked so indecent. Then there was that ridiculously huge banana poking through the whipped cream in a display too phallic to miss. Gawd, there were even nuts surrounding the banana. A bunch of little nuts instead of two sizeable ones, but it didn't matter.

Nope, it didn't matter a bit; she was already long gone.

Her mind raced to the previous night and going down on her knees to take Dusty's huge cock in her mouth. With any other man, oral sex was something she could take or leave. With him, she wanted to take it, again and again. Wanted to wrap her mouth around his luscious member and suck him dry.

Last night he hadn't let her savor long. Not that it had been any hardship to stop fucking him with her mouth so that she could do so with her body. He'd had her wet from the instant he'd pushed her up against the refrigerator. Hell, from the instant he'd bent down next to her and talked about biting, sucking, blowing, fondling . . .

Her panties grew moist with the memory of his rough voice so near to her ear. Her nipples leapt to attention at the thought of the cool cream sliding over them, followed by his hot mouth and that wonderfully coarse goatee. She held little doubt that if she hadn't ordered him to stop the nipple-play and get to the main event, he would have been able to turn her into one of those women who came from nipple stimulation alone. No doubt at all he could have popped her orgasm cherry.

"Something wrong?" Diane's soft voice piped in from behind her.

Yes. She was turning into a bigger head case than ever if she honestly found a sundae sexual.

Liz broke from her ogling to look at the late-forties, graying brunette dressed in the same tuxedo-style uniform she wore. The difference was her friend's ample chest combated the manliness of the outfit. "No. I was just thinking."

Diane's lips crooked in a knowing smile that brought small laugh lines to the corners of her mouth. "He musta been something."

"Who?"

"Whoever it was that left you with thoughts hot enough to melt ice cream." Amusement lighting her gray eyes, she nodded at the sundae in Liz's hand.

Liz groaned at the soppy state of the dish. With all that melted ice cream and whipped cream, it looked like the banana had just gotten off in a major way. How pathetic was that? Even fruit was more capable of getting off than her.

Yep. Definitely a head case, to be envious of the orgasm of an inanimate object.

"He was no one. No one important, that is," Liz corrected, remembering this was Diane, the woman who expected her to tell at least three wild sex tales a week, all of which ended with her coming so hard the force of climax left her temporarily blind. She forced a wicked smile. "But then, they never are."

And they weren't. No man was important enough to burn her pie over. Not even one who could conquer her jealousy over climaxing fruit. Not even one who, ever since he'd brought up his far-from-ideal youth, had left questions spinning in her mind. She wasn't asking those questions, and she sure as shit wasn't giving in to her jealousy by granting Dusty yet another try at providing her with a real orgasm.

So what if she never had her orgasm cherry popped? She would rather be an orgasm virgin who knew how to focus on those things that mattered than a hormone-driven slut any day.

"What are you doing here?"

Dusty bit back his laughter over Liz's murderous expression. He glanced around the community center classroom and then back at her, feigning confusion. "It's Wednesday night, right? The cooking class?"

She gritted her teeth, as if keeping her voice on a relatively calm level cost her dearly. "Yes, it's Wednesday night and the cooking class, but that doesn't answer my question. Why are *you* here? You got what you wanted."

Not even close. He wanted her quaking in his hands, too caught up in the throes of climax to consider faking it.

The last week had proven that Colin was partly accurate with his commitment assessment. Dusty was committed to Liz. Committed to giving her an orgasm that would remove any doubt of his pleasuring abilities. If that took a little time and patience, then he was in for the long haul.

He smirked. "Nice to see your ego's still healthy as ever, babe. But like I told ya last week, I'm taking this class to learn to be a better cook. Anything I got after class was a side benefit."

Liz studied him a few seconds, gaze narrowed, then said quietly, "I hope you enjoyed it, because that side benefit won't be happening again." She turned to the refrigerator to get out the ingredients for tonight's class, but then quickly turned back. A naughty smile curved her lips, plumping them enticingly.

Dusty's thoughts voyaged to the previous week and the feel of those satiny lips once again wrapped around his dick. His cock stirred to life, snugging his jeans tight in the front. He'd been an ass to speak words he knew would make her stop sucking him. From her hums of satisfaction, she'd enjoyed it a great deal. God knew he'd been ready to explode.

Liz retreated from the refrigerator to the counter he reclined against. Her hand settled on his forearm, stroking leisurely, while the muscles beneath her palm corded. Hundreds of women had touched him this way; never before had it made his pulse hammer. That hammering only intensified as she brought her lips to his ear and whispered, "I won't lie, Marr, you were good, but then so were the rest of the guys I screwed last week. There are way too many men out there to waste my time on one who can only finish the job a third of the time."

The feel of her warm breath warred with the cool accusation in her words. She was trying to piss him off. She was doing a damned good job.

As much as he would like to dismiss it, the roiling in his gut had nothing to do with the fact that she had yet to climax for him and everything to do with the mention of screwing other guys. It was because she was his friend's sister, he reminded himself. A woman he'd known, at least marginally, for years. It only made sense he would feel a certain amount of protection toward her. Why that protection level had risen in the last couple of months wasn't something Dusty cared to question.

"Right," he said nonchalantly. "You don't do relationships."

She reared back as if he'd slapped her. "You know damned

well I don't," she said loudly. Clearly too loudly, as she grimaced and sent a nervous look around the room. She shifted from foot to foot a few seconds and then returned to the refrigerator.

The hasty retort and her reaction further agitated his gut. Something told Dusty to change the topic. For the sake of figuring out what made her tick, he forged on. "Refresh my memory. Why is that?"

"*That* is none of your business."

"I can ask Colin."

Yanking the refrigerator door open, Liz shot him a glare. "Do I look like an idiot? No way would you bring my name and the word *relationship* up around him."

No way in hell, and that just meant he needed to probe her for an answer all the more. She squatted and pulled open the crisper drawer. He pushed off the counter and came up behind her. "So, what's on the menu tonight?"

Without looking at him, she handed out two cloves of garlic. "Shrimp scampi, and pull-eaze don't expect me to believe you're going to let that question drop. You're going to try to pull the same kind of crap you did last week. Forget it. I'm not interested."

He set the garlic on the counter. Still not looking at him, she stood, grabbed a stick of butter from the side bin, and held it out. Sliding his fingers up the stick, Dusty settled them over hers. He leaned inward, until he could feel the heat emanating off her body, smell her scent on the air, Ivory soap undercoated with a feminine musk that gave her away.

Not only was she interested in a repeat of last Wednesday night, she was wet for him even now.

Though he'd vowed to be patient, he couldn't resist rubbing his fingers over the smooth backs of hers. "Warm butter on hot skin isn't your thing, eh?"

Liz tensed. "I like it fine, with the right guy. You aren't him."

No? Then how could his touch get to her so completely?

That she was suggesting there was one right guy caught up with Dusty then. Releasing her fingers, he stepped back and set the butter on the counter, slowly digesting the idea that Colin's commitment theory could be dead on.

Was it possible that Liz could only climax when emotions were involved?

She had the reputation of a woman who loved sex and regularly partook of it with strangers and friends alike. What if that reputation was a sham? Colin complained about Liz sharing the details of her many sexual exploits with him, but had her brother ever seen her come home with anyone outside of Dusty, or were the men she spoke of as big of a lie as her mystery man Aiden had turned out to be?

He pressed the idea. "Thank God for that. In case you've forgotten, I'm not exactly Mr. Relationship. Makes me damned glad I'm a man."

"Yeah, because that big dick of yours would look pretty odd on a woman."

"I'm serious. A lot of women can't do the straight sex thing. They can sleep with every Ron, Mick, and Larry who passes by, but the odds of climaxing aren't good. They need the emotional connection."

Liz spun back so fast it was a wonder she didn't get whiplash. "You really don't know jack about women, do you, Marr? Of all the asinine things you've said, that has to be the biggest load of crap ever."

The words threatened to take a bite out of his ego. He pushed them aside to concentrate on her expression. Now it was amused, but for a second there he could have sworn he saw interest. "You don't have that problem, then? You get off whether you've been dating a guy for months or only known him a few minutes?"

"I got off with you, didn't I?"

No. She hadn't. Not for real.

Liz had nearly convinced him that the problem was his, that he'd become a failure at the one thing he was truly good at. It seemed that wasn't the case. It seemed the fault was neither of theirs, but a simple matter of him not being the right guy for her.

If Dusty wasn't as thrilled about the discovery as he should be, it was because he'd never gotten the chance to set his ego right. Then again, there was nothing to set right. He'd never stopped being a champion lover, just tangled with a woman who needed more than sex.

"Right," he said as she turned back to the refrigerator. "That isn't a problem for you. You're a regular coming machine." A coming machine he would never get to experience firsthand. And that was fine. So what if she gave killer head? That didn't mean a thing if, when all was said and done, he was the only one left sated.

Liz grabbed a package of raw shrimp and handed it to him. He accepted it along with the knowledge they weren't meant to be fuck friends. That being the case, they might as well try at platonic ones. Now that he'd signed up for the cooking class, Dusty couldn't miss the value in learning to be a better cook for the sake of the bar. Whether she liked it or not, Liz was stuck with him for the duration.

She'd shown an interest in his family the previous week. It followed she would be as interested in talking about her own. He knew Colin nearly as well as she did, but her mother was a mystery and her father almost as much so. "What are your parents like?"

"My mom's a slut." Audibly smacking her lips shut around the words and the disdain that dripped from them, she glanced tensely around the classroom.

If he'd been uncertain of her player reputation being a sham, he held no doubt now. Someone who got around even half as much as she claimed to would never hold such scorn for another's behavior. "Take it you guys don't get along?"

Liz crossed her arms and steeled her gaze. "I swear I've said like a hundred times that my life is none of your business, but no, we don't get along. It's hard to get along with someone you see once a year if you're lucky. And then if you're even luckier, she doesn't take off midway through the visit to fuck some guy who managed to get her panties wet from across the room."

Ouch. No matter how quietly she'd spoken, the hurt in her voice couldn't be masked. It was laced with a bitterness he knew only too well. The urge to comfort was automatic. Well aware of how she would react to his comforting, Dusty cast the urge aside to offer a grin, followed by a low, appreciative whistle. "Wet from across the room. Now, there's a guy I'd like to meet."

The response had the desired effect. The hurt evaporated from her expression, and she laughed loudly before slapping him on the arm. "Quit trying to get on my good side and get the damned skillet out, Marr."

6

Liz tossed aside the suspense novel she'd laid down on her bed to read an hour ago. She'd yet to make it past page one. With a disgusted sigh, she sat, moved up the bed, and sank back against the headboard.

Reading was as pointless as anything else she'd attempted that required a brain in the last three weeks. Her thoughts always voyaged to one man. One idiot who'd managed to take up residence in her head and refused to budge.

Then there was the effect Dusty had on the rest of her.

Since the night she'd faked orgasm, the man had been living in her dreams, doing things so erotic with those killer hands and mouth and dynamite body that they had to border on criminal. In her dreams, she was no orgasm virgin, but a woman who came hard and plentifully. In her dreams, Dusty couldn't get enough of her, needing to touch her, kiss her, impale himself inside her every few hours or risk insanity. In reality, he didn't want a thing to do with her, outside of friendship.

Friendship, hah!

She'd guessed that once he thought he'd given her an orgasm, his attempts at getting into her pants would end, or at least lessen. She never would have imagined in a million damned years he would want to befriend her.

How was such a thing even possible? He wasn't a man who had platonic friendships with single females under the age of eighty. And Liz didn't make friends with dickheads. Only, Dusty wasn't acting like a dickhead driven by his gonads but the gentleman the hired help had raised him to be.

Aside from a bit of initial flirtation during the cooking class three weeks ago, he no longer even looked at her suggestively. Instead he made small talk, telling her how he'd come to start up Dusty's Backroom and why he'd chosen Georgia for his home. He made her laugh at least a dozen times a class with his quirky and generally sarcastic remarks, and he never pressed for more information on her mother or her personality. The lone time he'd brushed her thigh with his, he'd apologized.

Apologized, of all the goddamned things!

"Ah!" Liz slammed her head back against the headboard.

Gawd, how she wanted to scream at him, "Just knock the fuck off and focus on getting me naked already!" She could ignore his seduction attempts, at least on the surface. She didn't have a defense against his sincerity. All she could do was pretend she wasn't listening, pretend she didn't care, pretend she didn't want to hear more each time he offered another snippet on his life that belied nearly every bad thing she'd ever told herself about him.

If he was any other guy, she would vent to Kristi and Fiona—it had been over three weeks since she'd chatted with the *G-Spot* ladies and, while she'd sent them an "I'm alive, just swamped" e-mail, they were bound to be worried. After the way she'd badmouthed Dusty and made it clear that she had no intention of sleeping with him again, she couldn't bring herself to share this latest development.

There had to be someone else to offer advice. Someone who could understand she needed things to return to the way they used to be, with her loathing Dusty and him making it his greatest quest to prove himself a modern-day Don Juan to every female from here to Tallahassee, present company included.

"Unless you plan to make love to my sleeping body, you'd best get your butt upstairs immediately!" Joyce shouted from the neighboring bedroom.

With a groan over the thought of yet another wall-banging, multi-orgasm sex-capade between Joyce and Colin, Liz closed her eyes and wished she'd found an apartment by now. Her eyes snapped back open with the knowledge of how her brother and his girlfriend had come to be. Colin had tried to pretend he didn't want Joyce again after a couple rounds of sex, but somehow she'd convinced him otherwise. Was it a somehow that would work on Dusty?

Liz climbed from bed and moved quickly to the door of the next bedroom. Colin would spot a red flag if he overheard her asking Joyce questions about sex, so she'd best make this fast.

The floorboard creaked beneath Liz's feet as she stepped into her brother's bedroom. Joyce looked up from where she lay beneath the covers, an expectant smile curving her unpainted lips and lighting her hazel eyes. That smile became guilty when she realized it was Liz who'd entered the room. "Oops. I woke you with my yelling. Sorry."

"I was already awake. I just . . ." Was out of her mind if she thought the petite blonde looking at her so sheepishly could really help. "Never mind. Col will be up any minute, so let me leave you guys—"

"No. Come in." Joyce pulled back the covers and climbed out of bed.

A little red nightie with nearly invisible straps and an even smaller hemline clung to a short but curvaceously feminine body that Liz could only dream of having. The slinky outfit shouted sex and reinforced Liz's reason for coming in here. Joyce might be sheepish at times, but the woman knew a thing or two about enticing the opposite sex.

"Colin's finishing a landscaping estimate for an early morning meeting. He'll be at least another few minutes."

Colin focused on his landscaping company a lot less since Joyce had entered his life. Still, Liz knew if he had a morning meeting, he would invest as much time as needed to be prepared. And that meant she had no excuse not to stay and seek advice from Joyce.

"It's just . . ." Liz looked down to find herself shifting from foot to foot. Damn, she hated that excited habit. Hated a hundred times more that Dusty could be the source of her restlessness. Forcing herself to stand still, she blurted, "There's this guy and—"

Joyce's eyes went wide and she gasped. "You're honestly asking me about a guy? You know my reputation with men is far from extensive."

"You're with my brother, aren't you?"

"Yes, but—"

"Why are you? What convinced him to let you back into his bed after he swore he was through with you? Was it a simple matter of getting naked and throwing yourself at him?"

"I didn't throw myself at him." Joyce laughed softly. "All right, I suppose I did, but not the way you're implying. Colin came around because, well, I guess because I was stuck in his head as much as he was in mine."

"So, you were driving each other nuts?" Now that was an interesting take on things. Was Dusty faking the whole friendship thing while in reality he still wanted her every bit as much as she wanted him?

Waaaait a minute!

She didn't want him. Okay, so maybe parts of her body gushed with wetness each time she thought his name, but that wasn't why she was asking these questions. She just wanted him to want her so that he would stop being so damned nice and friendly.

"We were both fighting our feelings for each other," Joyce explained, her blissful smile reflected in her words. "We share things in common that matter, things that drew us together and allowed us to understand each other in a way most people never could. It's really a blessing that we met."

And lovey-dovey in a way that made Liz want to stick her finger down her throat and make gagging sounds. That childish impulse aside, she couldn't stop from smiling back or stop the unwanted twinge of jealousy that sparked through her.

"You're lucky to have each other." Wistfulness she had no desire to feel sounded in her voice. Hoping she was the only one who'd detected it, she murmured a "thanks" and hurried for the door.

"Does this guy know how you feel?" Joyce inquired.

Inches from the safety of the doorway, Liz spun back to snap, "I don't feel a goddamned thing." Joyce blanched and guilt shot through Liz. She could be nasty around Dusty and have no qualms over it—at least the man-whore version of him—but Joyce and Colin she never acted so utterly mean around. "Sorry. I'm tired. Obviously it's making me an even bigger bitch than normal."

The color returned to Joyce's cheeks and she smiled. "You're not a bitch. Colin says you can be rough around the edges, but all I've ever seen is a strong woman who knows what she wants. I respect that."

"Thanks." Now, if only she was right.

"Everything okay in here?" Colin questioned from behind Liz.

Liz stepped to the side to let him into the bedroom. Joyce's gaze warmed as it landed on Colin, and Liz's jealousy spiked again. She rubbed a hand over her stomach, urging away the tight sensation. She had no reason to be jealous of their relationship and the obvious affection they shared. She didn't do relationships or emotions. Didn't want a full-time man in her life, now or ever.

Hell, it probably wasn't even jealousy she was feeling. It was probably gas from the broccoli she'd had at lunch.

"Everything's fine," Joyce assured. "Just having some girl talk."

"Right," Colin said dryly. "In other words, Liz is recounting yet another one of her breathless orgasm tales."

"Actually she was asking—"

"You don't want to hear about 'em, bro, don't bring 'em up," Liz cut her off quickly. Joyce mouthed an "oh" of understanding. "Speaking of orgasms, my vibrator's calling. You two kids have fun. And, Col, don't forget to wear a little rubber raincoat. Wouldn't want that baby carriage coming before the marriage."

He grimaced and then laughed. "Just what I always wanted, sex advice from my little sister." His amused look was replaced with sobriety. "Do yourself a favor, Liz, and don't let Penny's behavior shape yours. You aren't her, and you never will be. You *can* do relationships, and you *aren't* immune to love."

By mutual agreement, they hardly ever spoke of their mothers. That Colin brought her mom up now meant he'd overheard at least part of her conversation with Joyce. Either that or Dusty had asked him the question he'd threatened to ask three weeks ago: Why didn't Liz do relationships? It had to be the former because the latter would raise too much speculation. Either way, it didn't matter, because she wasn't in the market for a man and she sure as shit didn't do love, not even if opening herself up to the emotion came with the promise of not one orgasm but many.

With a parting "Don't do anything I wouldn't do," Liz closed their bedroom door and went back to her room. Sinking onto her bed, she shook away the idea of women who could only come when under the influence of caring emotions. It was a ridiculous notion Dusty had put into her head. One she had no intention of believing, since she never planned to get that wrapped up with any man. But she hoped to hell to experience at least one orgasm in this lifetime.

Blood gushed onto the bar in a crimson stream. Liz closed her eyes and tried not to breathe in the metallic scent. The throb of her cut finger was bad enough. Really, she ought to know better than to be holding a beer bottle when Dusty was bent over a pool table a mere fifty feet away. One look at his taut ass in the well-worn blue jeans and the bottle had become a two-piece weapon of broken, jagged glass.

"You really sliced it good," Jen said when the bar rag she tossed Liz's way failed to staunch the flow of blood. "You're going to need more than that towel." Over the slow-paced lyrics of a country song and the din and smoke of the usual Saturday night crowd, she shouted, "Dusty!"

He glanced over from the pool tables, blond eyebrows drawn together with curiosity. His gaze went to Jen, then, at the bartender's nod, skipped to Liz. Their eyes met, locked. Heat registered, warmed, spun out of control. Liz sucked in a breath as her heart took off. Oh yeah, he was *sooo* faking the friendship thing. No man who was after friendship alone would look at a woman with those wickedly lustful eyes.

Dusty started over. Sweat popped out on her palms. She inhaled another breath, dragged her sticky palms along the thighs of her jeans, and screeched like a banshee.

Jesus H. Christ! One hot look from the idiot and she'd forgotten all about the gaping hole in her finger.

Dusty was at her side before she could look back up. He

grabbed hold of her hand and turned it over in his, inspecting her injury. "What happened? Are you okay?"

Had his hand always been so warm, or why did it feel like hers was going to go up in flames where he touched it? Liz shut out the inferno of heat climbing up her arm to focus on his questions. He'd spoken louder than necessary, even over the boisterous crowd. The lust she'd detected in his eyes had faded to something else.

Worry? Was he worried about her? She didn't want him worried about her.

She attempted to jerk her hand free. He held firm, his eyes narrowing. "You can be bitchy all you want later. Right now you need help."

Her unease caved to a grin. He wasn't being nice. Okay, he was in actions, but not words. She'd come here tonight to get things back to the level she needed them on, and while she hadn't planned to start that out via slicing her finger open, karma was being its usual twisted self.

"We have a first-aid kit, right?" Jen asked.

"Yeah," Dusty answered without taking his eyes off Liz's face. "It's too crowded out here. I'll fix you up in back."

Her mouth fell open with his no-arguments tone, and she just managed to stop herself from voicing a crass denial. She had him where she wanted him. She would be an even bigger head case than usual if she let the opportunity slip past. At the same time, she couldn't give in without a little bluster. "Fine. I'll go, but only if you get your damned paws off of me."

A smirk flirted with his mouth that suggested he knew exactly how much she liked his paws on her. Instead of speaking the words, he let her hand free. Wrapping the bloodied bar rag around her finger, Liz followed him through the crowd to the galley door that led to the back of the bar. She'd worked in a number of restaurants and bars alike. While the parts of establishments the customers could see were generally neat and tidy, the kitchens were only clean enough to pass health codes. The kitchen of Dusty's Backroom gleamed from the silver cast of the ovens to the plastic tube rails that held the call liquor.

A thirtysomething guy in a white chef hat with a sable ponytail swinging from its back side said hello as they passed the hot food pickup area. It registered that he could be Matt, the guy who'd walked in on Dusty going down on her on the pool table several weeks ago. Liz was too in awe of the place to work up any shame. When the day arrived that she was done butchering recipes and ready to open her pastry shop, it would be run with the same tidiness and obvious efficiency.

"I'm impressed," she said when Dusty stopped in front of a closed door at the rear of the kitchen. "I've seen a lot of kitchens in my time, and this place really shines."

He opened the door to reveal a small bathroom painted eggshell white, trimmed with sage green. She moved inside, noting the curtained-off shower stall that took up much of the right side of the room. The *snick* of the closing door had her turning back to discover exactly how much of the room the stall occupied.

He eyed her skeptically. "Exactly how many shots have you had tonight?"

Zero. And suddenly that wasn't even close to enough.

Dusty took a step forward, and Liz's breath hitched in. She forgot all about the sparkling kitchen and concentrated on not shifting from foot to foot. No way would she let him think it bothered her to be alone with him in such an intimate setting. She mentally rolled her eyes. Really, the employee bathroom of a bar was *such* a romantic spot. But damn if it didn't feel that way, with him standing barely a foot away, eating up her personal space with that big, beautiful body. He wore a white linen dress shirt, sleeves rolled up to reveal mouthwatering biceps and the collar unbuttoned far enough to expose a dusting of dirty-blond chest hair over suntanned flesh. Stubble blued his square jawline and added to the rugged appeal of his goatee. His scent curled upward, some rich, earthy cologne that wafted on the air to do a number on her senses.

Heat unfurled in her belly, licked its way downward to spike as moistness between her thighs. Gawd, how she wanted to touch. No, she wanted to lick. Starting at his Adam's apple and working her way down to that magical instrument that even now was making itself known as an impressive bulge against the inside of his right thigh. Her sex throbbed in response, wetness leaking onto her jeans. It served her right for not wearing panties. But who knew she would be staring at Dusty's crotch?

Staring. At his crotch. Shit, she was.

Liz jerked her attention to his face, certain she would find a knowing smirk in place. There was no smirk, no sign that he'd even caught her ogling. He wasn't even looking at her but rifling through a first-aid kit. Good. Now, if she could remember what they'd been talking about . . . right, his awesome kitchen. "I would have thought compliments were your bag."

Setting aside gauze and ointment, Dusty returned the first-aid kit to the hook on the wall he'd obviously pulled it from during her staring session. He turned on the sink's cold water. She jerked when he took hold of her hand, tossed aside the bar rag, and guided her finger under the spray. His apologetic look said that he thought he'd caused her pain. It wasn't pain shooting up her hypersensitized arm and straight to her ever-slicker core, but more of the pulse-pounding awareness she'd experienced out front.

"I don't have a problem with compliments. I just prefer to be on the giving end." A slight rasp peppered his voice, suggesting that while he might not be acting aroused, the stiff state of his cock told the truth. He was thinking the same potentially dangerous thoughts she was. For the first time, Liz acknowledged how well those thoughts could work with her plan.

Turning off the water, Dusty patted her finger dry with a paper towel from the dispenser next to the sink. Gently, he applied a thin layer of clear ointment to the cut and wrapped the finger in gauze. He eyed her soberly then, as if his concern for her injury was all that mattered. For an instant, as she considered just how gently he'd taken care of the wound, Liz believed he truly felt that way. Then she remembered his erection and exactly what was at stake. He was rock hard for her, and she had to take full advantage of the condition and set things right between them once and for all.

She started to reach for him. His hands were at her sides before she could touch him. Hot, hard, masterfully his fingers ascended to brush the outer swells of her breasts. She hadn't worn a bra, thought it would be that much easier to tempt him without one, and her nipples made that fact obvious. The buds steepled against her shirt, and she sighed at the feel of the soft cotton caressing them.

"There's something about the way you wear a T-shirt, Elizabeth." The sobriety remained in Dusty's eyes, but his voice had dropped to a seductive whisper that sent a shiver racing through her. "Not too loose. Not too tight. Just enough to make a man ache to get his hands on your tits. Damned sexy." His hands skimmed downward until they settled around her hips and then dipped to spoon the curve of her ass. "And these jeans. I swear whenever you bend over, every man for a hundred miles around sports wood. Very hot." He let go of her bottom. One hand journeyed to her mouth, the first finger tracing her lips. The sobriety died from his expression, sexual hunger darkening his eyes to chocolate. "Then there's your mouth. Plump yet firm. Full of sass."

More like full of shit, which was what Liz's mind had just

become. A big pile of doo-doo. Or maybe that should be goo-goo, seeping from her female orifice.

He leaned forward, his breathing picking up, fanning soft and warm against her face. Her own breathing sounded like a tempest as she fought the desire to lick the finger tracing her lips, suck it into her mouth, and savor every delectable inch.

Fought and lost.

Liz flicked her tongue over the tip of his finger, moaning low as she recalled the velvety sweet taste of it coated in whipped cream. Her lips worked downward, nibbling at the long, thick digit, swirling her tongue around it. His skin didn't taste velvety sweet tonight, but warm and salty. Dusty's groan as she worked her mouth up and down, eliciting slurping sounds that hinted at something far more erotic, wasn't sweet either, but raw. Feral. Reckless with a want she felt all the way to her toes.

The plan wasn't to kiss him. The plan was simply to touch him a little, get his motor revving. Prove to him they could never be friends and prove to herself that he wasn't a nice guy but a man ruled by his dick. The plan was about to take a serious detour.

Liz leaned into him, placing her hands on his hard chest. She sighed at the blissful contact and cocked her head back, eyeing his mouth.

Kiss. She wanted his kiss. Now.

His lips parted slightly. The tip of his tongue winked at her. Her heart skipped a beat. She closed her eyes. Held her breath. Waiting. Waiting.

"You into brunettes with beards?"

The unexpected question snapped her eyes open and rocked her back on the heels of her sneakers. "*What?*"

Dusty's hands fell at his sides, and he stepped back until he was nearly up against the wall. He cleared his throat. "I have a friend I think you'd like. Name's Cord. He owns a beefalo ranch in Texas. Mentioned coming to visit in the next month or two, and—"

"And what?" Liz snapped. "You enjoyed fucking me so much, you wanted to give your friend the same opportunity by setting the two of us up?"

He frowned. "I want to see you happy."

And he'd been about to before he opened his mouth and failed to stick his tongue between her lips.

What in the hell was going through his head? Had he said that crap about her body to show her why his friend would like her? And why would he want her to date his friend if he was only playing at being nice? "Lovely. Tonight you're both a dickhead and a fruitcake."

"As much as that bitchy attitude does it for me, I have to wonder what I did to you to make you dislike me so much."

Where to start? There was . . . and . . . yeah . . . Okay, so at the moment the reasons were eluding her, but there were plenty of them. Liz jutted her hip out and planted a fist against it. "If I really have to tell you, you're even dumber than I thought."

His look said he wanted to voice a comeback. Dusty shrugged it off to ask, "So, what do ya say to meeting Cord?"

What did she say? Temper kindled and then quickly died as she realized the potential to be had in this conversation. The plan could still work, just slightly altered.

Crossing her arms under her breasts in a way that plumped the mounds and thrust their hard tips toward his face, she smiled naughtily and closed the distance between them by half. "He owns a ranch, eh? Guess that means he enjoys a good ride." She looked up at him from beneath half-drawn eyelids. "What about you?"

The muscle in his jaw worked. "What about me?"

Liz closed the distance by half again. Inches separated them now. Enough to keep their chests from touching but not their body heat from mingling. Damn, it was getting seriously hot in here. "Do you enjoy a good ride?" she practically purred.

"It's been years," he answered seriously. "I used to sneak out of the house to go riding with Cord on his parents' ranch—that's where I met Colin. Then one time I ended up breaking my arm. I'm not sure who was more pissed off, Mom being pulled out of her bridge club meeting, or Dad being interrupted during the workday to come to the hospital. Needless to say, it put an end to things fast."

We share things that matter.

Joyce's words on how she and Colin had ended up together sprang into Liz's mind and unsettled her belly. So what if she and Dusty had both had less-than-perfect upbringings? It didn't mean jack. Sure as hell not that they were meant to be together.

Shuddering over the ludicrous idea, she planted her hands on his chest. She spread her fingers over the delicious muscle and curled them in the linen of his shirt. "I'm not your mother, Marr. You wanna ride, I say go for it. Matter of fact"—she uncurled her fingers and smoothed her hands down his torso and past his zipper, connecting with his hard-on—"I'll join you."

His gaze narrowed. "Showing up here tonight, cutting yourself, complimenting the bar, it was all just a lead-in to my pants."

He sounded disappointed. When he talked about the bar during cooking class, his pride over its success always came through. Obviously the place was the equivalent of her pastry shop—a dream, in his case one realized. Just another thing they shared in common. La-di-flipping-da.

"I'm not a masochist, and I appreciate a good kitchen when I see it," Liz said truthfully and then reverted to focusing on the plan.

Lifting her hand from his groin, she pumped her hips against his. His rigid shaft brushed against her swollen pussy lips, and a heady sensation zinged through her. She didn't bother to stop her gasp or the urge to rub her sensitized breasts against his chest. Let him think it was all part of the act. After all, it was. Mostly. "I appreciate a good man even more."

"I'm not the right guy. You said so yourself."

Midway through a second hip pump, Liz stalled. That was why he'd acted so nonsexual toward her these last few weeks? She would never have believed him the type to let a little comment sway him. And she had to have been correct about that. He wasn't the type, just like he wasn't concerned with her happiness. He was an unscrupulous man-whore messing with her mind. Two could play that game, and she could play it better.

"You know damned well I have no intentions of settling on one guy." She ground her hips into his hard, each swivel of her sex against his bringing forth a new sigh. And new want. Real want. The kind she'd experienced three weeks ago before the pie had started to burn.

Her clit was hungry again. She could feel it throbbing between her juicy nether lips, aching to be let out to play. Poor little bastard would have to starve.

"So, what do you say?" She glanced at the sink. "You, me, and the sink?"

"You'll regret it."

There would be nothing to regret. All he had to do was admit that he wanted her on a purely carnal level and this would be over with. "In case you've forgotten, I'm a big girl." Liz moved back far enough to strip the T-shirt over her head. She pushed out her naked breasts and brought her fingers to her nipples, touching, squeezing, toying with the tight buds in a way that had her cunt thrumming.

Dusty's throat worked visibly as he watched her finger-play. His stoic edge vanished while his eyes grew heavy-lidded, his breathing intensified. The bulge beneath his jeans gave a noticeable twitch. Her heartbeat took off as she remembered the all-consuming thrill of his massive member impaling her.

He wanted her. He sooo wanted her.

And she wanted him. She sooo, sooo, sooo wanted him.

Expectancy fired through her, further dampening the crotch of her jeans. The impulse to widen her stance so that the rough denim would rub against her inflamed clit taunted her. She should ignore it, him. Stick to the plan. Demand that he admit he wanted her and then leave. Remember what really mattered.

"Touch me." Ah, wrong words.

Indecision warred on Dusty's face, shocking her. The want in her words should have been enough for him. He should be on her, inside of her, or at least teasing her in a way that made it clear he would soon be that way.

Unless he wasn't playing head games.

Seconds passed. Five. Ten. Fifteen. Finally, he moved, straight to the door. Liz's pounding heartbeat screeched to a halt. Damnit, she didn't want him leaving. But she wasn't about to ask him to stay.

He didn't reach for the knob, but pushed in the lock on the door handle. She breathed a sigh of relief. Some of her judgment must have slipped out with that sigh because her next words were, "Don't lock it."

"I'm not getting caught fucking in the staff bathroom."

She snorted. "As if it would be a first."

He looked back at her. "Until the night Matt walked in on me going down on you on the pool table, I've never done anything more than kiss a woman in this bar. That woman was you."

Liz blinked, taken aback. Was he being honest? His expression suggested he was. But why would he single her out to misbehave with on the job site, and did the reason have to do with his nonsexual treatment of her the last few weeks? He'd made it sound like he hadn't touched her because she told him he wasn't the right man for her. Did his admission now suggest that he wanted to be the right one?

Never mind. Even if the idea of him—not to mention her—in a relationship wasn't laughable, she wouldn't want to know the answer. She didn't want to get one iota closer to him on a personal level. She just wanted to screw. Wanted her one bona fide orgasm and then be done with him and on with the rest of her life. Amen.

"Fine, lock it. You'll have to find another way to give me a little added thrill."

7

He shouldn't be doing this, Dusty's conscience screamed as Liz rocked back on the bathroom sink and he buried his tongue in her mouth and filled his hands with her small, supple breasts. But since when did he give a shit what his conscience said?

The white bandage on her finger flashed in his line of vision, and he had his answer. He'd started giving a shit some time in the last few days, or weeks, or months. Hell, maybe it had been their first encounter eight years ago, when he'd given her a smile and in return she'd given him the finger. When wasn't important. His reaction to seeing her blood spilling onto the bar counter was.

The cut hadn't turned out to be as bad as the amount of blood seemed to indicate; still it had tightened his gut with concern. Because he'd known her for so long. Because she was almost like family. The little sister he never had. Damned good thing, too, since the desire to screw his "little sister" senseless wasn't bound to go over well.

Dusty indulged in a full minute of tongue-play, committing to memory the fervent way Liz stroked back and the sexy little sounds that erupted from the back of her throat. Then he lifted from the openmouthed kiss and emptied his hands of her breasts. He straightened, giving the high, firm mounds with their brown tips a long look, aware it would be the last. He was a man who could get off on pleasure alone. She was a woman who needed more—that one right lover—to achieve orgasm. Given the accidental insight into her mother's promiscuous behavior, he couldn't blame her for that.

Only, if her mother's promiscuous behavior stopped Liz from partaking in casual sex, why had she slept with him twice before and was even now attempting at lay number three?

Her fingers buried in the shoulders of his shirt, and she gave the material a rough jerk. "What are you doing, stopping?"

The right thing. Or was it?

He stepped back and looked at her face. He attempted to gauge her true feelings but couldn't see past her appearance. Even with her eyelids at half-mast, the blue of her irises showed startlingly bright, intense in a way that seemed to see right through his pretense of wanting to be friends. Her lips were no less powerful. Extra pink and plump from their kisses, they made him think of anything but friendship. Made his body throb with the desire to make them pinker and plumper yet. To do the same to those sweet lips hidden beneath her jeans. Shit.

Dusty buried his hands in his pockets. "This isn't going to happen."

Her eyes went wide. "What? Why the hell not?"

"You don't want it to. You just convinced yourself you do."

Liz's eyes snapped closed on a growl. She thrust her hands into her short ebony locks, looking like she wanted to tear them out. "What is it with you and your stupid-ass ideas lately?" She opened her eyes and released her hair, pinned him with a seething look. "Get it through your thick skull—I *want* this to happen."

It would be easy to believe her. Too damned easy to sink

into her warm, wet body and ride her to fulfillment. But if he was the only one able to achieve that fulfillment, it would also be a mistake. He shook his head and lied. "I don't."

With a grunt, she jumped off the sink and sent her tits swaying into motion. The whisper of material sliding against skin had Dusty's gaze going from her jiggling breasts to her thighs—her naked thighs. The breath snagged in his throat as he realized how much of her was naked—every tight, toned inch. He took in the shimmering black curls that covered her mound, and his cock pulsed savagely.

With her uninjured hand, Liz grabbed one of his and brought it to her sex, cupping their joined hands against her pussy. "Feel this and tell me you don't want me."

Cream seeped onto his palm. Wet heat rolled from between her pink folds to perfume the air. His index finger speared upward without his permission. He groaned as the slippery walls of her cunt welcomed him inside with a hug. "Christ, you're wet."

"No shit. Do something about it."

He wished he could. Wished to hell he was the right one for her.

The thought sneaked up to pummel Dusty in the gut. Pulse racing, he jerked his finger from her body and his hand from beneath hers, and he took a desperately needed step back.

The way her face had glowed when she commented on his kitchen had blindsided him. First, by making his pride soar with the idea he was a success at something other than sex. And, second, by making his heart warm with her honest smile. What her glowing appreciation hadn't done was turn him stupid. He didn't want to be any woman's right guy. The only reason he'd even considered such a thing was because, no matter how he tried to ignore it, his dick was clamoring to call the shots. The big guy knew that if Dusty was the right one for Liz, he would get to spend the next while out of the too-snug confines of his jeans and into the perfectly snug confines of her pussy.

The big guy was shit out of luck. "I can't."

"You're seriously earning that dickhead title."

"By not sleeping with you?"

"By making me feel like an idiot," Liz admitted with a quiet sincerity that shocked him. "How much harder can I throw myself at you?"

She sniffed. He tensed with the thought that she might cry, resisted the urge to soothe her with either words or actions. The Liz he knew would never shed tears over a man. But then, how much did he know about the real her?

"You really don't want me, do you? I should have known it the second I smelled you." She sniffed again, and this time he realized she was scenting him, not preparing for an emotional breakdown. "You never wear cologne unless you're wearing it for something special, someone special." She nodded at his groin, where his cock had yet to relax. "That's for someone special, too. You were already hard when Jen called you over to look at my hand."

She was right on both accounts. Dusty had been wearing cologne for the last week in the hopes of attracting a woman capable of challenging him on the levels that Liz did. As for the erection, he'd developed it the moment he'd realized a capable woman had finally arrived, in the form of Liz herself.

He couldn't tell her the truth without risking her jumping him. He was bigger, stronger, but brawn was no match for her current state of guilelessness and the weakness he never expected to feel toward it.

Giving a shrug, he smirked. "What can I say? Ya oughta know by now that my dick gets hard whenever the wind blows."

Embarrassment and anger flashed in Liz's eyes. She slammed her fist into his upper arm, wincing when her knuckles connected with bone. "Get your ass out of my way!"

He stepped to the side. She grabbed her jeans and hastily pushed her legs into the holes. The T-shirt was jerked over her head with the same haste, and then she scooped up her socks and sneakers and made for the door. She unlocked it and tossed it open, looked back at him, nostrils flaring. "You can pretend all you want, Marr, but we aren't friends. We will never be friends. Anything else, you just lost your chance at."

She needed coffee, bad.

Sitting up in bed, Liz scrubbed her hands over her face. Her supercharged morning persona was something she'd never had to fake. She was one of those people who didn't require much sleep and was energized both morning and night. Each day started out the same, waking at six o'clock without the aid of an alarm clock and getting in her two-mile jog before most of the neighborhood stirred.

This morning it was after eight and her energy seemed to have moved to another country, right along with her self-respect.

Unless last night had been a nightmare.

Maybe she hadn't thrown herself at Dusty only to have him turn her down cold for some hoochie whose blow-job technique clearly merited his wearing cologne.

Yeah, and maybe hell had frozen over during the few minutes of sleep she had managed.

She'd played such the fool over him. And why? Not because for a few seconds there she'd crazily thought he might care about her beyond the physical. And, damnit, for a few more seconds, as he kissed her so thoroughly it robbed her of sound judgment, she considered maybe the two of them being in a relationship was neither an absurd nor fictional concept. Oh no, that mistake wouldn't have been hard enough to live down. No, her behavior had been all about living up to her heritage, acting like the slut her mother would have raised her to be had the woman been around enough.

Liz pulled her hands from her face and scooted to the edge of the bed. Last night she might have fallen victim to her hormones, but today was a new day. Today she had hold of her common sense. She also didn't have to be at work until four.

Just as soon as she got some coffee pumping through her system, she would do what she should have done long ago and go apartment hunting. The sooner she got out of this house and away from the potential of running into dickhead Dusty, the better.

Slipping into the faded pink terry robe her father had given her for her eighteenth birthday—she'd never been able to part with it no matter how much it wasn't her style—she smiled. She'd managed to accomplish her primary objective last night. Dusty was firmly dislodged from her head as a nice guy.

Five minutes later, energy slowly pushed through Liz's body as she sat at the small, round kitchen table, sipping the still-warm coffee Colin had left behind. She was a firm believer in the idea that food off someone else's plate, or in this case drink from someone else's mug, tasted better. Her brother had had issues with her sharing habit when she'd first moved in, but now he made it a point to leave enough coffee in his mug for her to have a few drinks.

A thump sounded through the door that led from the kitchen into the living area. Liz frowned. Colin should have already left for work, and she hadn't seen any signs of Joyce when she'd made her way downstairs. Grabbing the coffee mug, she went to investigate. The door swung inward as she reached for the handle. Liz screeched and teetered backward, sending coffee sloshing over the rim of the mug. Two male hands, judging by their firm grip, grabbed her upper arms, stabilizing her.

"Jesus, Colin! You scared the shit out of—" The words died

on her tongue as she connected with Dusty's concerned look. The hands on her arms went from solid to steaming in a heartbeat. Her cheeks warmed just as quickly, both sets of them.

"You okay?" he asked.

For an instant, the sincerity in his expression and tone reminded her of the gentle way he'd bandaged her finger, and she almost smiled. Then her brain started functioning again. He didn't give a rat's ass about her welfare. If he did, he wouldn't have made her feel like a complete moron last night. She attempted to jerk from his arms, but he gave her a look that said she needed his support and held firm.

She narrowed her eyes. "What are you doing in my house?"

"It's *my* house, or ours." Colin appeared a few feet behind Dusty. He wore faded Levis and a tan chambray work shirt that suggested he would be spending the day with one of his landscaping crews instead of at the office. "I asked him to stop by to help me load the sycamores for Branson's backyard."

"The trees are out back."

"The coffee's in the house," Dusty said, bringing her attention back to him. Back to the fact that his hands were still on her arms, still burning through her robe and bringing wet need to life between her legs.

She remembered what she wore and groaned. It was bad enough he was seeing her in girly pink, but beneath the thin layer was nothing but her naked and quickly heating body. One little tug on the sash binding her robe and his hands would be on her skin, sliding down her arms, over the swell of her breasts, along the rise of her belly to bury in the liquid heat stirring in her pussy. Right where he'd had his finger last night . . . because she'd made him put it there.

Liz closed her eyes on the memory. Her brother had said that she wasn't her mother, but everyone knew actions spoke louder than words. Given her behavior with Dusty, she might as well change her name to Penny and write "whore" across her forehead in permanent marker.

"You're too late," Colin observed. "She's already confiscated your mug."

She opened her eyes to ask, "*His* mug?" At Dusty's nod, she swiped her hand across her mouth, barely resisting the urge to spit.

"Relax, Liz," Colin said. "If he had cooties, you would've had them by now."

She whirled on her brother, managing to catch Dusty off guard and dislodge his hands in the process. "What is *that* supposed to mean?"

Grabbing a coffee mug from the overhead cupboard, Colin shrugged. "Figured they were an airborne germ. He's over a lot."

Liar, liar, pants on fire. (Lovely, only Colin could reduce her to sing-songy childhood phrases.) That her brother lied was clear in the smile that crinkled at the corners of his eyes. He knew something. Or thought something. She wasn't about to question what that something was with the current undesirable company.

She thrust the coffee mug at Dusty so that he either had to take it or let it fall to the floor, then nodded at Colin. "I need to get moving. Have a good day, Col." She glanced back at Dusty and said in a voice that dripped with sarcasm, "Be careful with those trees, Marr. I'd hate to see one fall on your head."

"Liz, you have company."

"Thanks," Dusty said to Diane, the middle-aged woman with graying brown hair who'd led him into the kitchen of the restaurant Liz worked at. Liz stood punching keys on a computer system. He saw that she still wore his bandage wrap on her finger and thought to remind her to clean the cut with antiseptic. He snorted then, unsure which was stranger—that he believed she might follow his advice or that his first thought on seeing her wasn't about getting her naked but about her well-being. He would take it as a sign that they truly were meant to be friends alone, if his second thought wasn't how quickly he could get the tuxedo uniform off her body and his hands and mouth on it.

Liz looked up. Loathing flashed through her eyes. "What are you doing here?"

"He said it's an emergency." A teasing glint in her gray eyes, Diane let go a low whistle. "Another sundae in jeopardy of melting by the looks of things."

"Not even close," Liz assured as Dusty grinned at the other woman. Liz looked back at him in time to catch the grin, and her expression turned frosty. "Obviously this emergency isn't serious, so if you don't mind, I have a job to do."

He sobered instantly. What he'd come here to say was more serious than anything he'd said or done in years. He'd thought turning Liz down had been the right thing to do, that they could be friends. If the erotic role she'd played in his dreams the last two nights wasn't a sign of how wrong he'd been, then their encounter in Colin's kitchen yesterday morning was.

All it had taken was a touch and his body had reacted to her. The idea that her lips had been in the same spot as his on a coffee mug had shot his testosterone level through the roof. It was an asinine, pubescent reaction, and one that even now had him growing hard thinking about. Liz had been just as affected—that much was clear from the way her nipples jabbed at the surprisingly feminine robe that matched the color that rose in her cheeks.

He'd done some hard thinking on the idea that there was only one right guy for her, and what he'd come up with was the concept was bullshit, nothing more than a flippant remark on her part. She'd said as much two nights ago. That didn't change the fact that she held no respect for her mother's loose ways and, quite likely, suffered the inability to enjoy sex enough to orgasm because of them. That inability had to be the reason Liz had attempted to seduce him, because despite her accusations to the contrary, she believed in his reputation as a gifted lover. She believed he could deliver her from orgasm exile. And she was right, he could.

Dusty had vowed not to sleep with her again, but that was before he knew sex was the best thing for them both. Showing Liz that she had a working G-spot would get her out of his head while repaying the favor she'd done for him. Massacring his ability as a lover had accomplished more than make him reflect on his roots and feel like a once-again failure. It had opened his eyes, made him see he wanted more out of sex than to know he was the champion of the fast, easy fuck. That wasn't to say he wanted a relationship. Just to spend more than a handful of minutes chatting with a woman before he banged her. He wanted to know there was a little challenge involved in getting a woman into his bed and that she wasn't there solely because of his reputation.

"I need to talk to you now. Is there someplace private we can go?"

The need to move past his want for her brought unexpected desperation to his voice. Desperation Liz clearly heard, because she frowned but then nodded. "Fine. We can use the stockroom."

"Order up in three, Liz," a guy in a white sous-chef hat and matching chef's coat called from behind the hot food line.

"Which way?" Dusty asked.

She nodded toward a stairwell on the opposite side of the kitchen. "Down the stairs and to the right. I have three minutes, so whatever's on your miniscule mind, I suggest you share it damned fast."

Fast wasn't nearly long enough for the sexual awakening he

had planned. But fast could allow enough time to entice her into coming over to his house later.

Liz followed him down the stairs and inside the stockroom, flicking on the overhead light. He closed the door and twisted the lock, then turned to find her sinking back against a metal-rod-framed shelf of canned goods.

With a wary glance at the door, she crossed her arms under her breasts. He guessed she meant the move to make her look standoffish, but all it accomplished was plumping the soft mounds in an alluring way even her manly uniform couldn't hide.

She narrowed her eyes. "What do you want, Marr?"

"You."

Gasping, she shot to her feet. "*What?*"

She'd called for fast, so that's how Dusty moved. He grabbed her arm and spun her around so that her ass rubbed temptingly against his groin. Dropping his lips to her ear, he popped the button on her tuxedo pants, yanked the zipper down, and slipped his hand inside, past her panties, to find both the soft cotton and her curls dewy.

Pleasure to know that he got to her as thoroughly as she did him cruised through his body and had his cock expanding to new limits. Pleasure that was all about the physical, he assured himself. "Got the party started early, babe. Your pussy's already nice and juicy wet for me."

"I am not—" The denial died on a moan as he parted her curls to tease her clit. He circled his thumb around the bundle of nerves. She reared back, sliding her buttocks along the length of his dick, nearly eliciting a moan of his own. "Ohmigawd. This is sooo wrong. I work here. We could get caught."

He nipped at her earlobe, inhaling her scent. So many of the women he slept with covered themselves in perfume and body spray. Liz's scent was natural, the clean smell of soap and woman mixed with the musky tang of her excitement. He loved that about her. Loved, in the purely nonromantic sense of the word. "It adds thrill, remember?"

She wriggled around his finger as he sank it into the deliciously wet warmth of her sex. Her hips shot backward. He drew his finger out partway, then pushed it in again, repeating the act when she whimpered and contracted her feminine muscles.

One of her hands reached behind her, finding and squeezing his shaft through his jeans. "And, apparently, kills brain cells."

Something that felt too much like bitterness pushed through Dusty with her insinuation that she would have to be stupid to sleep with him. He laughed it off. "I owe you a little added thrill for the other night."

Liz stiffened. "I'm not one of your cheap-thrill flavors of the week. If you think you can leave me to screw someone else and then come back days later to finish what we started, you're wrong."

His finger stilled with the tone of her voice. Hurt, and beyond that, jealousy. But no. He had to have heard wrong. She'd just made it clear she thought their behavior was foolish, and beyond that, neither of them was in the market for a relationship.

Not as content with that truth as he should be, Dusty resumed the insert-and-withdrawal play of his finger. "Relax, killer. There was no one else. I was hard for you. There has only been you since that first night." She stiffened again with that last part. Words he hadn't meant to speak and ones he wasn't going to waste their precious time dwelling on. "Enough talk."

He shoved her forward so that she had to brace her hands against the shelving to stop from careening into the canned goods face forward. She screeched and then hissed out a breath as he jerked her pants and panties midway down her thighs, exposing her ass to the kiss of the air. Later he'd plant several kisses of his own upon her fine behind, then follow them up with some long-deserved spankings. Now, he brought his fingers back to her clit. He plucked at the stiff bud with one hand while he freed his aching cock with the other, exposing it between the vee of his zipper. He dipped into her sex with his fingers, found that she was still good and dripping, and then rammed into her from behind.

Liz puffed out a gasp and coiled her fingers around the shelf's metal framing while her pussy received him with a tight, wet, wonderful squeeze that could never feel the same encased in a condom. Savoring the raw sensation of skin on sensitized skin, he slid his free hand beneath her shirt and bra to her breast.

Two pumps of his hips, two tweaks of her clit, and a single nipple rub and she thrashed in his arms like a woman possessed. "Holy shit! I'm going to come. Like really, really soon."

Without the latex between them, Dusty could easily feel her tightening around him, milking his length, edging her ever closer to orgasm. The idea he might be the first to supply her with a real climax took a hit at his self-control. The lack of latex pushed that control to the snapping point, hurtling him too damned close to his own release.

Time to get out before he completely lost it.

He allowed one last thrust and then pulled from her body, conscious of the shaking state of his limbs. Direct connect was all that it was about. It had been years since he'd done anything as stupid as having sex without a condom, and then it had been with a woman he trusted enough to believe her when she said she was on birth control.

Ignoring the throb of his erection, he eased his hand from beneath her bra, then pulled her pants up over her hips and tugged at the zipper.

Liz rounded on him before he could get to the button. "You, bastard, don't you dare stop now!"

Because stopping was the last thing he wanted to do, Dusty focused on adjusting his clothes. "Your order should be up."

"My order? Forget my damned order and focus on my orgasm!"

"And let you lose your job? Not a chance, babe. You want to finish this, ya know where I live." He went to the door, turning back when he reached it. The unguarded need in her eyes was almost his undoing. When she looked at him that way, with every bit of her tough-girl edge stripped way, it made him want to do crazy things, not to mention think crazy thoughts he had no desire to have. The kind of thoughts that belied his vow never to settle on one single lover. The kind of thoughts she would probably coldcock him for if she found out about them.

Dusty shut out those dangerous thoughts and the acute urge to pull her back into his arms. He kept his voice even, if not a little on the cocky side—it was what she expected of him. "And, Elizabeth, bring an overnight bag. I don't care if it takes all night or all week, you're not leaving until you get off for real, several times."

8

"You need the added thrill."

Hey, how's it going to you, too? Liz thought nervously as she stepped inside Dusty's house. She'd dropped Colin off here before, when his truck had been in the shop, but had never ventured inside the ranch-style house. The décor reflected Dusty's Texas roots, from the knotty pine furniture finished naturally with shellac and stain to the tanned brown and white cowhide rug that centered the living room's pine floor. Country wasn't generally her thing, but here the theme felt right.

Liz brought her attention to the man who'd opened the door before she could knock. A pleased grin lit Dusty's face, drawing out the strong angles of his whisker-roughened jawline and spotlighting straight white teeth she had the sudden and burning desire to slide her tongue over. Aware that one more step inside would mean no turning back, she didn't budge.

She'd been uncertain about coming here. Afraid to know the reason he hadn't stayed true to his reputation and banged several dozen women over the course of the last few months.

Jesus, there had only been her.

Unless that claim had been a lie. Gawd, how she wanted to believe it a lie.

Not able to look Dusty in the eyes and keep up a composed front, she slid her gaze downward. To find his blue-black dress shirt sexily rumpled and open to reveal the hard, lean lines of his torso from neck to abdomen. Warmth unleashed in her belly and quickly spread outward, further wetting a pussy that had been damp since he'd shown up at her work. Shown up and, with just a few strokes, reduced her to a quivering mass of horny female.

She struggled to sound blasé. "Added thrill for what?"

"To come."

Her nerves frazzled a little more. She truly did have the IQ of a stick of Juicy Fruit to believe a man with his track record wouldn't be able to tell when a woman was faking orgasm.

Fighting the urge to shift, Liz met his eyes with a roll of her own. "Pull-eaze. I've come a gazillion times."

"Guess you aren't interested in my idea, then."

She should say no, explain that she'd only come here to tell him to stop messing with her head or risk losing his nuts to her Leatherman while he slept. Only, she didn't have a Leatherman. And she had plans for his nuts.

She shrugged out of her jacket and handed it to him. It was, either that or act like a complete chicken shit and make a break for her car. No way would she allow him the satisfaction of knowing he had the power to unnerve her. Planting a hand on her hip, she shrugged. "Fine. Humor yourself."

A smile twitched at Dusty's lips. She expected a sarcastic remark to follow. Or worse, for him to prove how badly she wanted to know his idea by tempting the words out of her with an expert caress. He didn't make a move toward her but turned away to toss her jacket on the back of the only piece of living-room furniture that didn't appear handmade—a faded burgundy La-Z-Boy that looked older than he was. He turned back to ask, "Do you trust me?"

His expression was as sober as she'd ever seen it. Liz snorted anyway. "That supposed to be some kinda joke?"

"I need your trust and your agreement to do whatever I ask." He moved into the center of the living room and took a seat on the couch. "You know I'd never harm you, Elizabeth."

Physically, yes. Emotionally . . . Damnit, she wasn't any longer sure.

She didn't do relationships. Had never even wanted to attempt one. Not until two nights ago in the staff bathroom of Dusty's Backroom when he'd led her to think he might care by admitting he hadn't so much as kissed another woman in his bar. And again this afternoon in the stockroom when he renewed that idea with his words on her being his lone lover. And now . . . Now his need to secure her trust before laying a hand on her seemed to hint that he cared a great deal.

Well, too damned bad. He might care, but it didn't change the facts. It didn't change how like her slut of a mother she'd become. The moment sex came into play, she couldn't focus on the things that mattered. If Dusty hadn't denied her demand to finish with her orgasm, she would likely be out of a job.

Regardless of how he felt, her emotions weren't getting involved. This was going to be a casual fuck that ended with her climaxing and then walking away permanently.

Nerves eased a fraction, Liz moved into the living room. She stopped when she spotted a pair of white takeout cartons on an end table previously hidden from view. She seriously doubted he had a sundae in one container and a bowl of whipped cream in the other and planned to live out her nightly fantasy via some kinky food-play. The odds were better they held regular food. And that was bad. Sharing dinner didn't hint at a casual fuck, but a date. "We're having dinner?"

"We're going to need sustenance to make it through the night." His sobriety caved to a wolfish grin as he gestured to a cushioned wood rocking chair. "Strip and have a seat."

Her heartbeat accelerated with his hot look and the quiet demand in his voice. Something told her he was through playing Mr. Nice Guy out to secure her trust. "Right, Marr. Like you think I'm going to take off my clothes just because you asked."

Dusty's grin deepened, edging into his goatee and looking entirely too smug and equally sexy. "No thinking involved, babe. I know you'll do it . . . if you want to come."

Liz blew out a hard breath. Lovely. He had her trapped into acknowledging that his belief that she'd never before climaxed was dead on and there wasn't a goddamned thing she could do about it. "You're an asshole."

He chuckled. "So you've said. A dickhead, too."

That he was—a dickhead who knew exactly how to get to her. Her sex did a pulsing mambo, letting forth fresh wetness at the rich sound of his laughter. Summoning her courage, Liz moved in front of the rocking chair. No matter the cost to her pride and the bolster to his already-inflated ego, she'd come here for an orgasm and she wasn't leaving until she had one. "I'm stripping because *I* want to."

Hastily, she pulled the T-shirt over her head and cast aside her bra. She ignored his eyes, but she could still feel them on her breasts, and it had her nipples leaping to rock-hard attention. Her pussy wasn't any better. It sped right past mambo terrain into what had to be a tropical rain dance for all the heat and moisture that gathered between her thighs the instant she was out of her jeans and panties.

"Now what, your royal pain in the ass?" She toed the pile of clothes and sneakers aside and looked up, ready to throw a glare his way to go with the snarky words. The breath snagged in her throat, killing any attempt at speech.

Dusty had undressed silently, and his big, beautiful, completely masculine body was on full display.

Sitting back on the couch with well-muscled thighs spread, he held his stiff cock in his hand, practiced fingers stroking from base to tip with slow, unhurried moves. Liz's pulse pounded madly while her mouth watered with the yearning to suck his long, luscious member. He heightened the pace of his fingers, and his shaft surged forward in his fist. Silky fluid oozed from the dark pink head. Inhaling the heady scent of his stimulation, she fought the urge to go down on her knees and lap greedily at the salty liquid, as if she hadn't been dying to do just that for three long weeks.

"Now we eat."

What? Was he out of his mind to think she could handle swallowing while he sat just feet away, fondling himself? "I ate before I came over. Can we just get to it already?"

"Relax, babe." His fingers moved past the thatch of thick blond hair at the base of his dick to cup his balls. He massaged their heavy weight, reminding her of their first night together, when she'd pulled the sensitive sac into her mouth and suckled. "You get worked into a dither and end up psyching yourself out."

She jerked her attention to his face. "I'm not in any damned dither."

"All but frothing at the mouth." With his free hand, Dusty grabbed the remote control and hit the POWER button. "You strike me as a *CSI* fan."

Incredulity shot through Liz. Yeah, the man was definitely out of his mind. "You brought me over here and ordered me to get naked to watch TV? *That's* your idea of added thrill?"

"You'll enjoy it."

What she would enjoy was cutting the crap. Since that didn't appear an option, she sat down on the rocker, crossed her legs, and turned to the television screen. She'd waited twenty-four years to climax. She could stand to wait a few more minutes, or however long the big idiot planned to keep her hanging. So long as she kept her attention off the maneuverings of his hand, she could.

"Why, Elizabeth, I never realized you were such a lady. Quit with the granny act and spread your legs; show me how wet you are."

She went rigid. Given her slutty behavior as of late, the granny comment should have amused her; instead it pissed her off. "Go to hell."

"I hate to break it to you, but the badass attitude doesn't work on me. The bitchier you get, the harder I get. You don't believe me, look for yourself."

Liz fought the dual impulse to toss another nasty remark his way and to give in to his bidding and her own desire and watch him masturbate. She didn't dare watch, not without risking the last of her patience. Unless his patience was just as thin, in which case giving in to his order could be the right course of action. "Maybe on the commercial break." Stomach tightening, she uncrossed her legs and spread them wide. "I can't stop watching once I start. I have this thing for Warrick. You don't believe me, look for yourself."

Dusty let go a low whistle. "Man must be good to get your pussy that wet from a flat screen. Part your lips and touch yourself."

Juice trickled down her inner thighs. Juice she knew had everything to do with the penetrating way he eyed her slick folds and nothing to do with his suggestion. "It won't do any good."

"Can't even come on your own. Poor thing. Whaddya say you humor me again and do it anyway?"

Whaddya say you drop the pitying note?

Though his words were light, the sympathy in his voice couldn't be missed. He sounded genuinely sorry for her. Next to affection, sympathy was the last thing she wanted from him.

Praying it would be enough to try his patience, Liz brought her right hand to her nether lips and used her first and third fingers to separate them. Her clit stood out, puffy and red, from beneath its hood. Playing with it was bound to set him on edge. She brushed her index finger over the swollen pearl and nearly shot off the rocking chair as a shock wave of carnal sensation rioted through her, all but robbing her of breath.

It had to be knowing that Dusty watched her every move at work.

She allowed herself to look at him. His hand was back on his staff, stroking the generous length as leisurely as if he had all night. His fingers stilled near the tip, and he rubbed his thumb in the precum glistening there. He slid his thumb downward then, until the right half of his cock glistened with his essence. The urge to make the other half just as shiny with her tongue vibrated through her, so she forced her attention up to his face only to be captivated.

Want sizzled in his every feature. She'd witnessed him eyeing various women through the years, women it was clear he planned to sleep with at the first opportunity. Not once had he looked at those women with such intensity. Her finger scraped back across her clit with this discovery, and she just managed to stifle her gasp.

"You're pink inside and extra juicy," Dusty observed in a rough voice that had his accent thicker than ever. "What's your nationality? Your skin's olive."

"My mom's part Indian."

"I can see why so many men want her if she looks like you."

Liz's fingers froze, loathing pushing through her. "Little hint, Marr. Talking about my mother's a guaranteed way to kill the moment."

He met her eyes, understanding in his own. "Same here."

"Right," she said dryly. "Just one of two things we have in common."

Amusement flashed in his eyes, followed quickly by interest. "What's the other?"

"Wanting to own a business. You already do." And that was enough about their commonalities. She was here for sex, not small talk.

"What do you want to own?"

She was here for sex, not small talk, and still she found she wanted to answer. Clearly the really-want-to-orgasm monkey had sneaked up and taken off with her better judgment. "A pastry shop. Laugh and die."

Good humor gleamed in his eyes. "What's there to laugh about? I know for a fact that you crack a mean egg."

She couldn't stop her smile. "Bite me."

"Later, I promise. Now, back to these things we have in common." He glanced at her crotch. "And keep playing with yourself. Your tits, too."

In the past, whenever something entered her thoughts during sex, her ability to feel pleasure would evaporate. Blame it on the sensual quality of Dusty's voice, the commanding hunger in his dark chocolate eyes even while he teased her, or a combination of the two, but as Liz dipped her fingers into the slick valley of her sex, she felt pleasure galore. Raising her left hand to her breast, she tugged at the hard nipple and her pussy responded with a core-deep throb.

"You forgot our egos," Dusty put in thickly, his attention returned to her fondlings.

She let her gaze wander back to the hand that petted his cock. Her breathing quickened as she studied the way he touched himself. Long, steady strokes. An occasional squeezing of the head. The trailing of his thumb down the vein that bulged along the underside. "You're suggesting we both have big ones?"

"No. We have egos that need constant strokes. And that leads to our fourth thing in common: We lead people to believe we're something we aren't."

Liz's gaze shot to his face. Tension filled her with how closely he'd hit on the truth, at least for her. What was it he led people to believe about him that was off? She shouldn't care. She should go over to the couch, take his shaft between her lips, and start sucking, make him forget they'd even been talking. But she did care. She had to know the answer.

"You really aren't a dickhead?"

"'Fraid not. And you really aren't a bitch."

She had to know the answer, and yet it wasn't worth the cost of revealing the truth about herself. "Damn, you're on to me. I'm actually a sweetheart in bitch's clothing."

"I know. But I promise not to tell." With a wink, he tossed her the remote.

She nearly jumped out of the rocking chair with her relief. Thank gawd! They were finally going to get on with it and not a moment too soon. "Tired of *CSI?*"

A bad-boy grin hitched up one side of Dusty's mouth. "Changing the channel's not what I had in mind."

Then what did he . . . ? The sensual challenge in his eyes registered. Holding out the remote like it was poisonous, she shook her head. No. No way. "I'm not sticking that thing in me. Christ, it probably has jizz on it from the last time you gave yourself a hand job."

"Do it, Elizabeth! And that makes number five—the fact that we both like to have our way. I can go on if you'd like, but I'd much rather get on with the seduction."

Seduction. That was what this night was about. Him seducing her enough to finally give her a bona fide orgasm. She wouldn't have believed jamming a remote control in her pussy could be the means to that end, but then he was the sexpert. No, the man-whore without a single moral. That was who he truly was. Any act of caring or claim of monogamy had been a pretense to get her to his home and this moment.

Concentrating on the heat that simmered in his eyes as he watched her, Liz brought the remote to her slit and slowly eased it in inside. She expected to tense up with the first brush, to feel vile. Instead her pulse sped and fresh cream filled her cunt with the feel of the controller spreading her in a completely hedonistic way she'd never before experienced. The protruding channel buttons brushed against her clit. Her breath wheezed out as a jolt of raw sensation sent a shiver racing through her.

He smirked knowingly.

She snarled, "I was coughing."

His smirk deepened. "Relax and enjoy the sensation."

Relax, he'd told her, but it was the last thing Dusty could do when watching her fuck herself with the remote. He'd never seen a sight more erotic or thrilling. And it was getting to Liz in a big way. If the labored sound of her breathing was a sign, she was already skirting the edge of orgasm and probably didn't even know it.

Time to change that last part.

"Enough! Get up and turn around." He didn't mean to bark the words, but he was close to his own climax, and it was having a serious effect on his mood.

Liz shot him a glare but stood. She turned and waved her tight ass in his face. Slowly, no doubt purposefully, she bent over so that her glimmering pussy lips peeked at him from between toned thighs. She tossed the remote on the seat of the rocking chair.

He wasn't in the frame of mind or body for asking permission. And she would respond better to action than words anyway. He'd told her that she needed added thrill to come. Thrill might help her plight, but the green-light way she'd behaved in the stockroom suggested the true problem was her mind. Every other time he'd had her on the verge of orgasm, someone or something had come along to distract her, bringing her out of the moment. Tonight he wasn't taking chances with distractions. Or giving her the time to think about her behavior.

Dusty moved to stand behind her. Palming her butt cheeks, he spread them to reveal her puckered hole slippery with desire. He considered pushing his tongue inside, showing her pleasure he could almost guarantee she'd never experienced elsewhere. The tensing of her rear suggested that would be too much too soon.

"Wh-what are you doing?"

He had her nervous again. Now that he understood her anxiety, he could remedy it.

Using his knees to apply pressure to the backs of hers, he felt her legs go weak. She allowed him to guide her to her hands and knees on the rug. That she gave in without any bluster said that while she hadn't admitted to trusting him, she did so completely. Exultation filled him. He'd found a challenge in Liz; successfully meeting that challenge brought more satisfaction than supplying a thousand women with screaming orgasms could.

Because he couldn't resist the temptation, he planted a wet kiss on the sweep of her spine and then returned to his ogling. "You have the greatest ass, Elizabeth."

Starting at the top of her crack, he worked his first finger downward, until he reached her hole. He eased the finger inside a fraction. Her breath caught audibly, and her rear once again tightened. Bringing his other hand to her sex, he massaged a finger over her clit until cream flowed from between her folds and her ass cheeks relaxed. He inched his finger farther inside and found the passage growing increasingly slick with her excitement. His cock twitched joyfully. She might have lied about her many climaxes and the surplus of men who provided them, but her passionate nature was a fact.

"You like to have your asshole fingered . . . and to be spanked."

Liz flinched as he pulled his finger from her body and smoothed his palm over her ass. "Jesus. You're a sicko."

"Trust me, you won't find this sick."

"Don't you dare—"

The words died on a huff as Dusty brought his hand down on her bottom with a solid thwack. His dick throbbed with the primal sound, the skin stretched impossibly tight, ready to burst. Her fingers curled into white-knuckled fists, but she didn't say a word. He took the silence as a good sign.

With a mental command to his cock to behave, he lifted his hand a second time. He allowed more pressure, slapping a bit harder, reveling in the pretty red that tinged her supple flesh. "Tell me you don't like it."

"I . . . I shouldn't."

No matter how much she wanted to climax, or even how much she trusted him, he hadn't expected the quiet yet candid admission that suggested her tough-girl edge was once more stripped clean. His gut clenched. Sympathy swelled to life along with a soul-deep desire to hold her close and assure her it was perfectly normal to enjoy the sensual play, that it didn't make her anything but a woman with a healthy sex drive.

Afraid what might come out of his mouth if he chose that latter route, he brought his palm back up and asked a single word. "Why?"

"I just shouldn't," Liz squeaked out as he spanked her a third time, allowing the side of his hand to come into contact with the rear of her pussy lips.

She thrust her hips back, clenching her buttocks, showing him how much she enjoyed the paddling. "It's wrong."

"Then why does it feel so good?"

"I-I don't know."

"Because it isn't wrong. It's right. Let your mind go, absorb the stinging sensation. Remember, I would never hurt you, not for real." Thanks to her mother's bad choices, Liz was a victim of secondhand sex to an extent he'd only just realized. There was only one cure for her ailment, and that was showing her nothing they could do was wrong, just so long as it wasn't hurting either one of them or anyone else in their lives.

Dusty pulled back his hand again, focused on the lips of her cunt, then struck the plump, pink edges with just enough force to make her whimper and squirm and build her up to the kind of blind-pleasure orgasm she'd never be able to forget.

A deluge of juices trickled from between her thighs with his next spank. He brought his finger to the rivulet, coating it with her cream. After taking a lick from it himself, he reached around to her mouth and held out his finger. "Taste your excitement. See how delicious you are."

He thought she might hesitate. Tell him he was a sicko again or give in to any number of creative put-downs. Whether it was simply implicit trust or she'd done as he'd suggested and gave in to the thrill of the sting, her anxiety suddenly seemed a thing of the past.

Liz flicked her tongue out, dabbed at his finger like a cat sampling fine cream, and then opened her lips to him fully. He slid his finger inside the hot wet confines with a moan of approval. She lapped at the digit, worked her mouth up and down its length, increasing and decreasing the pressure the same way she did when it was his cock pushing between her full, feisty lips. A visual of it doing just that threatened. His control already too thin, he withdrew his finger before that vision could take shape.

She released a throaty *mmm*. "It's good, but still only my second favorite cream. I want to taste my first."

They were a play on words from their first cooking class together. He'd said them as a form of enticement. Her admission didn't sound like taunting but fact. It made this seem like more than casual pleasure.

Was it more?

Dusty didn't tense with the question the way he might have expected, but he wouldn't allow himself to consider it either. No matter what this felt like, it was casual pleasure, payment for a favor she'd done him. His rash thoughts about settling on one lone lover were nothing more than thoughts.

He flushed them from his mind with a visual sweep of Liz's mouth-watering ass and splayed thighs. "I promise, babe, you can suck my cock all you want . . . after you get your orgasm."

"And when the hell will that—"

Gripping her hips, he pushed his tongue into her folds from behind, stilling her words on a gasp while he feasted on her delectable juices. He licked the length of her weeping slit, gliding upward until he reached her crack and then shoved inside to give her ass bud a tonguing.

"Oh. My. Fucking. Gawd." Liz thrashed beneath him. Panting, she reared back and sent his tongue deeper still. "Dusty!"

The name soared through him, tossed around inside his head and ceased his movements. She never called him Dusty. The word was stronger than any endearment she could have spoken. It smacked of intimacy, made this seem like it wasn't casual pleasure after all but the makings of something serious. He should hate that. Only, he didn't hate it. He liked it and the warmth it spread through him a whole hell of a lot.

She wiggled her butt cheeks. "Why the fuck are you stopping?"

"You called me Dusty."

"It won't happen again. Now get moving!"

She sounded desperate, too far gone to notice the change in his mood. Damned good thing, too. Now wasn't the time to explore that change, when his dick was calling the bulk of the shots.

"I liked it," he allowed, and then gave her the one thing they'd both been wanting since he left her in the stockroom this afternoon.

Pulling the condom from where he'd tucked it beneath the couch cushion in preparation for her arrival, Dusty quickly rolled it on and then pushed into her glistening sex from behind. Joint cries of ecstasy filled the air. He'd thought the feel of skin on skin had been intense. It had to be his off-kilter mood factoring in, but even with a condom separating them, Liz's hot pussy clenching around his cock felt better than anything he could remember.

Filling one hand with the softness of a tit and using the other to brace his weight, he came over, reclined his chest against her narrow, sweaty back, and thrashed into her.

Thrashing truly was the only word to describe the mad way he pumped. Animalistic, the wild need to bury himself farther than he'd ever been in a woman. There was no controlling the balls-to-the-wall speed, the fact that their grinding tempo wasn't even close to being in unison, or the painfully snug way his nuts hugged his body.

Climax built in seconds. Tautness corded his muscles, strung out the arm he used to brace himself with. Perspiration beaded on his forehead. A roar built in the back of his throat. And then died without a sound as reality punched him in the gut and jerked his hips to a halt.

Christ, he'd lost his goddamned mind.

At the cost of her pride, Liz had come to him for an orgasm no other man had been able to provide. She was counting on him to prove her G-spot was alive and healthy. And what was he doing but kneeling on the edge of coming without her.

The thought was no sooner out than her still-thrusting hips quickened their pace. Her sex fluttered, the muscles milking his cock with damp, delicious squeezes. Pants sounded. Loud, rasping pants. The kind of pants that were a prelude to climax. Maybe he wasn't kneeling on that edge alone after all.

"Dusty . . ."

With that one word, he knew what she wanted, for him to come back to her, to regain his tempo. To savor a mutual moment of ecstasy. That she'd chosen his name to get her point across ensured he would savor the moment to the fullest.

"Now, now, now!"

He resumed his pace. Seconds passed before her cunt unleashed turbulent vibrations. Her pussy clenched around his cock. Once. Twice. And then spewed forth a river of hot liquid desire.

He buried his face in the crook of her neck as his own cum shot forth, shaking his entire body with the magnitude of his release. Sexy little mewls squeaked from her lips as she continued to cream around his dick. And when it seemed her quaking would stop, Dusty slid his hand from her breast to her pussy and fingered her sensitized clit until another orgasm was shuddering through her, leaking a fresh course of juice onto his fingers and around his shaft.

He could have happily fingered her to climax all night, shown her she was born to be a passionate woman and that it was something to celebrate, not run from. But she trembled beneath him, and this time he could tell it was about weakness. Unlike the night she'd faked orgasm, Liz was all but breathless, too drained to hold her weight up. He was nearly as winded himself, and if one of them didn't do something about their position, both would end up doing a face-plant.

Holding her to him, he rolled them over. His shaft pulled free with the move, and for an instant he regretted the loss. Then he remembered it was early, barely even ten. They had all night, all weekend if Liz agreed to stay.

If Liz agreed to stay.

She'd let her tough-girl edge go the moment he laid his hand on her ass; she became a woman who could be as insecure as she was blatant. The tensing of her body now said her armor was back in place. Dusty didn't know what tonight meant in the long run, but he knew he wasn't ready to let her go yet. He tightened his grip on her middle and lay still, inhaling her natural clean scent mingled with the musky tang of sex.

Less than a minute passed before Liz started fidgeting. When he didn't let go immediately, she pried his arm from her waist and rolled to her feet. She looked down at him, her lips twisted in a wry smile. "Way to go, Don Juan. You did it. Now you can get back to your harem."

No. Now all he could do was watch the jiggle of her breasts and then the sway of her ass as she moved to her discarded clothes and started tugging them on.

She pushed her arms into the sleeves of her T-shirt and yanked the crew neck over her head. "Speaking of women who want you, I have a friend who's interested in hooking up. Blond and bubbly, with huge tits."

Fresh from the loving and she was already sure he wanted another woman.

Disgust assailed Dusty, all of which was aimed at himself. For the first time in his life, he didn't want another woman. He wanted to live out his plans for tonight, spend it making love with Liz, cuddling with her early into the dawn. Only, in the planning stage, he hadn't called it lovemaking, and there had been no cuddling involved. Hell, he'd never even considered the concept before. Judging by Liz's easy dismissal of him, he shouldn't have considered it now. She didn't want anything from him but sex, and he'd be smart to feel the same.

He pushed up on his elbows and leaned back against the couch, then tossed out, "You know I can't say no to blondes with big tits. Have her stop by whenever." But, shit, he wasn't a smart man. He couldn't leave it at that. "I planned to spend the night together. Have some dinner, maybe a few drinks. Show you how orgasmic you are."

Liz snapped her jeans shut and reached for her shoes. She pushed her feet into the sneakers, not bothering to tie them before she grabbed her jacket from the La-Z-Boy and shrugged into it. When she finally looked at him, her expression held a finality rivaled only by the aloofness of her voice. "Yeah, well, plans change."

Yeah, and so did people. But apparently Dusty wasn't among them. He was still the failure he'd always been for letting her walk out the door without another word.

9

Liz forced herself to answer the knock at the door, though moving off the couch and away from the oniony haven of an extra-large bag of Funyuns was the last thing she wanted to do. Her stomach clenched as she reached for the doorknob, half-afraid Dusty would be standing on the other side of the door, half-afraid he wouldn't be.

Two days had passed since he'd given her not one but two orgasms. Two days where she'd done little more than remember.

The previous two times they'd gotten physical, it had been her clit that hungered for his touch. Two nights ago it had been all of her. Every last inch of her aroused beyond measure, quaking to feel his hand swatting against her sweaty flesh, his tongue lapping at every bend and curve of her body, his cock spearing into her again and again. And her heart. Her goddamned heart had been involved, had had her longing to feel his big, hard body spooning up against hers, holding her in a way that said she truly mattered after he'd finally delivered a release over two decades in the coming.

What a complete moron. How many times had she told herself he didn't care, that he just talked a good game to get her where he wanted her? Then, just as soon as he had her there and his big-ass ego placated, he'd happily moved on to another. Okay, so he hadn't moved on to Kristi immediately. He'd wanted Liz to spend the night, or weekend, or whatever. That didn't change the eventual outcome or the way he'd jumped at the idea of getting a hot blonde with big tits wrapped around him.

Growling her frustration, Liz yanked open the door. Dusty had the stupidity to show up now, and he would be lucky to leave with his balls intact. She still didn't have a Leatherman, but there were plenty of sharp knives only a kitchen away.

It wasn't Dusty who stood on the front porch, though, but a strawberry blonde. A strawberry blonde with serious personal-space issues, Liz thought as the woman tugged her into her arms with a chipper, "Surprise!"

Liz tensed. As a kid, she'd gotten hugs from her dad and Colin, but no way had she ever gotten one from a stranger. This stranger happened to be a good six inches shorter than Liz, and her chin pressed against Liz's breasts. "Um, do I know you?"

The woman released her and stepped back. A grin spread across a pretty face a shade on the plump side, centered with an upturned, freckled nose. "I'm with the prize patrol from the Instant Millionaire Contest. You're the big winner."

"I am?"

"Yep. Your millions will be paid out as Swedish Fish. A supersized box a day for the rest of your life. Ready to sign on the dotted line?"

Swedish fish? Liz frowned, searching the street for a prize-patrol van, or more likely, a stolen bus from the mental ward.

The blonde laughed. "Oh, c'mon, Liz. How many people do you know who could come up with a joke that pathetic? It's me. Kristi."

Kristi? Kristi! "Ohmigawd. What are you doing here? I mean, I'm glad to see you, but what are you doing here?"

"Dusty."

What? A sick feeling settled in Liz's stomach. She rubbed her hand over her belly. Too damned many Funyuns. "What about him?"

"I came to do him."

"Oh." Her stomach did a slow roll. Her heart hurt. So much for the Funyun haven. They'd obviously gone straight to work on clogging her arteries. "He's all yours."

"Yum." Kristi's smile grew, lighting gold-brown eyes. She looked past Liz. "Please tell me that's him."

Liz turned to find Colin standing feet away, his gaze narrowed in a way that said he'd heard the entire conversation. Great. "That's Colin and, as you know, he's taken."

"Bummer. So, when do I meet Dusty? I know he's going to be the one. Just thinking about him on the plane was enough to have me wet."

"You flew here to sleep with Dusty?" Colin's words rang with disbelief.

Liz glared at her brother while her stomach and heart continued their painful tirades. "Don't you have a meeting or a huff-and-puff session with Joyce to get to or something?"

He glared back. "Or something."

Lovely. He was going to make a big deal out of this. It wasn't a big deal. She couldn't give a rat's ass if Kristi wanted to get naked with Dusty, even after she'd told the woman on numerous occasions what a dickhead he was. She waved from her brother to her friend. "Kristi, Colin. Colin, Kristi. She's a friend from Seattle."

"When were you in Seattle?" Colin asked.

"We met on-line," Kristi supplied.

He looked stunned. "Since when do you get on-line?"

"Since I have to spend my nights listening to you getting

your rocks off and Joyce telling you what a god you are in bed." Liz turned back to Kristi. "Dusty isn't working today. I can drive you over to his house and introduce you." Her stomach clenched, and she brought her hand back over it, pressing hard.

"Not necessary. Just give me directions and I'll call you post-O."

The turbulence of her belly worked its way upward, making her throat ache. She should take the time to remind Kristi what a terrible idea sex with Dusty was, but she felt too damned bad. The sooner she got the woman out of the house, the sooner she could ease her pain by stuffing her head in the Funyun bag and forgetting to breathe.

Liz invited Kristi inside. After shooting Colin a dark look, she went into the kitchen for a pad of paper. She scribbled the directions on the first sheet, tore it off, and went back into the living room. Her fingers curled around the sheet as she handed it to Kristi. "Are you sure you don't want me to drive you over there?"

"Absolutely. We'll get along explosively, if you catch my drift." She smiled hugely and gave herself a whole-body hug. "Hey, do you mind if I borrow your lipstick and maybe a dress if you have anything that will fit me? I'd unpack my own stuff, but I just can't wait any longer to get my hands on Mr. Happy! Oh, and his daddy, too," she added with a twittery giggle that Liz would never have imagined coming out of Kristi's mouth. Bad sense of humor aside, she'd sounded so normal on-line, intelligent even.

Fifteen minutes later, Liz felt ready to explode from chest and stomach pain as she waved good-bye to Kristi, who was climbing into a cab. The taxi moved down the street, and she closed the door. She started for the couch, the smothering-by-Funyun-bag-idea fast gaining merit.

"You're honestly going to let her have him?" Colin asked.

Frowning, she collapsed onto the couch. "Let who have who?"

"You know damned well what I'm talking about. The idea of a relationship scares you so bad you're going to throw someone else at the man you love."

A gasp barreled up Liz's throat. *Love?* He thought she loved Dusty? Hah! What a riot! She didn't love Dusty. She, in fact, hated him so much that she would be elated to hear that Kristi's cab driver ran him over by accident.

She rolled her eyes. "Pull-leaze. You are sooo far off, Col."

"Am I? Then why did you look ready to stick your fist in your friend's face when she said she couldn't wait to get her hands on Mr. Happy and his daddy, too?"

A few months ago, Dusty would have been thrilled by the bubbly blonde bouncing in his doorway. Now it took all his effort to keep a smile on his face, knowing he was expected to sleep with her. Upon hearing he was interested in doing her, Kristi had flown in from Seattle for the sole purpose of climbing between his sheets. For both of their sakes, he felt obligated to deliver. Fucking another woman had to help in getting over Liz and over the idea that letting her walk away believing she was just another casual screw in a long line of them was his biggest failure yet.

"I'm so excited to meet you," Kristi chirped. "Liz has told me all about you. And I do mean all." Waggling her eyebrows, she glanced at his crotch.

He'd had his dick stared at hundreds of times. This was the first time he felt the urge to seek cover. Resisting the urge, he gestured for Kristi to come inside. He owed her a fuck, and he would provide it. "Forget about Liz. Tell me about you."

She pinched her first two fingers together and dragged them across her lips. "My lips are sealed. No mention of Liz at all."

She ran her hands along the outer swell of generous breasts to ample hips. "Do you like my dress? I realized after I landed that I didn't pack anything worthy of a man with your reputation, so I borrowed something."

Dusty recognized the electric-blue dress as the one Liz had been wearing the night she'd tried to go home with the metrosexual only to end up with her thighs spread and Dusty's head buried between them. On Liz, the dress had been seductive in a hiding-the-goods sort of way. On Kristi, it hugged every inch of her generous curves, leaving nothing to the imagination. He'd never realized how much he appreciated hidden goods until this moment. "It looks good on you."

"Thanks, but you can tell it was made for Liz." Her smile turned from friendly to naughty. She closed the distance between them, rising on tiptoe to twine her arms around his neck. Even then, she had to tip her head back to meet his eyes. Now was a hell of a time to discover he preferred his women tall. "Where were we?"

"You were about to kiss me." Damn, he needed to try a little harder. He sounded like kissing her was like having a tooth pulled.

Kristi didn't seem to notice. Rubbing her tits against his chest, she used his ears to pull his head down. She brushed a kiss across his mouth that should have been casual but ended up feeling sloppy, like a puppy was licking him. Only, she was no puppy but a woman with a dynamite figure he needed to focus on.

Before he could give her a real kiss, she squealed and pointed at the aerial photo of Turner Field stadium on the wall behind him. "I can't believe you have that picture! Liz has it, too."

Liz was a Braves fan. *Just another thing we have in common,* Dusty could hear her saying, all the while looking like she wanted to kill him for daring to love her sports team. He started to smile with the thought, then realized what he was doing and frowned. "Did you come here to fuck or pay homage to Liz?"

Kristi regained her hold on his ears and licked her lips. "I came here to fuck, bad boy. What's your favorite way?"

"Any way that involves sticking my dick in a warm pussy."

"What about a warm mouth?"

He looked at her lips, hoping to find some encouragement there. He groaned at the familiar ruby-red shade. "Is that Liz's lipstick?"

"Yeah. My coloring's too pale for it, but she said you liked it."

"She said that?" In other words, she'd gone out of her way to see that he liked her friend. That pretty much shot to hell any chance that Liz regretted walking out on him.

Why should she regret it? He hadn't said anything to make her want to stay. He'd consoled himself the last two days with the idea he'd kept his mouth shut as not to scare her. The truth was he'd been looking out for his own sorry ass. He'd failed her by letting her walk out without revealing she meant something to him, but that failure would be nothing compared to what he'd feel if they didn't work out.

"'Nough about Liz. Tonight's about you and me." Kristi's hold on his neck tightened to a near-painful level, almost like she wanted to strangle him. She hopped up his body and worked her legs around his waist. He held her to him reflexively. She took advantage of his grip, releasing his neck to bring her hands between their bodies.

"This is going to be so good, bad boy. You'll never want another woman again." Yanking at his shirt, she wrenched it from the waistband of his jeans. The warmth of her fingers touched down on his chest at the same moment her lips found his neck. Her tongue came out, teasing his ear with wet promise.

If he tried, he could probably feel more of that wetness where her crotch met his waist. If he tried hard enough, he could probably even get in the mood to develop an erection worthy of fucking her. Dusty wasn't about to try. There was a woman who made him want to be with her alone, but it wasn't the one attempting to seduce him.

Angling his neck away from Kristi's mouth, he captured her roaming hands in one of his. "Stop."

Giggling, she wiggled her fingers in his. "Ready for the bondage games?"

"No bondage. I can't do this. I'm sorry."

Her mouth pulled into an O. "You can't do it? But I heard you have a huge dick."

"I can fuck, and I do have a big dick—"

She tugged a hand free of his and reached beneath her legs to grab hold of his cock through his jeans. "Lemme see."

"Son of a bitch. Stop!" Prying her from his body, he set her on her feet and took a few steps backward. "I don't want to sleep with you."

"What? I'm not good enough for you?" She looked angry for all of two seconds and then sniffed loudly. "It's my size, isn't it? I'm too big."

Dusty ran a hand through his hair. Shit. He'd never had to dole out rejection before. It felt damned bad. "You have a great figure. It's not. It's . . . shit. I can't do this to Liz. I can't cheat on her."

"Cheat on her? You guys aren't even an item."

"We might be if I hadn't been too much of a candy ass to let her know how I feel." The guilt he felt over rejecting Kristi turned bitter with the reminder of how he'd handled things with Liz. He'd probably always known she was different than the rest of the women who made him look twice, and not in a sisterly way either, like he'd tried to convince himself. Hearing her speak his name had just brought the truth to the surface.

"Maybe it's not too late to tell her."

The sorrow was gone from Kristi's voice. She sounded happy. He looked down to find her smiling in a way that had nothing to do with sex and everything to do with making him see the light. It occurred to him then the slim odds of Liz having a friend who acted the way Kristi had moments ago. "You didn't come to fuck."

She shook her head. "I came here to see if you were worthy of Liz."

"And did I pass?"

Her smile grew impish. "If that's how your cock feels flaccid, I'd say with flying colors."

Death by Funyuns wasn't a bad enough fate. Liz deserved to be cannibalized for allowing Kristi to go over to Dusty's house. She'd always known that when Kristi fell, it would be hard and fast. She just hadn't realized how fast. Kristi had called twenty minutes ago in tears, saying she'd locked herself in Dusty's bathroom when he got mean after she told him she thought she was falling for him.

She couldn't imagine Dusty raising a hand at the other woman in anger, but when his attitude was bad, he could be scary. To other people anyway. Personally, she enjoyed pissing him off just to rile his temper. Personally, she ought to bypass Dusty's house and check herself into the local mental hospital for some serious evaluation for even thinking of him in nice terms.

Her nice thoughts vanished the instant she pulled into his drive, got out of her car, and heard the shouts coming from inside the house. They were loud and, though the words were indistinguishable from outside, Dusty sounded angrier than she'd ever heard him. Maybe he was capable of raising a hand at a woman and doing far worse things. Maybe she didn't know him at all.

Racing to the front door, she pushed it in and froze dead in her tracks. Kristi and Dusty stood a foot apart in the living room. They were shouting, all right—over who had to take off which item of clothing next using what part of their body. They were already down to their underwear, and her imagination went wild with ideas of how they'd removed the rest of their clothes.

He'd probably used his teeth, what with the way he was always offering to bite Liz. Probably used his mouth, too, had his lips all over Kristi's body, his tongue stuck in her mouth and everywhere else he could get it.

Liz's stomach clenched. Damnit, she thought she'd gotten past the Funyuns. "I guess you worked things out."

If Liz were the one caught in her underwear, she would have been embarrassed, attempted to write it off with bluster. Kristi smiled so wide it was a wonder she didn't break any teeth. "You were right about him. Totally dee-lish and totally hung."

How could she tell when he still had his boxers on? Liz glanced at his groin, and Kristi laughed. "This is round two. Round one only lasted a few minutes."

"You've already . . . I mean you . . ." She couldn't say it. Couldn't get the words out. Couldn't believe they'd actually gone through with it. Kristi was supposed to be her friend. And Dusty was . . . a bigger dickhead than she'd ever realized.

Pain splintered through her. Pain she could no longer pretend was caused by an overdose of Funyuns. She'd thought she couldn't lie to herself. But she'd been wrong. Looking at the real source of her pain, she knew she did give a rat's ass that he'd slept with another woman. She'd fallen for his games and allowed herself to care about him, to believe he cared in return. She'd wanted a relationship with him. And here he was, screwing her friend, because Liz had pushed that friend at him.

Oh yeah. Karma was having one big fucking laugh at her expense now.

"I have to go." But she couldn't. Not until she set Kristi straight on exactly what kind of man she was dealing. No, not man. Unscrupulous man-whore.

"I'm sorry I let you come here and sleep with him." Her voice shook, but she couldn't make it stop. "He's an asshole. He doesn't care about you. He just makes you think that he does. The second he gets what he wants, you'll be out of here and he'll be screwing someone new. You're just another flavor of the week. We all are."

Dusty snorted. "Like you wanted to be anything more. All you were after was a man who could locate your G-spot. You got your orgasm and were out the door so damned fast, I still have whiplash."

Up until now she'd avoided his face. His cynical tone gave her the strength to meet his eyes. He'd always been an open book, easy to read. Now she had to be reading him wrong. No way could he be upset over the way she'd left. "That's not true."

"Then what is?"

Gawd, he sounded sooo upset. Like he really did feel that way. But that was impossible. She'd been just another flavor of the week, just a game. "You wanted me to leave."

He shook his head. "I never wanted you to leave. I told you as much."

"Not right then, but in the morning." After they spent the night sharing dinner, conversation, more amazing sex. Getting closer in a way she'd refused to even consider because . . . she'd been afraid. Not that he'd been playing a game with her but that he hadn't. That he might actually feel something for her, that he'd been serious when he'd told her there hadn't been any woman but her for months.

"I never wanted you to leave," he repeated, not offering anything further in words; but his expression said plenty. He wanted her to trust him. She'd done that once already and look where it had gotten her . . . with a working G-spot.

The pain subsided a bit, but she refused to feel hope. He had slept with Kristi, after all. That wasn't the action of a man who cared. Needing her front now more than ever, Liz rolled her eyes. "Yeah, right. I was just gonna stay here forever. Shack up with you and raise babies."

"I never wanted you to leave."

And that meant what? That he wanted to shack up and raise babies? No. No way. It was just too much to believe of a guy with his reputation. But, damnit, she wanted to believe it. "Then what are you doing with her?"

She hated the way her voice squeaked. Apparently, Dusty found it amusing because he smiled in that cocky way that drove her nuts and made her horny all at once. "Pissing you off so you'll tell me the truth for once."

"But you slept with her." Nice. Now she was not only squeaking but whining.

Kristi smiled, apology clear in her eyes. "He didn't sleep with me, Liz. He wouldn't. And if he would've, I wouldn't. I didn't come here to do Dusty. Fi and I knew something was wrong when we didn't hear from you in so long. We thought you needed in-person guidance. I'm sorry, but this seemed like the only way."

They didn't sleep together? No sex. Just some bonding time in their undies. Relief bubbled up, threatened to come out as laughter. "You came here to push me at Dusty?"

"We care about you, Fi and I. We want to see you happy."

Liz let her laughter free. "You think he makes me happy? What are you, nuts?"

Kristi shook her head. "You are if you can't see how much he cares about you."

Dusty came toward her until he was almost too close for comfort. Given both his and Kristi's blatant disregard for personal space, she should let them have each other. Only, she knew she couldn't. She might not be a carefree sexaholic, but she could be a huge bitch, particularly when it came to some other woman pawing her man.

"I should have said something the other night, Elizabeth." All trace of Dusty's arrogance was gone now, replaced with a humbleness she hadn't known he possessed. "I was afraid you wouldn't want me beyond sex. That we wouldn't work out. I don't do failure well."

"I don't do relationships at all."

"And why is that again?"

He'd asked her the question before. The difference was now she wanted to answer. It was time to put her faith in him for real. "Because my mother is a slut who can't stay with a man longer than a handful of orgasms, and I don't want to be her."

Sympathy flashed in his eyes as he pulled her into his arms. "You aren't her, babe. The more I think about it, the more I know Colin was right about your orgasm problem."

Liz had never felt so right being held before. That didn't stop her from wanting to punch him. She settled on swatting his arm. "You talked to Colin about my orgasm problem?"

"I didn't say it was you."

"Yeah, like he couldn't figure it out." Obviously he had figured it out, considering how many times in the last couple weeks he'd mentioned her ability to do just fine with relationships. "He's the one who told you I had to care about a guy to come?"

"Something like that, and now I know he was right. You care about me, Elizabeth, and I care about you. So we're just going to say to hell with our relationship issues and move in together." Dusty punctuated the words with an openmouthed kiss.

She sank into it gladly, hungrily, greedily, all the while aware he was trying to shut her up so she wouldn't turn down his offer, which he'd made sound more like fact. She would punish him later. Men had to be susceptible to spankings, too, right?

Liz pulled back from the kiss, every cell alive with happiness and her sex moist with need. He grinned at her in a way that said he expected one in return. She glared in the direction of the living room. "You honestly expect me to live with a cowhide?"

"You can redecorate. A little."

Letting the glare slip away and her happiness shine through, she gave him his smile. "I like the cowhide."

"You do?"

"It works." She fanned her hands over his chest, thrilling in the hard muscles and warm flesh. All hers. To lick. To lust over. To love. "I like you, too."

Kristi piped in from over Liz's shoulder, "Awww . . . I think I'm going to cry."

Liz traveled her hands down his body to his defined abdomen and then lower still, to discover she hadn't been the only one affected by the kiss. His cock was rock solid. She took great pleasure in grabbing it through his boxers and squeezing.

She was over feeling guilty about sex. Over every one of her hang-ups. Well, all but the one about her friend playing voyeur. "Do it in my car on the way back to Colin's house. I need to have sex now."

Dusty laughed. "You have such great manners."

"Thank God you're a gentleman, huh?" Kristi moved past them, clothed once again. "I promise to be over in an hour," Liz said. "We have a lot to talk about."

"You plan to tell her everything that happens in the next

hour, don't you?" Dusty asked the moment the door was closed with Kristi on the outside.

Liz nodded. "Damn straight. So you'd best be good."

Not only was he good, but he was also fast. He had her on the floor in an instant, her jeans and panties stripped away and his face buried between her thighs, his masterful tongue licking her toward ecstasy. She was quaking nearly as fast, her pussy thrumming with the need to explode. She was an atomic orgasm bomb, and she went off in a major way, screaming his name without fear of who might hear or how much more it might bring them closer together.

Grinning, he stood. "Good?"

"Ohmigawd, yes! So good I'm going to let you do it whenever you want."

He laughed and pulled her to her feet. She kissed him hard, the taste of her juices on his tongue igniting fresh need. As if he could scent her renewed arousal, he tugged her down the hall and into his bedroom; no cows here but silk sheets she sighed over the moment they touched her skin. "Did I ever tell you how much I respect you?"

The reality of how much he needed to hear the words reflected in his eyes as he came over her. He removed her shirt and bra, then kissed her long and hard, exploring every inch of her mouth until she was aching and wet with the need to feel him inside her. "So you respect me, eh?"

Holding her hips, he eased slowly into her. She closed her eyes, savoring the raw sensation tumbling through her. She opened them on a moan as he began a gentle rhythm that had his pubis brushing her clit with each stroke. Tremors were already building that told her another orgasm was just around the corner.

Damn, she loved her G-spot.

And she loved him, naughty tendencies and all. "You not only rose above your obviously idiotic parents and realized your dream of owning a successful bar, but you also landed this woman who is *sooo* amazing she's going to create a breakfast menu for your bar and do all the cooking herself."

"Do I get to help break the eggs?"

"Only if you help me live out my sundae fantasy. It involves whipped cream and cherries and great big monster bananas and lots of tongue action and . . ."

SEXLESS IN SEATTLE

1

"Touch him! Touch him!"

Kristi Hill had many aspirations. Being surrounded by a throng of drunken, screaming, horny females—most of whom were barely dressed and all of whom seemed to have made getting Kristi to touch the naked guy thrusting his cock in her face their goal for the night—wasn't one of them.

At least the club was darkened, the main source of light a trio of pulsing yellow flashers ascending from a stage at the front of the room to center on the beefcake of the moment. And said beefcake's cock was covered . . . by a leopard-print loincloth bound to fall off with the slightest provocation.

"C'mon, honey, grab his nuts!" someone shouted over the pelvis-undulating music from the row of high-top minitables on the level behind Kristi.

The raven-haired Tarzan wannabe responded to the suggestion with a hip roll and shift that had his member inches from her mouth. Expecting the next shout to be "suck him," Kristi diverted her attention to the early thirtysomething, twin Asian beauties sitting across the table from her. The women's styles were polar opposites, from Kim's elegant hair twist and sensible, slim, red, pantsuit to Cai's long, loose black hair shot with pink streaks and body-hugging fuchsia miniskirt coordinated with a cleavage-baring top. Their amused grins, however, were identical. And the words coming out of their mouths, in chorus with every other woman in the club.

Kristi grabbed her screwdriver from the table and smothered a groan into the glass's rim. How had the evening come to this?

She'd agreed to meet up with the Ngo sisters at Shenanigans for a business meeting. Having lived in Seattle since her freshman year in college nine years ago, she should have known that Shenanigans was not a restaurant but an upscale, female-targeted strip club. But she hadn't. And now she was forced to make a move toward Tarzan's gyrating crotch or suffer the consequences of looking like a woman who wouldn't put her mouth where her money was, so to speak.

The Ngos owned Wild Honey, one of the largest adult toy and outfitter chains on the West Coast. Their stores were impressive, from the inventory to the clientele. Kristi had never ventured inside, but the pictures and testimonials on their Web site said plenty. What Wild Honey didn't have was Kristi's unique variety of pleasure gadgets. She'd never planned on selling the toys apart from the small-time on-line business she'd started two and a half years ago after quitting a life-consuming product-design job with a Fortune 500 company; however, the generous figure the Ngos offered to exclusively carry her products had changed that. She was in debt up to her eyeballs from supplier and distribution expenses. She could sign a contract with the twins tonight and bring her finances into a very healthy shade of black.

Unless they realized she was a sham who could only vouch for the immense satisfaction derived from her solo-user apparatuses.

To be fair, the last time she'd tried out one of her toys in the company of a man, he had been turned on by it. So much so that he'd come in his jeans. It was for the best. Even if he'd waited to find his release inside of her, she wouldn't have gone along for the ride. When it came to a guy locating her G-spot and making her climax, not even a detailed map and directions could help. She'd long since given up on test-driving her couples' toys. As such, she couldn't personally speak for their effectiveness. The Ngos wouldn't have a reason to expect that if she followed the universal suggestion, which was becoming more like an annoyingly obsessive mantra, and touched the beefcake.

Kristi slammed back the remainder of her drink and slapped the glass onto the table. To a chorus of raucous cheers, she reached for Tarzan's sweaty thigh. A little brush and she would save face with the Ngos while appeasing the horde of female piranhas surrounding her.

Her fingers touched down on glistening, rock-solid muscle, then quickly slid upward with the momentum of the beefcake's next shimmy. She sucked in a stunned gasp as her fingers kept going, disappearing beneath the loincloth until they connected with another naked, sweaty muscle. Warmth swept into her cheeks as her knuckles grazed a semierection. Moisture dampened her panties, reminding her that while she couldn't come with a man, she had no problem getting wet with one.

But she wasn't getting wet over Tarzan—at least, not any more so. He was a prop. And she would treat him as a prop. She had to if she wanted the Wild Honey contract.

Kristi turned her hand around and his cock slipped into her palm. Silky smooth but interestingly not fully erect. With so many female admirers, she'd assumed he would have a massive hard-on. Maybe he was gay. Out of sheer curiosity, she folded her fingers around his cock and squeezed. His shaft gave a twitch and expanded in an instant, the extensive girth making it impossible for her thumb and fingers to touch.

Oops. Guess he wasn't gay.

But she was suddenly dying of thirst. With her unoccupied hand, she fumbled on the table behind her for her drink. Someone placed a glass into her hand, and she took a long swallow, remembering too late that she'd finished her screwdriver. Something far more potent singed its way down her throat.

A whistle sounded in the near distance. Tarzan lifted her hand from beneath his loincloth and brought it to his lower torso, gliding it over sculpted abdominal muscles and up to a broad chest waxed free of hair. He traced her fingers over his small male nipples until each puckered, and then pulled her hand higher still. She had no choice but to rise to her feet. Instinct had her tipping back her head and meeting his eyes, seeing the sinfully wicked invitation burning in them. A smile every bit as naughty curved full lips. He had a crook in his nose that suggested it had been broken at some point in time. She'd always been a sucker for broken noses—it gave the owner's face a whole new level of character.

Kristi's attention shot back to his mouth with the damp swipe of his tongue across the tips of her fingers. Her pussy clenched as he closed firm lips around her first finger and sucked hard. His free hand settled at the small of her back, urging her closer, until his erection prodded into the softness of her belly. His hot mouth began an erotic dart-and-thrust game with her finger, and her nipples stabbed to aching awareness.

Oh boy. He was good. And it was hot.

The hand at her back moved lower, cupping her ass through the fabric of her modest black business skirt, squeezing an ample butt cheek. He jerked her to him at the same time he brought his pelvis forward. The plump head of his shaft slid past the confines of the loincloth to press into her belly button. She could feel his precum soaking through her thin pink cotton shirt. Smell his primal scent on the air. Or maybe that was hers. Her panties were drenched with her essence, her thighs throbbing with jealousy for the sensual treat her belly button received.

Sliding her fingers from his mouth, Tarzan began working his way down her body. His tongue replaced the press of his erection. He circled her belly button, licked over the wet cotton. The look on his face as he tipped back his head to eye her was sheer and exquisite pleasure. It shouldn't excite her so much that he liked the taste of his own cum, but it had the blood sizzling in her veins. She balled her fists to stop from reaching for his hair, curling her fingers in the thick raven locks.

Oh yeah. It was hot in here. Getting hotter all the time.

He lifted up the hem of her shirt a few inches, blew on her sensitized skin. Drawing in a hard breath, she reached behind her, fumbled to find a glass of something. Anything. "Need. More. Drink."

Laughter was followed by a glass being placed in her hand. Kristi gulped back the unknown drink like a dying woman. Tarzan's tongue settled on her bared skin, moved in sinuous circles. The rise of her belly wasn't enormous, but it had never been flat a day in her life. He didn't seem to mind her fuller figure. Didn't seem to mind at all that she was dressed completely wrong for the hedonistic atmosphere, the last woman in the club who should want his attention. He just eased her back onto her chair and fell to his knees at her feet as if he planned to worship her.

He lifted her foot into his lap, and she bobbled in her chair. Using both hands, Kristi held on to the sides of her seat. She watched through a haze of liquor and desire as he slid a black sling-back from her foot to curl his tongue around her big toe. Her pussy gushed with juice, and she heard herself cry out as distantly as if she was a voyeur watching the scene play out through someone else's eyes.

She blinked as another face swam into view. Another dark-haired beefcake, working his big, magical hands up her leg, along her burning inner thigh.

But, no. It was the same guy. Not two. Just one. Couldn't be two. Not with so many other women anxious and screaming for attention.

She had to quit drinking. It was messing with her head. Making her forget she was here on business. That all she would achieve by allowing a man to get her wet was the need to go home and finish the job on her own. Her throat too dry to bear, she grappled behind her for a glass. She would quit drinking, just as soon as her thirst was quenched enough so she didn't feel like she would go up in flames.

Was it a bad sign that her tongue felt like used toilet paper?

Against an unsettling sixth sense that she would live to regret it, Kristi opened her eyes. Sunlight streamed onto her face from a part in the curtains on the other side of the bedroom. She squinted against the light as ache ratcheted through her head.

The toilet-paper effect had definitely been an omen.

A leg brushed against her left one—a hairy leg. A hairy leg that didn't feel like it belonged to her Jack Russell terrier, but a man.

A man. With her in bed. And she had no recollection of how they'd gotten that way.

The hairy leg rubbed up against hers again, followed by an arm wrapping around her middle and a groggy, "Hey."

"Hey," she returned quietly.

"Hey," he said back. From her right side.

How was that possible? He couldn't be lying on both her right side and her left side.

The bed shifted to her right, and a broad back, tanned and

toned to perfection, appeared in her line of vision. A deep male voice asked, "Jack?"

The arm around her middle moved away, and another broad back, this one not quite as tanned but equally toned, appeared. A second deep male voice questioned, "Spencer?"

So that was how he'd been on both sides of her. Because there wasn't one man in bed with her but two. Perfect explanation. If she was a frigging mutt!

Oh. My. God. There were two men in bed with her! Not one, but two. And they were naked. And . . . Kristi peeked under the covers. Yep, she was definitely naked. Naked and sore. It felt like someone had rammed a toaster between her thighs. And her ass . . . nope, not even gonna go there.

She sat up, glanced at each of the men, and noted they were vaguely familiar, definitely attractive if you were into that whole dark, built, hot-as-sin package, and opted to leave it at that. "Kristi." She wriggled from beneath the covers and crawled quickly down the bed. Her head spun as she slid off the end onto her hands and knees. "Now that we've figured out who we all are, I really need to be going."

Clothes. Clothes would be good. Ignoring the throb between her temples, she searched the garments scattered about the floor. Two pair of men's pants. Two pair of men's boxers. Two men's shirts. How convenient, since she'd slept with *two* men.

Jesus. She had to get out of here. Like now. Even if it meant leaving naked.

Then again, leaving naked was probably a bad idea. The alarm clock on the stand next to the bed revealed it was almost one. People were bound to see her rather healthy, very pasty figure jiggling down the sidewalk as she ran off in search of her sanity and lose their lunch.

Kristi didn't want to stand up and face the guys and the reality of what she'd done to end up naked and sandwiched between them. But she did so in the hopes one of them could direct her to her clothes. They sat exactly how she'd left them, having a stare down that reminded her of some animalistic alpha-male face-off to see who won first rights to the prime-breeding female of the pack.

The joke was on them because neither was getting her. Nor were both. Not again.

Hysterical laughter bubbled out before she could stop it. The guys quit staring to look at her. Two sexy smiles formed. Two hard male chests puffed out. Muscles had never done it for her any more than bravado. She had to still be drunk because her pussy squeezed with excitement over the idea they were silently warring over her.

She sighed. When she decided to give men another chance at locating her G-spot and providing that all-consuming O, she did it in a big way.

"It was fun," she managed when they continued to look her way; then she wondered, Was it? She'd never been so sloshed as to forget the bulk of an evening. She'd definitely never forgotten sleeping with someone, though there had been several encounters she might as well have slept through.

Jack tossed back the covers and slid from the bed. He stood, towering nearly a foot over her five-foot-two frame, and stretched, running his fingers through tousled raven hair as muscles rippled from his ears to his glutes. There was action between his legs, too, but not of the rippling variety. More of the bobbing. "Don't you live here?"

Kristi stared openmouthed at his enormous erection. Good Lord, the guy looked like he'd just stepped off the pages of *Playgirl*. Guess it wasn't a toaster to blame for her soreness.

His question registered then. Heat suffusing her body from her perusal, she looked around, noting the familiar peach, lace-trimmed comforter atop a late Victorian, mahogany, four-poster bed. A white wicker hamper set off to one side of the room, the open slats revealing a kaleidoscope of color. That explained where her clothes went.

She struggled not to cringe over the reminder of her naked state. She was comfortable with her body when it was one man eying her. Two men . . . two men, both of whom were equally naked, eyeing her felt sinful. In the kind of wickedly carnal way that had her sex tingling and her nipples standing on end. "I meant you should be going. Both of you."

Jack's gaze moved to her aroused breasts and his smile grew, showcasing a dynamite set of pearly whites. She said a little thank-you prayer that he was gentleman enough not to comment, instead turning away to pluck a pair of black boxers and khaki pants from the floor.

The roguish gleam in Spencer's eyes and the way he openly looked his fill suggested he didn't suffer from a gentleman complex. Finally, he, too, looked away. Scrubbing a hand over a face centered by a neatly trimmed, dark brown mustache and shadowed with stubble, he glanced at the alarm clock. "Shit. I didn't realize it was so late. I gotta be on stage at two."

The sixth sense Kristi had experienced upon waking returned. "On stage?"

"I requested extra shifts this month," Spencer explained, slipping from bed to yank on red boxers. "They don't normally schedule us back-to-back otherwise. Dancing's a lot of fun, but it's also a helluva lot of work."

Kristi had noted more than the fact that he, too, surpassed the six-foot mark; she'd caught a flash of his cock before he'd covered it. Not only was it just as big as Jack's, but it was pierced with a ruby stud that the mere sight of had her clit throbbing. She'd designed more than one toy to simulate a pierced penis. The sensation of a piercing scraping over an aroused clit was orgasmic to the max.

Had she climaxed last night from the brush of his stud?

She forgot about the question as Spencer's words caught up

with her. Her belly did a slow roll. He'd said dancing, but what he meant was stripping. As in she hadn't slept with two random guys she'd picked up after leaving the strip club. She'd slept with two strippers who probably went home with a different woman every night of the week.

Oh boy. Her parents would be so proud.

Ultraconservative, tighty-whitey wearers through and through, they were the reason she'd planned to keep her sex-toy business small-time—she didn't want to run the risk of her name being tied to her merchandise. Her parents were just too proud of her product-design position. Her father, a high school career counselor back in her small Oregon hometown, used her as the example for success. If he knew the truth, that she'd left the well-paid and respected position behind to make orgasm-inducing goodies, he would never look at her the same. Then there was the way her folks would react to finding out she'd slept with two men at once—two men who were strippers, at that. It would make her reaction seem like just another of the bad jokes she was known for.

She had to get them out of here now, when hopefully the bulk of her neighbors were at work. "I'm sure you guys do this kind of thing a lot, but it's a first and last for me. So, not to be rude, but if you can be gone when I get out of the shower, I'd really appreciate it."

2

"This never happened," Spencer said to Jack the moment Kristi closed the door on the bathroom that adjoined the bedroom.

Fuck no, it hadn't, Jack thought as he pulled on a wrinkled short-sleeve polo shirt. He refused to entertain thoughts he'd had his dick anywhere near Spencer's last night. For the sake of the job, they had to get relatively close, do some minor touching, but that was where it ended. "Agreed. Whatever 'this' is."

Spencer smirked as he tugged on his T-shirt. "You don't remember?"

He'd been working with the guy too long not to know when he was full of shit. "Neither do you. I'd say Cai slipped something into those shots she bought us."

"Kim was acting just as naughty last night. Not her style." Pulling on his jeans, Spencer nodded toward the bathroom door. "I'd say hers either."

Despite the fact that she'd boldly slid her hand beneath his loincloth and grabbed hold of his cock—a move that earned her a misconduct whistle and could have gotten her thrown out of the club if he'd wanted—Jack had to agree. Kristi didn't seem the naturally naughty type. From what he remembered of last night, she'd been wearing clothes more suited to a mild-mannered businesswoman who'd been thrust into a scene she wasn't entirely comfortable with. Her shoulder-length, strawberry blond hair had been twisted into a classy style just as out of place. He blamed her contrasting appearance and actions on his response to her handling.

When he had first taken a part-time, second job with Shenanigans two years ago, he'd developed an erection within seconds of going on stage. These days, it rarely happened. The same could be said for his behavior. In the beginning, he'd gone home with a woman every other week or so. Nowadays that was never the case. Cai's after-dance shot and whatever secret ingredient it held had to be responsible for his being here now.

He spotted his loafers and Spencer's tennis shoes lying haphazardly in front of the closed bedroom door. He tossed Spencer's shoes at him. "The way Kristi's acting, she doesn't remember what happened either and doesn't want to."

"Then let's get the hell outta here."

Jack slid his feet into his loafers, then opened the bedroom door. A streak of white and brown fur shot past him, coming to a stop in front of Spencer. With a series of high-pitched yips, the dog wrapped its front paws around Spencer's leg and started dry-humping it.

The bathroom door clicked open, and Kristi came rushing out in a mint green robe that only covered an inch or two of her creamy white thighs. Her cheeks were tinged with pink, suggesting she'd either been scrubbing her face or was embarrassed about the situation. Jack would guess the latter.

"Climax!" She grabbed the dog by the back of its collar and pulled it off of Spencer's leg. "Bad dog. Down, girl."

Jack took a moment to appreciate the teasing flash of a generous breast from the neckline of her robe. He didn't have much time for dating between a full-time job as an electrician and his part-time gig with Shenanigans. When he did find the time to socialize, it was with real women like Kristi, the kind who had more than skin and bones to wrap his arms around. He laughed. "Her name's Climax?"

"I can see why," Spencer said. "And that she has great taste in men."

Jack snorted while Kristi gave a laugh that sounded more brittle than amused. "That's not why. But you don't care why. Did you guys want breakfast?" Her gaze shifted to the door, making it clear she didn't want to provide it.

Her behavior backed up the idea she wasn't naughty by nature, despite her dog's name. Hoping to relax her, he nodded at Spencer. "We were just leaving."

"Yeah. Thanks for the offer, but I really gotta get to work." Climax secured in Kristi's arms, Spencer led Jack out of the bedroom and down a short hallway, stopping when he'd reached the front door and pulled it open. "Damn. Looks like we didn't drive here."

A glance outside revealed a blacktop driveway edged on either side with a blossoming hawthorn tree and no vehicle in sight. Jack turned to find Kristi had followed them out of the bedroom. Squatting several feet away, she scratched Climax's head. He would be the first to admit to an active imagination when it came to sex, but generally he could contain those thoughts for the right moment. The way her position made her short robe ride up and the sides part to provide a captivating glimpse of her mound, he didn't stand a chance.

Her sex was shaved, the plump lips parted just slightly with her stance. He couldn't remember if he'd had any part of his body in or on those lips last night. The way his cock, which had only just begun to soften, instantly stiffened made it clear he would have found no hardship in fucking her.

"What's the matter?" Kristi asked.

From behind Jack, Spencer said, "Do you have a garage?"

Jack urged his gaze upward. He hadn't taken the time to look at her face much, thought it pointless since they would never again cross paths. Now he couldn't help but note her lush pink lips and the cluster of freckles on her upturned nose. Her eyes were wide, an appealing shade of golden brown fringed in thick, dark blond lashes. Right now, her eyes held a massive dose of unease. Anxiety that would only grow if he allowed his attention to wander back down to the delicacy of her bare, parted sex. But, damn, how he wanted to do just that.

"No garage. Why?" Her nerves reflected in her tone.

"There's no car out front." Jack glanced around, distracting himself from looking at her body by searching out a phone. "Can I use your phone to call a cab?"

"Yeah, sure." Kristi struggled to sound casual as she stood and ushered Climax into the nearest room with a door. After closing the dog inside, she started for the kitchen to grab the phone. She stopped halfway there and turned back. Though she told it not to, her attention zoomed to Jack's crotch. She hadn't considered that the way she'd been squatting while petting Climax would put her sex on full display until after she'd realized Jack's gaze was fixed there. One lingering hot look on his part and the idea of offering the guys breakfast in the form of herself had superglued itself to her brain and had her pussy damp with desire all over again.

Sheesh! Maybe she was a mutt, after all.

She focused on the reason she'd turned back. "Where's my car?"

Jack shrugged. "We must have caught a cab last night."

"Kim or Cai might have dropped us off." Spencer's eyes warmed with the mention of the twins. Earlier Kristi had noted those eyes were a shade or two lighter than navy blue. Now they were closer to midnight.

"You know the Ngos? How well?" She heard the tone of

her voice—it sounded jealous, as if she thought one night together meant she owned them—and bit her tongue. "Never mind."

She wasn't jealous and definitely didn't care who the men slept with, though the idea of doing the beautiful and perfectly petite twins' sloppy seconds wasn't exactly comforting. What she did care about is how much of a scene they'd caused coming home.

The subdivision she lived in had a noise curfew. Then there was Mrs. Johnson, her sweet, elderly, but entirely too nosy neighbor. The old lady had made friends with Kristi's mother last time her parents visited and now regularly called to update her on Kristi's comings and goings. She'd already had to lie to her parents once when Mrs. Johnson had noted Kristi rarely left the house. She'd told her folks that, to save on gas and office space, the company allowed her to work from home. "Do you think anyone saw us come in?"

"Your guess is as good as mine," Jack said.

She hadn't realized how tense she was until her shoulders sagged with his words and a huge sigh of relief escaped her. "You guys don't remember last night?"

Spencer's lips curved into an enticing smile. He gave her a quick once-over that lingered an instant on her breasts and groin area. Kristi held her breath in wait of his answer. "Enough to know you're quite the woman."

She looked to Jack, hoping for a less-enigmatic response, but he only nodded in agreement. For her first and last ménage, it sounded like she'd done a good job. That had to be something to smile about. In retrospect, say ten or twenty years from now, she was sure she would, too. Now she just had to get them the hell out of here.

Forcing a smile, Kristi went into the kitchen and grabbed the phone. She needed a minute alone to do some deep breathing, so she called the cab place for them. She popped extra-strength Tylenol, took a few more deep breaths, and then went back out into the other room. "Cab will be here in a few minutes."

She used the time until the cab arrived to dress. Since her car appeared to have been left at the strip club, it made sense to share a cab with the guys to pick it up. It made sense, but the instant she was in the backseat of the taxi, she regretted the decision.

There was a tall, dark, sexy stripper guy on either side of her, the warmth of their big bodies emanating into her outer thighs. His scent wrapping its way around her senses. She felt like the meat in a particularly big-bunned Kristi-burger.

Had either one of them eaten her pickle?

Ooh. Now was not the time for her bad sense of humor.

What seemed like an hour, but was closer to ten minutes, passed before they pulled into Shenanigans' parking lot. She spotted her lime green VW Bug. Thank God. Jack got out of the cab, and she slid out behind him, trying to look like the urge to run to her car and drive far, far away wasn't hounding her.

Jack smiled down at her. She struggled for words. At her home, the guys had been the ones leaving. Now she felt like a good-bye on her part was in order. "Bye. Have a nice . . . life."

Amusement passed through Jack eyes, drawing her into their green depths. There were little flecks of amber mixed in. Very appealing.

Apparently she'd stared too long because Jack didn't respond with words but leaned down and brushed his lips over hers. No tongue. Just a soft caress of full, firm lips. It shouldn't have gotten her heart kicking against her ribs. And she definitely shouldn't have missed his mouth the second he lifted it away.

Spencer's face came into view, followed quickly by his arms.

Through his T-shirt, the hard muscles of his chest crushed against her breasts. His mouth settled over hers. No soft caress, but a full-bodied commanding kiss that ordered her to respond. She parted her lips and his tongue pushed inside. Rubbed against hers. Once. Twice. And then was gone. His arms left her, too, and she felt cold. Given, it was early June and the sun was currently behind a cloud. But, no. Not that kind of cold. The kind that told her going without a man for over two years was a very bad idea.

"Good-bye, doll. Thanks for everything."

"Right. Everything." None of which she remembered.

Kristi had told herself it was for the best that she didn't remember, but suddenly she wanted to know every detail. Even if she hadn't climaxed, the memory of being loved by two such awesome specimens of masculinity would surely be enough to warm her through however many years she went without a lover this next time.

Jack's kiss helped in that department, too. Without warning, he returned to her, swooping down and pulling her against him, lifting her into his arms as if she was a ninety-pound waif. His mouth came over hers hard, his tongue sliding smoothly inside, stroking over her teeth, rubbing against hers, licking at her soft inner cheeks. Leaving her breathless and squirming for more by the time he finally pulled away.

He set her down and she instinctively looked to Spencer. It was his turn, after all. But he didn't make a move toward her. Just said a last good-bye and started for the club's entrance. Jack followed his lead, saying good-bye and heading toward the other end of the parking lot where his vehicle presumably waited.

Kristi licked her lower lip, tasting both of them. Both. Two. Two gorgeous men, with incredible smiles and really tight asses. Shamelessly, she watched them walk away, her attention fixed on the play of their pants across their taut backsides. Then they were gone from sight, one gobbled up by the club's front door and the other by the driver's door of a silver Caprice.

On the inside, the cold returned. On the outside, her cheeks felt more than a little hot as she slipped into her Bug. And as she sat down, her thighs brushed together and she realized she was also more than a little wet. From nothing more than kisses. To think what they might have been able to accomplish with more time. What they might have accomplished last night . . .

On second thought, she was better off not thinking about that. The only good course of action here was to forget the last twenty hours entirely and concentrate her efforts on what to say when she called the Ngos. Not only did she have to convince them that she hadn't been completely intoxicated during their business meeting, but she also wanted to ensure that her name would remain apart from her products.

3

Kristi closed her eyes against the exquisite tension barreling its way up her body, starting at her curled toes and ending deep in her burning core. The tongue lapping at the wet folds of her pussy licked harder. Crying out with the electric thrill of impending release, she buried her fingers in the hair of the man between her thighs. The man whose large hands held her legs splayed wide. Who ceased the assault of his tongue only long enough to nibble at her clit.

Tiny explosions went off in her cunt with the scrape of his teeth over the inflamed bead. Stars danced before her eyes. Her head spun. From the liquor, maybe a little. From the orgasm cresting over her, definitely. His tongue returned to her sex, shoved inside with a demanding thrust, and feasted as she came with a scream of triumph.

The ringing of the phone jarred Kristi from the memory. And what a memory it had been. Just a glimpse of the night before. A glimpse that didn't show her the owner of that magnificent tongue. But a glimpse that showed her something even better. She had climaxed last night. With a man. No toys needed.

The knowledge was enough to ease her misery over what else had happened last night. One of the guys had shaved her pubic hair. It had to have been one of them. Whenever she decided to go without, she went the waxing route. It stopped the urge to itch her crotch in public and the knowledge she looked like a poorly planted Chia Pet when the hair started growing back in.

Only, her current misery wasn't over an impending day or two of itching, but because she would never be able to forget the guys until the hair grew back.

Ignoring the phone, Kristi plunked down on the couch and accepted the truth. It didn't matter if she was shaved. She would never be able to forget the guys anyway, not now that she knew one of them had done what she'd believed impossible. If the brief memory was a sign, then last night's orgasm had been more powerful than anything she'd ever experienced with one of her pleasure gadgets. It made her want to rush over to Shenanigans for a repeat performance.

Almost repeat. She wasn't up for another ménage, now or ever. She just wanted one man. Whichever one had buried his head between her legs and expertly devoured her pickle. Unless her memory provided further insight, she had no idea how to figure out which man was responsible.

What she needed here was advice. Thankfully she knew the people to give it: two women who, up until last night, suffered the same affliction as her—the disappearance of a working G-spot whenever a man entered the equation. Fiona still suffered that fate anyway. Several months ago, Liz had gotten lucky in a big way and found a man who could make her come a river.

Kristi had stumbled upon the women while researching new toy design ideas on-line. Soon after, they'd created a private

Web group appropriately termed *Operation G-Spot*. Scattered across the United States as they were, the group allowed them to gather and chat with regularity. Though the *G-Spot* creed effectively said each woman was responsible for dating and doing every man who came her way in the hopes of finding one capable of getting her off, Kristi had never taken it seriously. Had never even planned to put any effort into asking a guy out. And apparently she hadn't needed to make the effort, since two men had seemingly arrived in her bed by magic.

Two men who had her hot thinking about them even now. But, no. It wasn't the two of them that had her hot. It was the one of them who had given her an orgasm.

Shivering over the memory of the powerful climax, Kristi went into the spare bedroom she used as her office. She sat down at her iMac, hit the Internet icon, and logged into the *Operation G-Spot* chat group. She breathed a sigh of relief when she spotted Liz's name highlighted as being on-line.

Kristi: Thank God you're on. I did something bad last night to the tune of 138.

Liz: 138?

Kristi: 69 x 2.

Liz: Nice, twice in one night. So much for Fi's claim you aren't trying.

Kristi: But that's just it! I didn't get lucky twice, and I also wasn't trying. I got lucky with two guys at the same time by accident. Just call me a drunken mutt.

Liz: Ohmigawd! No way.

Kristi: Way. And I didn't remember a friggin' thing.

Liz: Then what makes you so sure you did it?

Kristi: We woke up naked in my bed this morning, and both sides of me feel like they were visited by the Toaster Fairy. These guys do not have teeny weenies.

Liz: I'm seriously not laughing. Oh, who am I kidding? LMAO!

Kristi: They strip for a living, Liz!

Liz: You slept with two strippers?

Kristi: Yes! And I said I didn't remember. I do remember now, at least a small part. A really good, small part. I had an . . . get ready . . . orgasm.

Liz: You dog! That's *sooo* awesome. Are you seeing them again?

Kristi: Them? Am I seeing *them* again? They aren't a package deal. And, no, I am not seeing them again. I still can't believe I ever "saw" them in the first place.

Liz: But they gave you an orgasm. That has to mean something.

Kristi: Yeah, that I was drunk enough to mistake them for a double-headed dildo.

Liz: What makes you think one of them didn't give you the orgasm and the other was just there as a bonus?

Kristi: Actually, that's what I'm hoping for. But how am I supposed to figure out which one did the job? They don't remember much either.

Liz: Fi would suggest the obvious. Do them both individually until one comes through for you, literally. Who knows, maybe one of these guys is your Mr. Right.

Spencer finished his routine and returned out front to where he'd seen Cai talking with Linda, Shenanigans' manager, at a table in the back of the semidarkened room. Cai sat alone now, looking over some papers. Out of habit, he took in her outfit: neon green hot pants and a matching tank top that exposed the bulk of her cleavage through a strategically placed open metal ring. He'd been friends with the Ngos in high school. Fate had reunited them a few years ago when Wild Honey started up a small shop inside the club's entrance. Cai had dressed as modestly as Kim in school. He couldn't say he minded the transformation. What he did mind was Cai slipping shit into his drink that landed him in bed with another man.

Reaching Cai's table, he jerked a chair out. He turned it around and sat down, with his arms folded over the chair's back.

Cai looked up, a feline smile curving lips that matched the pink highlights in her hair. She arched a black eyebrow and supplied an answer before he could ask a question. "You offered to try out Wild Honey's new products every other time I asked. This time I just didn't ask. I wanted a guaranteed authentic reaction."

"You got it, doll. I not only wound up naked in bed with Jack, but I also can't remember a goddamned thing."

"Sorry about the memory. It sounds like all the bugs aren't worked out yet." Amusement shone in her eyes. "As for waking up naked with Jack, you've obviously wanted him all along. 'Tiger' doesn't make you do things you don't want to do; it just gives you the courage to make a move."

Spencer growled in the back of his throat. Cai had a reputation for fucking both women and men, and he was fine with her choices. Personally, he would rather be castrated than stick his dick up some guy's ass. "I didn't wake up alone with Jack, Cai. I woke up with Jack and that woman you were with last night. She was in between us. I never touched any part of Jack's body." He hoped.

She smacked her lips together. "Mmm . . . lucky boys. What I wouldn't do to get my face between those big, beautiful tits."

He wanted to forget last night, but the mention of Kristi had him remembering certain parts in a big way. He made it a point not to get involved with sweet women. They wanted things in the long term, and he wasn't at that stage in his life. He couldn't deny how appealing she'd been this morning, though, scrambling off the bed, waving her round, dimpled ass in his face. He couldn't forget the hungry way she eyed his cock either, licking her lips as if she found his shaft scrumptious.

Christ, he hardened now with the memory.

Adjusting his erection under the table, he observed, "She seems more Kim's type."

Cai barked out a laugh. "As if Kim would be caught dead with another woman. She's practically a virgin, for chrissakes. Kristi, now she has potential, but something tells me she doesn't want anyone to know about it. You enjoyed sleeping with her. Who wouldn't enjoy licking all that creamy white flesh, lapping at her hot, wet pussy until she's coming all over your face?" She shivered. "I could climax just thinking about it. But I'm not going to climax—you are. I need you to do Kristi for me again, Spence. This time when she's sober." Batting thick, black lashes, she leaned forward so that her cleavage pressed together and risked popping the metal ring. "For me."

Spencer's cock throbbed, not over Cai's behavior—he'd known her too long to feel anything but friendship toward her. It was the image of Kristi, with her legs spread wide and another woman licking her pussy that had his body humming with arousal. As much as the idea excited him, he could never see Kristi allowing it to happen. "I don't get it. You want me to screw some chick to convince her that she's bisexual?"

"I don't think she's bi. I just think she has a lot of untapped potential of the sexual variety. Kim and I noticed how hesitant she was about signing a contract with Wild Honey—she turned red when I started stroking a dildo in front of her. If she hadn't gotten hammered the other night, she might not have gone through on things at all." Her expression became the serious face of the owner of a company that had something to lose. "We won't have her backing out because she has some complex about being associated with sex. I need you to show her how good getting dirty can be."

The way Cai described Kristi fit with the woman he'd met the other morning. What didn't jive is what Kristi was doing working with Wild Honey. "What's the contract for?"

"To exclusively carry her product line. She designs sex toys."

Spencer straightened in his chair with his surprise. "You're kidding! She designs sex toys but is afraid to use them?"

"Maybe. I don't know. Do me this favor, Spence, and I promise to be a good girl and not add anything special to your drink again."

He snorted. "How kind of you." He should call the request what it was—blackmail—and turn her down. He wouldn't because he knew where the Ngos had come from, how hard they'd worked to make Wild Honey a success. If it was in his power to ensure Kristi stuck with the contract, he would do it. To have the career she did, she couldn't be as sweet as he'd thought anyway. "All right. I'll do it. But you damned sure better hold up your end of the bargain and keep your Tiger by the tail."

Cai groaned. "That might have been your worst joke yet."

"You deserve far worse than bad humor," Spencer said darkly. He stood and gave her a playful pinch on the butt before starting toward the front.

A nicely rounded strawberry blonde dressed in casual slacks and a knit top caught his attention midway to the stage. Kristi. The woman turned, and he shook his head and kept walking. Not Kristi. But the telling twitch of his cock made it clear that when it was Kristi in his presence, he'd enjoy carrying out Cai's request to the fullest.

Kristi cast a sidelong look at Jack. His big hands cradled the steering wheel of the Caprice, and his attention lay fixed on the road unfolding ahead. He gave total dedication to driving. Just as he gave his all when it came to stripping.

And to sex?

Trying to force another memory, she took in his profile, the slight curl of his thick, raven hair. The bump in his nose. A full, sensual mouth with a tantalizing tongue—if that kiss he'd given her in Shenanigans' parking lot was a sign. As exciting as the prospect was of that tongue and the secret joy she took in his imperfect nose, neither feature was the reason she'd chosen to invite him on a midweek getaway to her favorite B & B along the Washington coast. It was the fact that he seemed a gentleman. At least, much more so than Spencer.

Jack didn't seem the sort to mention their accidental ménage once she made it clear it wasn't up for discussion. Spencer appeared the devilish type who would take great pleasure in teasing her with reminders. Of course, she could be entirely wrong about both guys, since all she knew for certain about either was the size of their package.

Oy! What had she been thinking following Liz's advice?

I still can't believe I'm doing this.

Jack glanced over with a hesitant smile. "Despite what happened the other night, I don't normally go on vacation with someone I've only known a few hours."

Oops. Had she spoken that last thought aloud? "Then why are you here?"

"I have a thing for antiques. The way you described the Victorian bed-and-breakfast, I couldn't resist." His smile became a grin. "And you're right about our chemistry—there was definitely something in that kiss."

Kristi invited him on this getaway with the understanding that it was to get to know each other better. When he grinned that way, so his lips parted just enough to show her a glimpse of his tongue, she wanted to get to know him better, all right. She wanted to order him to pull over to the side of the road and show her exactly what he could accomplish with a few strategically placed licks.

Just in case he did turn out to be the keeper of the map to her G-spot—mmm, maybe he had it stored in the glove compartment even now—she wasn't about to risk coming off as a mutt again. First, they would get to know each other; that he shared her passion for antiques was a great start. And then she would demand he show her his tongue technique. "I don't normally think of strippers and antique-lovers as being one and the same."

He leveled a serious look at her. "I'm not a stripper. I'm a dancer. And it's a part-time second job I'll soon be leaving behind."

"I didn't mean to imply stripping is a bad profession."

Jack's smile returned as he focused back on the road. "It didn't come across that way. I'm just saying, it's not what I do for a living."

"What do you do?"

"Residential wiring. The last thing you want to hear about in any detail. How about you?"

Heat spread into her cheeks, and Kristi looked out the passenger-side window. She had no reason to feel anything but pride over her toys and the pleasure they brought to their users. Maybe it was the way they'd met, his admission to a day job that was anything but sexual, or just the fact that she hadn't spent time with a guy she was attracted to in almost three years, but she suddenly wished she'd never left her product-development job behind. "Nothing worth mentioning. Very boring stuff."

"Try me."

"I invent things."

"Things?"

She shrugged. "For women. To use alone or with someone else."

"Are these the kind of things that require batteries?"

She heard the amusement in his voice and forced herself to look at him. She was spending the next two and a half days with this man, sharing a room with him. And, really, he'd already seen every inch of her pale, ample posterior, quite possibly was the one responsible for shaving her pubes. Still, she couldn't get out a straight answer. "They might be."

Jack laughed, the sound rich, deep, and seeping moisture into her panties. The gush of wetness had her gaze instinctively going to his lap. Laughing harder, he lifted a hand from the steering wheel to give her leg a squeeze. "You're a puzzle. One minute you're blushing over your career choice, the next you're checking out my crotch."

Her cheeks hotter than ever, Kristi zipped her attention back to his face. Sheesh! If she was going to accomplish anything this weekend, she needed to start acting like an adult. "I enjoy my work. I just don't often discuss it with men."

"No boyfriends?"

"Do you think I would be here with you if I had a boyfriend?" Not to mention would have jumped into bed with two strangers? One of whom she wasn't going to think about. Just one man would be on her mind the next few days. Not two. Just one.

"I meant in the past."

Deep breaths. She inhaled three long ones before she felt relaxed enough to respond. "No one significant."

"You're free to use me this weekend."

So much for deep breathing! Kristi tensed so quickly and rigidly she thought she might have heard a bone snap. Or maybe that was the sound of her pussy clapping over the prospect of finding release much earlier than planned. "I can use you?"

"To discuss your inventions with. I thought you might like a male point of view."

"Oh. Thanks." Her inventions. Just discussion. Not sex. Phew! What a relief.

She really did want to use the next few days to get to know him better. Or at least tonight. Twenty-four hours had to be plenty of time to get to know someone. She hoped so. As wet as she was right now, she wasn't sure she could hold out any longer than that.

Kristi stood at the foot of an early Victorian, queen-sized walnut bed, its four-poster design similar to the one Jack remembered from her bedroom. He'd heard the expression "wringing one's hands" many times but had never seen anyone do it until now. She looked around the room—at the fainting couch detailed in regal shades of red, ivory, and gold that matched the throw and the pillows on the bed—and then at him and frowned. "I swear this room used to have twin beds."

And he could swear she was becoming a bigger puzzle by the moment. Did she have a split personality, or how could a woman who came across so nervous about the mere thought of sex be a success at designing sex toys?

"What's the big deal? We've shared a bed before. Then we were both naked. Now . . ." He swept his gaze over her, lingering on the plentiful rise of her breasts beneath a bright yellow V-neck T-shirt and her rounded ass and thighs hugged alluringly by black jean shorts.

Now they didn't have a third party.

She'd chosen him over Spencer, had asked him to keep silent about her decision for now so as not to hurt Spencer's feelings. She was as considerate as they came, and Jack had the burning urge to get her naked and show her how much he appreciated that trait by tasting every inch of her smooth, creamy flesh.

Kristi sucked her lower lip into her mouth, nibbled on it a few seconds. "I don't want you to think I'm only after sex."

He tugged his attention from her sexy little nibbles and the resulting effect they had on his groin to concentrate on her admission. So that was the reason for her anxiety. Sex didn't rattle her; she just feared it was all he was after. He had no doubt he would enjoy loving her—had enjoyed doing so two nights ago—but he also had a good feeling about the whole package. Not only was she built as if she'd been made exclusively for his full-bodied tastes, but any woman who knew her way around antiques impressed the hell out of him.

"But you are after it?" he teased, hoping to ease her nerves.

"No. Yes. Like I said on the phone, I want to get to know you better. First."

Actually, she hadn't added that "first" part on the phone. Neither Jack nor his cock minded hearing it, though. He smiled. "How about a walk?" Before he forgot his intentions to relax her and put the antique bed to use. "The sun will soon be setting."

Tension visibly drained from her body. She gave him an appreciative smile that had his own kicking higher. "That sounds nice."

He slid open the glass door that led from their room to an open terrace and extended his hand. "This way, m'lady."

She gave him an odd look but came to him, taking his hand and letting him guide her out to the terrace and on to a small beach a couple hundred feet in the distance. In the middle of the week in early June, one other couple occupied the bed-and-breakfast. Right now, that couple was nowhere in sight. Only a handful of squawking seabirds and the sound of the incoming surf broke the quiet sanctity of the beach and the emerging reds and purples of the sunset.

Reaching the sand, Kristi shook her hand from his. Kicking off her sandals, she started toward the water and proceeded to wade in.

Jack shivered. The temperature had to be dipping into the

sixties with nightfall, and the water would be colder still. "You must have ice in your veins. The water has to be frigid with the tide washing in."

Knee-deep in the surf, she turned back and smiled at him before looking down. "Oops. Guess you were right."

He followed her gaze to find the hard points of her nipples jabbing at her T-shirt. His shaft gave a telling twitch as he looked back at her face. Was he imagining things, or was that an invitation in her eyes? It looked like an invitation. He toed off his loafers and started toward her. She sucked in her lush lower lip for an instant, just long enough to expose the damp pink tip of her tongue.

He groaned. Oh yeah, that was definitely an invitation. She might not be wholly naughty, but clearly she had the ability to be so when the timing was right. Now that she knew he wanted more than sex from this trip, the timing appeared perfect.

He walked into the water wearing his socks and pants. She laughed. "What are you doing?"

Reaching her, Jack pulled her against his chest. He pleasured in the sensual cradle of her plump breasts against his hard pecs as she ran her palms along his back. She was a good deal shorter than him, and kissing her meant getting wetter yet. The blood pumped through his veins, hot and fierce, urging him on. He barely noticed the cold waves breaking against his legs as he slanted his mouth over hers, tasted the flavor of strawberry lip gloss and warm, delicious woman.

Her lips blossomed beneath his, parting on a throaty sigh. He moved inside with relish, feasting on her as her breasts rubbed in a tauntingly erotic rhythm. Thumbing his fingers over the rigid nipples, he eased from her mouth to feather damp kisses along her neck, down to her earlobe. He teased a wet path into the dip of her shirt's V-neck, where her cleavage sweetly pressed.

Kristi's hands moved from his back to his shoulders. Another breathy sigh escaped her. His heart rate kicked up several notches, his dick throbbing to full, aching-hard awareness. He went down on his knees in the water and brushed his mouth across a nipple through her shirt. The contact not even close to enough, he fit his lips over the crown and drew it into his mouth, cotton and all.

Her fingers tightened on his shoulder. She arched against his lips, releasing a sound that could be a cry of displeasure as easily as one of ecstasy.

Though it was the last thing he wanted, Jack murmured, "Want me to stop?"

"Mmm . . ."

With a last damp suckle, he lifted his mouth from her nipple. The sound she'd made was indefinable, but considering her earlier admission, he wasn't about to push things.

She whimpered discontentedly as he stood. Her lower lip pushed out in a pout that was as sexy as it was endearing. "I said no, don't stop."

On second thought, it was definitely more sexy than endearing. Relief cruising through him, Jack chuckled and swept her up into his arms. He started toward the shore, barely able to resist the temptation of her full, kiss-reddened lips. He settled on caressing the tilt of her freckled nose with his lips as he placed her on the sand.

Bracing his arms on either side of her, he let his lust reflect in his voice. "Is that what that sound was?"

Her tongue slipped out, dabbed at her lips. Her pupils dilated, irises turning dark amber beneath half-drawn lids. "Yes." The word came out a little breathless.

He took it as all the invitation he needed. He came over her fully, his mouth finding hers in an instant. His tongue pushed inside, stroked, tangoed. His hands moved down her sides, touched down on warm, damp skin peppered with the salt spray of the ocean. Her fingers met with his, and she tugged at the hem of her T-shirt. He didn't take it off but went beneath it and the silky cups of her bra, filling his hands with her full, soft breasts, wishing his tongue was licking between her ample cleavage.

Kristi's hips rose beneath his. Her knees came up as her legs spread around him, bringing his swollen shaft into closer contact with her mound. His pulse sped as he moved his hand beneath the leg of her shorts and upward, felt her wetness on her panties. She moaned into his mouth, and he went higher, finding her hairless mound, fingering her slick, dewy pussy lips until she was dripping with excitement.

His cock clamored for release. He loved her several more times with his fingers and then pulled his hand free and reached for the waistband of his pants. He stopped with the give of the button, let her harsh pants fill his head and clear out the cobwebs of desire that had fogged his common sense.

Fuck, he had taken things too far. If he didn't end things immediately, he would be screwing her right here in the sand. As thrilling as that sounded, he wouldn't do it. Not at the cost of sending her fears soaring again the moment they were finished.

Jack refastened his button, then lifted himself up on his forearms. He skimmed each of her closed eyelids with a kiss and then sat back to find her lip gloss replaced with a natural sheen that was damned hard to resist. Smiling, he stroked her flushed cheek, brushing a blowing strand of hair from her face. "You're dirty."

Kristi's lips curved into a siren's smile. "Thank you. I try."

He chuckled while his body gave an impatient throb. "I meant that literally. You have sand in your hair." He traced a gritty pattern along her cheek. "And on your face." He rolled off of her and stood out of self-preservation. One kiss would only lead to a whole lot more. "They're going to quit serving dinner soon. If you want to eat, we'd best get cleaned up."

Her smile drooped and she opened her eyes. "Okay. Food's always a good thing."

Food was a good thing, but she didn't sound like she wanted it. She sounded like she wanted to feel him buried inside her as badly as he ached to be there. He pulled her to her feet and brushed a reassuring kiss across her mouth. "You know the best part about dinner? Right after comes dessert."

4

Jack shouldn't be thinking about spoiling his dinner by having dessert first. Not at the risk of ruining what could become a lasting relationship. As he'd told Kristi, he soon planned to leave the dancing job behind, and that meant he would have time to dedicate to a woman. But it was damned hard not to think about dessert when Kristi's shockingly bawdy, slightly off-key singing floated to him from beneath the bathroom door, along with the sound of splashing water.

The B & B owner had told them dinner was available until nine-thirty during the late spring and early summer months. Kristi had decided to take advantage of the extended time by indulging in a bubble bath in the claw-footed tub. She was naked less than ten feet and one door away. Considering the aroused state he'd left her in, she might be doing more than sloshing in the water. She might be using one of her inventions or sticking to old-fashioned methods and partaking in a pre-dinner fingering.

His cock pulsed with the erotic image that threatened. He

sat down on the fainting couch and stared out the patio door into the encroaching darkness. Time to think about something else. Anything else.

Kristi stopped singing. "Jack?"

He tensed. That didn't sound like an everyday Jack, but a husky, horny, come-n'-get-me Jack. "Yeah?"

"C'mere."

Not a good idea. Not if he was going to keep his hands to himself. He went to the door but didn't open it. "Do you need something from the front desk?"

"I can't hear you."

Shit. He pushed the door in and winced at the sight of her pale breasts bobbing in the sudsy water. Her nipples skimmed the surface, the dusky pink shade of her areolas drawing him in like lightning to a downed wire. "Did you need something?"

Her lips perked up at the corners, forming an impish smile. "I thought we could help the environment and save some water. You're dirty, too."

Man, was he ever. If she had any idea of the wicked thoughts barreling through his head . . . "You want to share your bath with me?"

She lifted a milk-white shoulder, exposing the bulk of her left breast. "We did already see each other naked."

Jack swallowed hard. He was right before—coming in here had been a bad idea. Terrible. And he had every intention of taking her up on the offer. His feet already moving, he asked, "You trust me to come in there with you and not touch?"

"You can touch. Yourself." He stopped dead and she laughed. "It could be fun."

"Somehow I don't think you watching me masturbate and fun belong in the same sentence. Sexy as fuck is more like it."

Her eyes registered something, maybe shock he'd spoken so frankly. Probably expected the words to come out of Spencer's mouth instead. His gut tightened with thoughts of Spencer, of the man with his hands on Kristi, with his tongue in her mouth, his dick God only knew where.

Kristi patted the water. "Join me. I want to see you get Jack off."

He chuckled at the quip but didn't feel amused. He felt like getting in that bathtub and making her forget that Spencer existed.

Quickly he undressed, letting his clothes fall where they might, and hopped into the tub. He looked up in time to see her eyes on his erection, just before he sank midway to his waist in the water. Her gaze moved to his chest, perusing several lingering seconds, long enough to have his small nipples erect.

"You have the body of a stripper."

"Dancer." Not that he had a problem with strippers. He just wasn't one.

"I know what you do is dance. I meant you could strip for a living. You have the goods." She leaned forward. With his attention on the way her breasts pressed together, he didn't notice where her hand was going until it was wrapped around his cock.

Jack flinched as she gave a squeeze. She laughed. "No teeny weenie here."

If she kept squeezing, there was not going to be a hard-on for him to take care of for her viewing pleasure. "What happened to not touching?"

Uncurling her fingers, she sat back and looked at him from under thick blond lashes. "I was helping you into the tub. Things have a way of getting slippery when wet."

He didn't miss the innuendo or the sly look in her eyes. To think he'd believed she was a sweet girl. She wasn't sweet, at least not right now, and he didn't feel like being a gentleman.

Shifting his right leg, he skimmed his toes up along her inner thighs, until his big one met with the tender folds of her cunt and sank inside a fraction. She gasped and he grinned, let it become feral. "Are you wet?"

Contracting her sex around his toe, Kristi glanced at the water. "Sure looks that way." Her hand disappeared beneath the surface. Her fingers brushed against his foot and then parted the folds of her pussy, encouraging his toe's exploration. She tipped back her head and closed her eyes. "Why do you dance if you have another job?"

Her voice was throaty, low. Jack let the seductive tone wash over him as he followed her lead and relaxed in the tub. He kept his eyes open, though, as he fisted his cock and began stroking. He didn't want to miss a minute of climax exploding over her features. "Punishment for a misspent youth. I'm repaying my debt to society, literally."

She opened her eyes. "You don't enjoy it? From what I remember of the other night, you seemed pretty . . . happy to be there."

"I was happy to see you." He continued the ministrations of his toe as she curled her first finger toward her clit. She must have found the sensitive bead as she sucked in a sudden breath. He quickened his strokes, wanting to be right there with her when the moment came. Or, rather, when she did. "Clearly, I knew you were special at first sight. I don't normally have that reaction to women in the audience."

Her fingers stilled and color flushed her cheeks. "I don't normally fall into bed with two guys I've never met. Or two guys at all, for that matter."

He jerked his toe free of her body reflexively. "What do you say we keep Spencer out of the tub?"

Kristi's relieved smile made it clear she had no longing for a third party. Though she'd seemed to be of that mind-set the other morning, he was elated to know it for certain. Pulling her hand from the water, she leaned over the side of the tub. She sank back against the tub's end, holding a small, wandlike object that sported a bristled round head and had him rethinking his observation. Apparently she did want a third party, just not in the form of another person.

She twisted the wand and the bristles spun soundlessly to life. "What do you say we let Mimi in?"

"That thing isn't going to electrocute us, is it?"

"Not a chance. Mimi has had hours of tub time." The wand moved beneath the surface, momentarily churning the bubbles. "She's one of my best-sellers. How Cai fo-ound me." She stopped talking for a second, and her eyes widened and then, went to half-mast. Mimi had clearly hit her mark. Kristi continued, her voice on the verge of breathless. "One of her friends came across my business site and . . . tri-ied out Mimi. I guess she enjoyed her as much as . . . I do."

Jack's cock jumped in his fist. He thought he would be turned off by the toy, wanted to imagine her fingers doing the fondling alone. Instead, he was turned on in a big way. The only thing better than envisioning those bristles spinning over her engorged clit and dipping into the tender folds of her cunt would be to watch. Tonight he would settle for the vision. Tomorrow, if things continued as well as they'd begun, he would ask for a visual demonstration. He had offered his point of view, after all.

The heightened sound of Kristi's breathing filled his ears and had his senses going into overload. The sight of her big breasts bouncing on the water with her vigorous play had his hand pumping without relief. Tension gripped his body, snugging his balls.

"The Ngos are . . . business associates?"

Kristi's words sliced through the haze of impending orgasm. "Yeah. But I don't think there's room for them in the tub either."

He was damned close to gone, and still he hadn't missed the tinge of jealousy in her words over the idea the twins could be more than colleagues. It made his release all that much more intense. As did the pleasure of watching her lips firm together and her eyes squeeze tight as her own climax pushed through her. She whimpered as her body visibly shook, her knees drawing up to poke out of the water. He pumped and pumped and pumped, then let go and groaned aloud with the hot, hurried push of his cum.

Seconds passed, turned to nearly a minute, before she lifted Mimi the Miniwonder from the water and dropped the toy onto the rug next to the tub. She sighed. "Mmm . . . Mimi has a way with pickles."

Jack grinned over her euphemism and how it somehow fit her character perfectly—suggestive, but not bluntly so. He opened his mouth to comment on his own pickle-handling skills when she stood and stepped from the tub. Grabbing a towel, she bent to dry her legs. Her ass jiggled inches from his face. His fingers itched to reach out and grab hold of her cheeks, his shaft to caress their part. "You're stunning."

"Have a thing for big buns?"

He frowned. "Don't tell me you think you're fat."

She straightened and turned toward him, providing a full-frontal, X-rated view that had his erection back in an instant. "Actually, I have a very good self-image. I'm not sure where that came from."

He stepped from the water. Her gaze shot to his cock, and his unvoiced words returned. "When it comes to pickles, I'm hands and tongue above Mimi."

Kristi's nipples stood at attention. Cream dribbled down her inner thigh. "I'll relish finding that out firsthand." She winced. "Sorry. That was bad even for me."

"It seems I have a soft spot for bad humor." He glanced at his bobbing dick, already so eager for more. "We both do."

The heat simmering in her eyes made it clear she wanted to

find out about the skills of his hands and tongue and all the rest of him this moment. She didn't reach for him but wrapped her towel around her body and tucked the end between her breasts. With a, "Then I promise to supply loads of it over dinner," she left him standing, bobbing dick and all, while she walked out the bathroom door.

Erections and horses didn't mix. Jack willed away his hard-on as he followed Kristi's mare along a line of evergreens. Last night had been torture. He hadn't gotten a second helping of dessert. They'd returned to their room after dinner and shared conversation that had him liking her all the more, but when it came time to crawl into bed, all he'd gotten was one hot kiss.

Having her so close, her body covered in a short, snug nightshirt and a skimpy pair of silk panties he'd had to endure witnessing her pulling on after their shared bath was torture, pure and simple. And just in case it hadn't been enough, he'd woken this morning to find her in his arms, his erection pushing through the slit in his boxers to cradle in the crack of her ass.

His cock had been rock solid ever since. That they were on their way to a private cottage for the day and night didn't help. The cottage was less than a half mile from the bed-and-breakfast, but the thickness of the trees made it seem much farther. It made it seem they had their own little private wilderness where they could do anything they wanted, moan and scream as loud as they pleased and no one would be the wiser.

"We're here." Kristi tugged on the mare's reins, drawing the animal to a halt, and nodded toward a small, rustic-looking cottage nestled in the trees fifteen yards ahead. They had come up on the building's rear. A three-sided, wooden shower with a hand-primed water pump stood several feet from the back door.

"Great shower." She sent him a naughty look and moved a hand beneath the hem of her baby-blue tank top. Her knuckles whispered against the cotton as her fingers massaged her breasts. "It's warm riding in the woods. No breeze comes through the trees. I feel sticky."

"I'm rather sweaty myself." More like hot as a goddamned live wire.

Jack slid from his horse. Kristi gave a sigh that said she thought relief from the internal fire that plagued her was near. The sigh turned to a pout as he grabbed her mare's reins. "Check out the shower while I take care of the horses and our packs."

Her lower lip stayed pushed out a few seconds, and then she sucked it back in and dismounted. "Okay. Thanks for being such a gentleman."

Gentleman his ass. He could be one. But that wasn't his intention here.

Jack made quick work of stabling and watering the horses, then tossed the packs into the cottage and sneaked around to the rear. Kristi stood with her back to him, letting the water cascade down over her head and along her spine. It slid in a rivulet down her crack, and his cock gave an anxious throb. Shucking his clothes, he moved up behind her and cupped her heavy breasts. "You look cold again." She squeaked and her nipples spiked into points against his palms. "Definitely cold."

He lowered his mouth to her neck, nibbled at her cooled flesh. She *mmm*ed and craned her neck to the side. "The shower was too much to pass up?"

"I can't resist communing with nature. The gorgeous woman doesn't hurt either."

One of his hands traveled down the swell of her stomach, dipping into her belly button and reminding him of their risqué encounter at Shenanigans before continuing on its downward journey. From their first touch, he'd somehow known she was special.

Kristi covered his hand with her own centimeters before he reached the silky softness of her bare mound. "Not yet, Jack."

The words were spoken quietly. He might have thought he'd heard them wrong if not for the tensing of her body. Damn, he was still trying to take things too fast. It wasn't his style to rush a woman who needed time, but she had him wanting her bad.

Letting his hands fall at his sides, he stepped back. "Sorry."

She turned to give him an apologetic smile. "Don't be. It's my fault. I acted like I wanted your hands all over me. I do want your hands all over me. How could I not? You are this totally dee-lish beefcake, and I want to lick every inch of you. But not yet. Tonight. I promise."

Jack might have been offended by the beefcake comment if she hadn't tacked on the word *tonight*. He could hardly feel offended when thoughts of loving Kristi and letting her make good on that licking desire clouded his mind and had his overactive, and suddenly incredibly dirty, imagination working overtime.

Kristi had never been so nervous. She stood behind the shelter of the outhouse door as twilight settled, trying to relax enough that Jack wouldn't suspect something momentous was going on.

There was something momentous going on.

The next few minutes—okay, hours would be really great . . . would predict the future of their relationship. She really, really, really liked him and the way he warmed her in places she hadn't realized had gone cold until that morning in the parking lot of Shenanigans. And it had nothing to do with his self-proclaimed pickle-handling skills. Not much anyway. She was into the entire package, and she wanted him to make her climax so badly she could cry.

Please let him be the one. Please let him be the one.

Deep breaths. She took five long ones and then pushed open the outhouse door and started for the cottage. She stepped inside the back door to find Jack seated on an overstuffed chair in front of a fireplace accented with an antique mantel and brass trim. No fire crackled in the hearth, and for good reason. The small, two-room cottage stayed plenty cozy nestled among the trees, so cozy she could feel sweat trickling between her breasts. Or maybe the perspiration had to do with the anticipation of finally allowing his touch.

Denying his fingering during her shower had left her horny and miserable. Now she was jump-out-of-her-skin anxious. But when he brought her to orgasm the first time, she wanted it to be with either his body or his tongue. Both in succession would be awesome.

He looked at her, frowning. "What's the matter?"

"Nothing."

He studied her a few seconds. Between his astutely narrowed green eyes and windblown raven hair, he reminded her of a panther on the prowl. "Something's on your mind. You're nervous."

"I'm horny." It wasn't a lie, just an omission of the complete truth.

Jack stood and came around the chair. He glanced meaningfully at his crotch where his monster member prodded against knit gray shorts. "It appears contagious."

Kristi stared at the bulge of his cock, recalling the first time she'd seen it that fateful morning in her bedroom. It wasn't as big as a toaster, the way she'd first surmised, but it was plumper and longer than any kielbasa she'd ever seen. As for the man himself, he'd turned out to be nothing like she'd first guessed. Oh, he was a gentleman at times. But he could be a scamp just as often.

With a wiggle of her eyebrows, she appealed to his scamp

side, tugging the tank top over her head to reveal she wore no bra. She twirled the shirt on her first finger, hoping she didn't look like a complete dork. Or if she did, then at least a moderately sexy one. "Care to join me in bed?"

He went down on his knees on a plush royal red rug. "I'd rather you join me on the floor. There aren't any lights in the bedroom, and I want to see everything."

Oy! Not good.

If he, God forbid, didn't give her an orgasm, she could have been able to fake one in the dark and give him a second chance. In the light, she could never fake it believably. She also couldn't act like she wanted to hide her imperfections in the darkness. It would only have him believing she'd lied about her strong self-image. Kristi had no longing to prance her bared bubble butt down 5th Avenue, but when it came to getting physical with one man—not two—she was plenty comfortable.

Dampening her lower lip with a hasty swipe of her tongue, she moved to stand in front of him. "The floor's good."

Jack grabbed her arms and tugged her down. He had her on her back on the rug in a heartbeat. Looming over her, huge and hard, he grinned, wicked intent burning in his green eyes and amplifying the amber flecks to the nth degree. "It's even better from this angle."

His mouth swept down, cloaking a stiff nipple, dragging it into warm, delicious wetness with a fierce suckle that took her by surprise. Her hips shot upward. Liquid desire jetted through her body. Bringing a hand to her other nipple, he tweaked the tip, rubbed it expertly between his big fingers until it was rosy red and throbbing with painful pleasure; then he drew that nipple into his mouth with the same carnal fierceness he had taken the first.

She cried out, her fingers fisting in the rug. "You're right. This angle is way better."

He lifted his mouth to laugh. The deep, rich sound faded

away as he brought his fingers to her shorts. He eased down the zipper, then lifted up her legs to aid in removing the remainder of her clothes. Her shorts and panties were gone in seconds. He didn't release her legs, instead bending and pushing them wide to expose her naked, open pussy.

Jack eyed her slick sex, his eyes dilated with lust, his mouth tugged into a licentious grin that only grew as he dipped his head toward her slit. His hot breath brushed over her intimate folds, weakening her limbs as rapture built, spiraling through her and making her quiver with anticipation. "How about this one?"

The quivers turned to a whole-body tremble of euphoria. Oh. My. God. Yes! He was going for it. He was going to lick her pickle.

Kristi's heart felt as though it would burst with the forceful push of his tongue into her hole. Her pussy gushed with a flood of cream. Little tingling explosions went off in her core. He was her O-man. She just knew it. "Better yet."

His fingers teased along her legs, from the apex of her thighs to her kneecaps, enlivening every cell to a fever pitch of need as he tongued her with hard strokes. She spun a little higher with each long lick. Her breasts ached with the exquisite pressure building within. He turned his mouth on her clit, alternately brushing his lips and scraping his teeth over the inflamed pearl. The pressure continued to build until she could feel it pushing through her in a near-blinding crescendo. Any second now.

He brushed, licked, shoved inside her and lapped. She teetered on the edge. She teetered. Teetered. Tottered. Teeter-totter.

Oh no! She was not a teeter-totter. And the crescendo was receding. This couldn't be happening. He was the one! How could her pussy not know that?

Jack's tongue stilled its torment, and he lifted his head to look at her through the vee of her legs. "What's the matter? You're stiff as hell and not in a good way."

She couldn't give up yet. "It's just . . . too soon for that, I guess."

He released her thighs and sat back on his knees. He dragged a hand through his hair, looking guilty. "I pushed it."

"No. You didn't push anything. Let's just stick with regular sex tonight, okay?"

Shock replaced his guilt. "You still want to have sex?"

"Of course!" Regular sex would work. They were too good of a fit in too many ways for it not to. She smiled. "Dibs on the top. I still haven't gotten my licks in."

He reached for her again, filled his palms to overflowing with her breasts. "Like I'd complain about getting to watch these beauties jiggling in my face."

Kristi laughed, the sound cut short by a gasp as he grabbed her around the middle and spun them. She ended up on top. She lifted off of him far enough to allow him to remove his shorts and boxers and then quickly returned. They'd never been this close, skin on heated skin, his coarse pubic hair tickling her juicy folds. At least, not during a time she could remember. She'd teased him with the idea of licking him from one end to the other. Earlier it had been exactly what she wanted. Now she just wanted him inside of her, had to know the answer once and for all. He would be her miracle man.

He looked up at her with a tight smile that said he couldn't wait much longer. Thank God. "Condom's in my shorts pocket."

She dove for his shorts, grabbed out the little foil packet, and ripped it open with her teeth. She sheathed him in an instant. Took hold of his cock and centered it with her opening. Sucking her lower lip between her teeth, she slid on to him. Her eyes watered. The air pushed out of her throat. Holy toaster!

"We never did this," Jack breathed. "I would've remembered something this incredible."

It didn't seem likely she would have been able to forget the hedonistic sensations shooting through her body, the frissions of desire sparking at her slick core and cruising to her throbbing nipples. Could he be right? Had she not slept with either him or Spencer? Maybe the three of them had come home and passed out. Maybe her oral-sex memory had been nothing more than a fantasy caused by wishful thinking. Her sore body the morning after a side effect of something else—strenuous dancing, perhaps.

This definitely was not a fantasy. This was real.

Splaying her hands over his hard, hairless chest, Kristi sat back so that his pubic bone hit her clit at just the right angle. She rode him then, fast, furious, gliding the length of his dick and thrilling in the flutter of her clit with each downward thrust. Her pussy contracted. Cream seeped from between their joined bodies. The musky scent of sex hung heavy in the air. It was about to get stronger yet. Bursts of pleasure rocketed deep within her cunt. The big O was coming fast.

She waited. Waited. Waited. Waited. Kept waiting. Jack moved his hand between their bodies, found her clit and applied pressure. It should have sent her over the edge. But she just kept waiting. For nothing.

Kristi whimpered when what she wanted to do was bawl.

No. No. No. This had to work. But it wasn't. Maybe if she could reach her backpack, she could still salvage the moment. Slip her little red rabbit in place.

His fingers left her clit. The rocking of his hips ceased. "Too soon for this, too? You're stiff as hell again."

Oops. Too late for the rabbit. Damn. She sent him an apologetic smile. "I want this to work. At least, let me help you get off."

He lifted her from his body, muscles bunching in his arms

with her weight. He set her down beside him and reclined to a sitting position. Gave her a reassuring smile. "We don't have to have sex, Kristi. I like just spending time with you."

"You do?" How could he when his swollen cock was twitching inches from her face? He wanted more. A more she couldn't give no matter how badly she wished it. Coldness settled over her body and soul. Her heart hurt. Kristi bit her tongue to quell her fast-rising emotions.

"Of course I do."

She warmed a little. Friendship was better than nothing. She could use a male point of view on her sex toys. So what if he would be testing them out with someone else? Her belly gave an angry little flip. She ignored it. He could sleep with other women, and she had no right to be jealous. "So, it's cool that we're just meant to be friends?"

"Friends. Sure. Cool."

5

Kristi: I suck.

Fiona: Why am I thinking you don't mean that in a good way? BTW, Liz told me about your threesome. Can we say jealous with a capital *J*?

Kristi: Don't be. I've been miserable ever since.

Fiona: You didn't take Liz's advice and try them on one at a time?

Kristi: I spent the last two and a half days with Jack, and we totally clicked. And then it came time for the big O and I couldn't get past the friggin' tingles! I can't even work up the energy to make a bad joke about it. I'm so bummed out. I thought this guy was going to be the one. I could see myself with him.

Fiona: You know, woman, orgasms aren't everything. If you're happy with him and you can get yourself off, what's the big deal?

Kristi: You really think a guy would want a relationship with a woman he can't give an orgasm? And even if he would, I wouldn't. It wouldn't be fair to him. I feel broken. Again! What is wrong with me, Fi?

Fiona: You're asking the wrong person. I spent the entire weekend with King Simon. By far your best invention ever!

Kristi: You spent the entire weekend playing with your vibrator? Sheesh, that does make me feel better.

Fiona: Well, not every second, but I wasn't with a man either. I am just as pathetic as you are. And, hey, at least you did have a man-induced orgasm once in your life, if memory serves.

Kristi: For all I know, that memory was nothing more than a fantasy.

Fiona: Or maybe you spent the weekend with the wrong man. If you aren't going to sleep with Jack again, why not give hot stuff number two a try?

Kristi sat back in her office chair and mulled over the question. She hadn't allowed herself to consider giving Spencer a try since returning from the bed-and-breakfast because she liked Jack too much to hurt his feelings that way. At the same time, he had agreed to be friends. And if things didn't work out, Jack would never have to know she'd been with Spencer. And if they did work out . . . Her inner thighs heated as the possibilities warmed her to the core.

She had to give Spencer a try. The happiness of her pickle, and quite possibly her future, depended on it.

Kristi closed her eyes and inhaled a few deep breaths. When she opened her eyes, the brochure was still in her hand. A full-color spread overnight-mailed direct from Wild Honey headquarters in Los Angeles. A spread that detailed her top-ten best-sellers and that bore her name in letters too huge and loud to miss. Her name. On a sex-toy brochure. One that was already being shipped.

Stuffing the brochure back into its envelope, she closed her mailbox and glanced around the subdivision, lingering on Mrs. Johnson's front windows. Sunny yellow curtains fluttered in the breeze pushing in through the raised panes, but the old lady was nowhere to be seen. It didn't appear anyone had witnessed her getting her mail. Not that they would have been able to read the brochure from more than a foot or two away. Not that the knowledge relaxed her.

"Fuck, fuck, and triple fuck."

She couldn't blame the Ngos for using her name. It was her own fault. Instead of spending their business meeting setting down her terms, she'd gotten sloshed. Since the meeting, she hadn't been able to get hold of either woman. The twins' assistant had informed Kristi that they were in and out of Wild Honey's various locations, seeing to the final preparations of the new product-line launch.

"And here Jack and I thought you were a nice girl."

She jumped at the sound of Spencer's voice. Her mind on the family fallout this latest turn of events would generate if her parents got word of it, she hadn't even noticed him pull in the driveway. She noticed him now, in sin-tillating detail.

She stood eyes to chest with him. Though Kristi had once sworn muscles didn't do it for her, her body reacted to the white tank shirt hugging defined pecs and showcasing dynamite biceps so completely she lost her ability to think.

His words settled then, and her heart went into her throat. "You discussed me with Jack?"

"Not since the morning we woke up in bed together."

"Oh. Right." Thank God.

Before her mind could roam to the morning in question and turn her into the same blushing twit she'd first been with Jack, she tucked the mail under her arm and started for the house. "I got some bad mail, but I'm over it. Let's grab my stuff and go."

She'd packed and repacked for the two-day excursion to a place Spencer wouldn't confide the details of. All she knew was that it involved sleeping under the stars. Hence the reason for her packing problems. He struck her as a man who preferred his women on the wild side. It had been a long time since she'd done anything truly wild—accidental threesomes noninclusive.

Two weeks ago she was sure she had no use for men, that one couldn't find her G-spot with a detailed road map. Now she felt certain that her fantasy had been more than wishful thinking, that Spencer had gotten her off for real. And she felt wild, not to mention damp as all get out, at the thought of parading around in the woods in some skimpy lingerie while he caressed her with wickedly dark eyes, then grabbed her up and let his hands and mouth take over.

And his tongue.

Her pussy fluttered. Oh boy. She couldn't wait to finally feel the gifted tongue from her fantasy and experience a man-induced orgasm. But she had to wait, and that was the whole problem with packing lingerie.

She'd told Spencer the same thing she'd told Jack—this trip was meant as a way to get to know each other better because she sensed they had some major chemistry. Though she hadn't expected Spencer to accept an offer that sounded like she was thinking in relationship terms, he had. She wouldn't risk that little step in the right direction by having him spot lingerie in her camping duffel and assume her true motive was to get him out of his clothes and into her sleeping bag.

Looking at him from across his big black truck's cab over an hour later, she had to admit his assumption would be accurate. He was cocky in a way she never expected would call to her. Even now, the truck's interior running lights revealed his mouth set in an arrogant smirk that had his lips curving toward his mustache, making it look like he held on to some private joke.

Some private, naughty joke, Kristi amended as he glanced at her, his smirk becoming a devastatingly sexy grin. He brought his right hand to her leg, touched his fingers down above her kneecap. It reminded her of the way Jack—who she wasn't going to think about—had subtly squeezed her leg when he'd been driving them to the B & B.

Spencer didn't do subtle. His warm palm, roughened in a way that suggested he spent his time away from Shenanigans doing manual labor, skimmed along her bare thigh, inching upward until it reached the hem of her tan canvas shorts. One finger went beneath the material, brushed lazily back and forth as his gaze slid the length of her. The perusal lasted less than a second and was hindered by the darkness. It shouldn't have left her shifting in her seat as anxiously as if her little red rabbit was buried inside her sex and happily vibrating away. But it did. Left her stimulated and rubbing her thighs together to combat the sensual ache.

His finger left her shorts, and her pussy gave a disappointed throb. He looked out the windshield, where the blacktop had faded to a winding stretch of dirt road void of other vehicles and surrounded by woods, then back at her. His attention went to her breasts. She held her breath with the idea he might continue the upward journey of his hand, until it was her nipple he stroked, taunting it into a point so hard it hurt. Only he didn't need to touch her to accomplish that. All he had to do was look at her with his blue eyes weighed down with lust and demand and her nipples leapt to hungry, aching life.

"You look hot, doll."

Hot. Wet. And seriously considering saying to hell with it and jumping him here and now.

Kristi took in his profile as he again concentrated on the road. Strong straight nose; a thin white line above his right eyebrow, remnants of an old scar; angular jawline with a stubborn chin; a sensually detailed mouth that evoked a dimple in his cheek when his grin really sparked, the way it was now. "You look . . . scrumptious."

And like his naughty secret had just gotten naughtier yet, she thought as he shot her a look that said he could read her mind and liked the direction it had taken.

Would it hurt to hurry things along a little and give in to her urge to jump him? It would if he turned out to be her O-man, then refused her another date because of the way she'd acted like a mutt who climbed onto the lap of every guy who looked at her twice. Something told her plenty of women who fit that description came his way. Something also told her he slept with a good share of those women and never saw them again. She wasn't after a one-night stand. Once she found the guy who held the map to her G-spot, she was playing for keeps.

Small talk would be good here. Anything to get her mind off of sex. "You said dancing was fun the other weekend. I take it you like your job?"

"Mostly. The hours can be a bitch, but I get a kick outta the women. You'd be amazed what some of them will do to get your hand on their ass."

Or your tongue in their pussy. Oops. So much for getting her mind off of sex. "I can imagine."

"It's not something I plan to do forever, but for now it's paying the bills and getting my kid brother through college."

"It's sweet that you're looking out for him." And unexpected. They were words she would have expected out of Jack's mouth. Jack, who she was not going to think about again and wonder what or who he was doing. She had her man. Didn't need another one.

What would she even do with two guys? Let one lick her pussy while the other went to work on her backside?

Spencer laughed. "Sweet. That's a new one for me."

And it was new for her to be fantasizing about two guys having their way with her, but her mind was suddenly going bonkers with possibilities.

Three sets of tangled limbs, slick sweaty body parts locking in every way imaginable, the scent of sex triply magnified thick in the air. Hands all over her body. Hot, hard male hands. Stroking her breasts, her sides, the dip of her navel. Dipping into her pussy, fingering her dripping sex. Bringing her to the peak of ecstasy again and again, until she was insensate with her need. Finally pushing into her, from the front, the back, joining in a trio of arms and legs and torsos until they were a pumping grinding, slippery sliding masterpiece that had her sex heavy with the urge to come just thinking about.

Kristi forced words out through dry lips. "You prefer the bad-boy image?"

He looked over. His eyes narrowed in an accusing way that said he'd detected her arousal. "You do. You're thinking about being bad right now. Go ahead, doll. Be naughty."

Be. Naughty.

The tender lips of her cunt pulsed with the invitation. Her fingers tingled to reach over and grab hold of his cock, find out if he was prepared to be naughty right along with her. His mouth tilted higher on one side. His eyes reflected every bit of her want. Oh yeah, he was prepared. All she had to do was make a move.

And risk so much way too soon.

Releasing her pent-up tension with a sigh, she looked ahead, out the windshield. And screamed.

A bull moose stood in the middle of the narrow dirt road less than fifteen feet away, and that distance was fast gobbled up by the truck's heavy-duty tires.

"Son of a bitch!" Spencer's curse was followed by another of Kristi's screams as he wrenched on the steering wheel to avoid hitting the huge animal. The truck jerked to the shoulder, then fishtailed its way down into the ditch, stopping with a hollow thunk as the truck collided with the embankment and the air screeched from her lungs.

Deep breaths. One. Two. Three. She willed the beat of her heart to slow and gave herself a mental check. Toes and fingers all wiggled. Nothing appeared to be broken.

"You okay?"

"Yeah." She looked over, thankful to see he was concerned but not injured. Too bad the same couldn't be said for the truck. Past the windshield, the glow of the headlights reflected off the side of the ditch to spotlight steam rising from the hood. "I don't think your truck's doing so great."

He climbed out into the ditch and surveyed the damage. Frowning, he climbed back inside the cab, grabbed his cell, and flipped it open. "Shit. No signal. Looks like we found our campsite earlier than planned. As far in the boonies as we are, I doubt anyone's gonna find us tonight."

Kristi looked out into the blackness of the woods. She shivered. She'd gone camping plenty of times as a kid and loved it, but it had never been in a place as secluded as this. Anything could be hiding in those woods: a grizzly bear, another gigantic moose. Bigfoot and his abominable friends. Whatever was out there, she would have to deal with it. Not only did she feel partly responsible for the damage to the truck, but also her time away with Spencer was burning up fast.

Time to wipe that frown off his face and remind him how glad he was to be here with her. Wherever "here" was. "I've slept in worse places with guys far uglier than you."

His grin returned, edging into his mustache and budding a dimple so yummy it took all of her self-control not to stretch across the seat and lick it. "You suggesting I'm ugly?"

She wouldn't lick him—not when her pussy was still damp from her preaccident fantasies—but touching had to be okay. She reached out, palming the side of his whisker-roughened cheek, and stroked her thumb along the sexy divot. "You probably wouldn't like it if I called you pretty either."

The intention hadn't been to sound like a well-petted sex puppet. Not only did Kristi sound that way, but she felt it as well. Every cell in her body seemed to have joined in with the female piranhas from Shenanigans, only her cells weren't chanting "touch him," but to give into Spencer's suggestion and "be naughty."

Just in case her supercharged cells weren't loud enough, he shifted toward her, bringing his mouth into temptation's way. His breath warmed the air between them and sent a quiver of anticipation racing through her. If there was one thing she remembered from the strip club, it was how unbearably hot and thirsty she'd been. She was that way again, sweating despite the fast-cooling night and parched for the taste of a hard male body beneath her tongue.

"Would you punish me?" It was said life-and-death situations had a way of leading to great sex. The accident had definitely brought out the naughty in her.

"Is that what you were thinking about? Getting punished?"

Her toy line included several whips, flogs, and one very special paddle. She'd never been inclined to use any of them. Until now. "It might be, for the right guy."

6

Spencer watched Kristi lay down the thermal-lined sleeping bags as he warmed up a makeshift dinner over the campfire. He'd never wanted to be any woman's right guy. Not until a half hour ago, when she'd looked at him with eyes that were dirty as a girl could get them and he'd taken the pansy way out by acting like her talk of punishment was nothing more than a ruse to make him forget about his damaged truck.

She was unexpected—as seductive as she was sweet—and in that way she'd gotten past his radar. He avoided women like her, the kind who offered the whole package and had what it took to get to him on more than a physical level. Not forever, but until he was ready to take on the responsibility of a family again. His dad having passed away from a heart attack when Spencer was sixteen and his younger brother barely five, he'd been thrust into a grown-up role that hadn't ended until his brother became a teenager and no longer bought into Spencer as a father figure. Not that the kid turned down his monthly checks to help pay for college tuition and food.

Kristi shifted, leaning over to smooth out the sleeping bags and waving her curvy behind at him in the process. He groaned as his dick grew impossibly harder. It had been on the threshold of pain since she'd brought up that whole punishment thing.

He should never have agreed to this trip. He'd done so for the Ngos' sake. Kristi's unexpected invitation had worked perfectly into Cai's request that he help bring Kristi's inner vixen to the surface permanently. Even if it wasn't for helping out the twins, Spencer would have been tempted to say yes. Kristi had sounded ecstatic to hear his voice over the phone and, sorry sap that he was, he'd been just as happy to hear hers. Given the way she'd stayed in his head despite his best attempts to dislodge her, sleeping with her was the last thing he should do. If he buried himself between her supple thighs, he wasn't liable to come back out.

She straightened and turned toward him. The light of the fire rearranged the shadows of night that fell across her face, masking the freckles on her nose and removing all trace of sweetness. She looked hungry, in a way that had nothing to do with food. "I zipped the sleeping bags together. It'll be warmer that way."

Warmer. Right. He would believe that was why she'd zipped them together the same day he convinced her that he was a virgin. "Good thinking, doll. It's gonna get cold tonight." It already had cooled enough to require sweatshirts, which worked in his favor by camouflaging her bountiful breasts.

He lifted the enamel camp pot from the fire. "Dinner's ready. Beans and franks a la mode."

Smiling, Kristi settled in a lawn chair. "Ooh . . . one of my favorites!"

Spencer snorted as he moved into his own chair, resting the pot on a hotpad on the chair's arm. He handed her a spoon. "Wouldn't have guessed you for sarcastic."

"I have one of the corniest senses of humor ever, but I was a being serious. Dad and I used to go camping a lot when I was a kid. We always had pork and beans for our first night's meal. Brings back a lot of good memories."

The woman had more angles than he ever would've imagined. Each new one had him liking her a bit more. For that reason, he should be hightailing it to the road and walking until he got a signal on his cell phone. But this was the first time in a very long while he'd been able to get away from the chaos of city life and the first time ever he had such intriguing company. "You're close with your family?"

She scooped up a spoonful of beans and franks, swallowing them with a hearty moan of approval. "My parents live in Oregon, so I don't see them a lot, but yeah, when it comes to everything but my job, I am."

Spencer had never believed in love at first sight, but lust at first bite seemed a thing of fact. His cock pulsed with the way she made eating camp food sound like a carnal delight.

Ignoring the sensation, he spooned in a mouthful of food and focused on his conversation with Cai. She feared Kristi would dissolve her contract with Wild Honey because of a complex about being viewed as a sex advocate. If Kristi's parents didn't approve of her career choice and Kristi let their opinions influence her, then Cai had a reason to be concerned. "Your business dealings with the Ngos aren't going the way you'd hoped?"

She looked up midscoop. "*What?*"

"You said you got some bad mail. I noticed the only thing you opened was a package from Wild Honey."

"Things are going great. Cai and Kim have gone above and beyond what they promised. They just . . . used my name." At his questioning look, she continued. "I didn't want my name associated with my products, but I never got a chance to tell them that before I signed a contract and haven't been able to get hold of them since that night. It isn't a big deal."

Then why did she sound more anxious than a priest in a room full of hookers? He'd soothed both his brother's and mother's anxiety on numerous occasions. The urge to do so for Kristi was automatic. Redirecting the conversation toward sex was dangerous, but if it turned her tension toward the positive, it would be worth it.

Spencer put on the bad-boy smile he'd perfected for the stage—the one he'd been told by more than one woman had the power to make a girl come on sight. "That night? The one where you got sloppy drunk and begged me to lick your pussy?"

The spoon fell from Kristi's hand to clatter against the side of the pot. She turned a red so bright even the dark couldn't hide it. "You remembered?"

He didn't want to like her so much, but her personality swings were charming as hell. "Nah. Just teasing about the pussy licking. I do remember you were feeling rather good earlier in the night."

Her unease gave way to a sultry smile that made him want to tackle her to the ground and lick her pussy for real. She leaned toward his chair, settling her hand on his thigh as she spoke in the sort of low, throaty voice reserved for bedroom talk and X-rated secrets. "Blame it on the entertainment. They had me too hot to bear."

Spencer's gut tightened with her word choice. He looked up from where her palm heated his leg through his jeans. "They?"

She moved her fingers in sinuous circles, edging toward his erection with a slowness meant to get a man's dick throbbing while driving him gradually insane. "You."

And Jack. The truth was clear in the momentary wobble of her smile. He liked Jack. Could see where he and Kristi had a lot in common. That didn't make Spencer's gut lighten up any at the thought of the two of them in bed together. He'd never felt possessive over a woman, particularly one he barely knew, but then he'd never shared a woman with another man the way he'd shared Kristi last week. It made him want to say to hell with Cai's request and give in to Kristi's caresses for his own reasons.

Since he wasn't about to dupe her into sleeping with him believing he was after a relationship, he stuck with fishing for information that could benefit the Ngos while appeasing his own interest. "How'd you get into the sex-toy business?"

Her fingers stilled. "Did Cai tell you what I do?"

As pillow talk. The implication was clear in Kristi's tone. He should let her think what she wanted, but the idea of feeding her more lies, even those by omission, made him feel guilty. "Yeah, but not how you think. She'd rather sleep with you than me."

Kristi's eyes widened. "She's a lesbian?"

"Bi, and I'm not kidding about her wanting to sleep with you. She was green as hell over your doing Jack and me."

She shifted in her chair, but then restarted the slow circling of her fingers along his inner leg, climbing ever higher and sending his pulse rate into triple time. "I'd rather talk about us."

And he'd rather a grizzly barreled into their camp and swallowed him whole. Fortunately for Spencer, she was lying. From the anxious way she rubbed her thighs together to the sudden dilation of her eyes, she was wet over the thought of Cai fucking her. That she tried to hide her stimulation further backed up Cai's theory she wanted to keep her enjoyment for sex behind closed doors. "Most people don't know what you do. At least they didn't before you signed that contract with Wild Honey."

Kristi tensed. Lifting her hand from his leg, she stood. "Not everyone's as liberal as you are." She moved to the bed on the other side of the fire and pulled her duffel bag in front of her. After working the jeans down her legs and pulling her sweatshirt over her head to reveal a T-shirt that ended before her panties began, she rolled the clothes into a ball and tucked them inside the bag. "I'm going to bed."

Spencer pulled his attention from the jiggle of her pale, dimpled ass beneath a scrap of ivory silk to check her expression. The hot look she sent him before she slid into bed said she was hoping for company. He could still make the trek back to the road and attempt to get a signal on his cell. And spend the rest of his life regretting the decision to act like a pansy afraid of a woman barely tall enough to reach his armpit.

Kristi was half dressed in that sleeping bag, waiting for him to slide inside and ease her arousal. His cock had been hard for hours, hell days, with the desire to do just that. His cock was shit outta luck. He would climb inside and hold her, even touch her and breathe a hot word or two meant to get her off, but full-blown sex was not happening so long as she believed he was here to see if they had something between them.

Setting the pot on a flat stone near the fire, he rounded the campfire. After toeing off his hiking boots, he removed his jeans and sweatshirt and slid in behind her, careful to keep his hard-on from prodding into her back. He was good with intentions, but if she turned around and started petting his cock, he wasn't making any promises about stopping himself from pulling aside her miniscule panties and shoving inside her welcoming heat.

Spencer teased his fingers over the warm, smooth skin of her hip, brushing the thin strap of her panties with each pass. He moved her hair aside and rubbed his mustache against her nape, eliciting a sigh followed by a shiver. "Everyone might not be liberal, doll, but you are. The idea of sex with Cai excites you." He slipped his tongue out and laved her earlobe, dipped the damp tip inside the shell. "The thought of her tonguing your tight little pussy has you so wet you're dripping with it."

Her breathing grew harsh, fogging the air. "I don't want to sleep with a woman. That's not even close to my style."

"Never said you did. I just said the idea excites you." He toyed with the strap of her panties a few more seconds, then walked his fingers beneath the silk and toward her naked mound. With no hair to absorb her dampness, he could feel her excitement even before he reached her slit and brushed it with his fingertips. He parted her pussy lips, and she sucked in a hard breath. Cream seeped onto his finger, sending a thundering pang through his shaft.

He allowed a cocky smile. "Like I said, dripping."

Kristi shifted in his arms, dislodging his finger from her body as she turned to face him. She brought her legs up, wrapping them around his and locking their bodies together so that her breasts rubbed against his chest and her mound provided a hedonistic distraction for his dick.

Two thin pairs of underwear were all that separated them. Never had temptation been so bittersweet.

Gliding her hands over his chest, she nipped at his chin before moving her mouth higher. "I'm wet for you, not Cai. I want your hands on me, not hers. Your fingers inside me. Your tongue."

What about Jack? Would she want the same from him?

Spencer flushed the question from his mind with the feel of her soft, full lips against his mouth. She applied pressure, and he parted his lips, letting her tongue inside to explore. Like the day he'd kissed her in the parking lot of Shenanigans, the sweet taste of strawberries exploded over his senses while need clawed at his gut.

If she was any other woman, he would do something about that need by taking over the kiss and then all of her. With Kristi, he waited to see her next move. Would she let her liberal half out to play, or revert to her blushing, conservative side?

She pulled free of his mouth. "Finger me, Spencer. Please."

His blood burned with the breathy words. Her liberal half was alive and kicking, and making a request he had no intention of ignoring. He brought his hand back between her thighs and dipped his first finger into her folds, petting the length of her sex until he reached her swollen clit. He pressed his finger against the bead. Her hips shot forward, thrusting against his cock with sizzling force.

Adding a second finger, he moved them together, felt the slick walls of her sex expand to accept him. He'd described her pussy as tight and he'd been right. Outside of her fucking him last week, he would guess she hadn't been with a man in some time.

Outside of fucking him and Jack, he corrected with a grunt.

Christ, he had to quit thinking of the other man. But he couldn't. And something told him he wouldn't until Kristi was riding his cock and letting him know he was all the man she needed. That wouldn't be happening tonight. Likely not ever. And that meant he had to end things now, before he took advantage of how little separated them, by spearing his shaft through the slit in his boxers and deep inside her warm pussy.

"I have to get something." Spencer felt guilty uttering the words, knowing she'd take them wrong and assume he meant a condom.

The hot, wet, eager way she kissed him before unwrapping her legs from his said he'd guessed accurately. He stood and looked down at her, his body too primed with desire to be touched by the cold. She lay with her eyes closed, the firelight dancing over her face and bringing out the reddish highlights in her blond hair as it showered over his pillow. She looked sweet again, in a wood-nymph-he-wanted-to-fuck sort of way.

Shaking the thought away, he grabbed her duffel bag and shoved his hand inside, hoping he'd be right about what he found inside. His fingers connected with a contoured, cylindrical arm that could only belong to one thing.

Pulling it out, he grinned at the sex toy. He might not get to experience the ecstasy of Kristi's hot pussy milking his cock with her climax, but watching her come around a dildo of her own creation was a decent second.

He sat with his back to the fire and tossed the dildo next to her head. "Open your eyes and spread your legs, doll. It's punishment time."

Kristi flicked her eyes open with Spencer's taunting words. Disappointment cruised through her followed quickly by relief as she spotted the Double Diamond lying beside her head. As much as her sex thrummed with the need to feel his monster member inside, driving her to her first man-induced orgasm, she'd known it was too soon. She would totally come off as a mutt if she did him already. Allowing him to bring her to climax with one of her gadgets was another story.

She wriggled out of the sleeping bags, barely noting the drop in temperature as she turned around and lay back so that her feet came to rest near his own. She spread her thighs and bent her knees. The intensity of his gaze on the crotch of her damp panties chased a shiver through her.

Sheesh, she felt like she might come from his eyeing her alone. "Bring it on."

Spencer laughed darkly. "Now, what kind of punishment would it be if I did the work for you? You're going to torture yourself with that beast while I watch. No stopping until I hear screams and see your pussy explode with juice."

Disappointment threatened to return. She wanted his hands on her, expected him to want the same, to already have used his bad-boy charm to get her naked and panting. Maybe he wasn't the guy she believed him to be, or maybe he was just into voyeurism. Hoping for the latter, she looked at her duffel. "There's enough toys to go around."

"I don't want any distractions." He moved to his knees and crawled up between her legs. Hovered over her, just out of reach.

Kristi's breath dragged in. Her sex clenched. Warmth charged through her. Had he changed his mind? Did he want all of her now?

The right side of his mouth quirked up, revealing the sexy dimple. He brought a hand to her panties and tapped the damp silk with his index finger. A mass of little tremors went off deep in her core. "All my concentration's gonna be right here."

He moved back, reclaiming his spot in front of the fire. She whimpered. The idea of giving him the same treatment Climax had and dry-humping him in order to get her way surfaced. Only, there wouldn't be anything dry about it.

"Quit pouting and get vibrating, assuming that's what that beast does."

Fine, she would get vibrating, get torturing. It wouldn't be herself she tormented, though, but Spencer.

Smiling in a way she hoped was as naughty as it felt, Kristi sat up to remove her bra and panties. She worked her fingers in her sex, wetting them with her juices, and then brought them to her nipples. They stood at aching hard attention with the damp swipe of her fingertips. She sighed with the erotic play, and her cunt stabbed with desire. Coasting her fingers downward, she trailed a wet path of arousal over the rise of her belly and then coated her shaved mound with a fresh dipping of cream.

She looked up with Spencer's groan. "Distracted yet?"

His eyes gleamed with approval. "Hell, yeah. Keep it up."

With pleasure.

She grabbed the Double Diamond, her second favorite invention and first design. The short, two-headed dildo simulated being entered on both sides at once but to a lesser degree. Two purple vibrating heads were each centered with a diamond-shaped buzzer, one to stimulate the clit, the other the anus.

Almost as good as doing Spencer and Jack at the same time.

Oh boy. Where had that thought come from? Wherever it was, it was a fluke. She was with Spencer alone, and things were about to get really hot.

Wetting her lips, she pulled both of their pillows behind her head so that it was elevated enough she could watch his face through the vee of her legs. Spencer flashed a sensual but lazy smile that spoke of how completely he had control over his body. If the situation was reversed, watching would never be enough. She would be touching herself, fondling her breasts, parting her pussy lips . . .

Following her thoughts, Kristi spread her lips. His throat worked visibly, his eyes reflecting raw want in the firelight. Her sex gushed with moisture. "You like juicy pickles. Just wait and see how juicy I can get."

"I'm all eyes," he said thickly. "Remember, doll, I want to hear you scream."

Spreading her lips wider with her left hand, she used her right to switch on the Double Diamond and bring it to her pussy. She touched the front vibrating chamber against her sex. A shockwave of carnal pressure sizzled through her, shooting her hips nearly off of the sleeping bags. The diamond buzzer touched down on her clit then, and she almost came on the spot. It had never taken much for this particular toy to get her off. Knowing Spencer watched her every move made it that much more intense.

Before she climaxed without the full effect of the toy, she wetted her fingers with fresh juice and pressed them into her asshole, gasping with the rapid entry. Then gasping that much louder when she replaced her fingers with the vibrating shaft of the anus stimulator and hit the switch to vary the vibration cycle of the chambers. The rear buzzer pressed against her ass bead at the same time the front buzzer hit upon her clit. The breath screeched from her lungs, and every nerve in her body went on red-hot alert.

Kristi saw Spencer's eyes become lust-dazed slits and then nothing but the white lightning of ecstasy as the almost painful pleasure slicing through her became too incredible to keep inside.

Her head fell back in rapture. Her eyes slammed closed. With the first wave of orgasm, she screamed loud enough to send Bigfoot and all his furry friends scurrying for cover. The second wave hit. Bliss spiraled through her so acutely she thought she heard the windows in Spencer's truck shatter with her scream. The third and fourth waves had her thrashing, unable to hang on to the toy, to keep her knees up and her legs parted. The dildo fell from her hand. She crashed onto the sleeping bags like a rag doll and lay in a barely breathing pile of highly sated female.

Jesus. It had never been so intense. If Spencer could accomplish so much just watching her masturbate, he was going to be a god when it came to taking part. He was beyond a doubt her O-man.

"Need help getting into bed?" he asked seconds later from somewhere above her.

"I . . . yes." She fought for normal breathing. "It's never . . . been so . . . good." He picked her up and helped her into the sleeping bags. She found the strength to open her eyes and look up at him. His own eyes were wild with hunger. "What about you?"

"Watching you was damned near as good as experiencing it firsthand."

She slid her gaze to his cock. It pushed hard against his boxers, tenting the front as far as the cotton would allow. Precum seeped through to darken the front panel. She dragged in a few more breaths, slowing the mad beat of her heart as her mouth went dry with the urge to take him inside and provide a well-deserved release.

"You can't sleep like that," she reasoned as he pulled back the corner of the sleeping bag. "It's like you have an entire breadbox stuffed in your shorts. We won't even fit in the sleeping bags."

Laughing, Spencer slid inside the bed, managing to somehow fit, enormous erection and all. He pulled her close, trapping her body in place with a heavy, hairy leg. "Thanks for the concern. But it won't be the first time or the last."

7

Spencer dug his booted heels into the forest floor to keep from moving to Kristi's spread thighs and burying his tongue in her center. He'd had plenty of erotic experiences, had slept with women of every shape, size, and color. He'd never known the painful extent to which his cock could swell until he watched Kristi fucking herself with the double-headed dildo.

As if she couldn't get enough of the toy, she had it back between her lush thighs, the dual ends pumping in and out of her pussy and ass, the diamond buzzers humming in tune with her high, throaty moans. Her eyes snapped suddenly shut, and her lips parted on a scream. The primal sound speared through Spencer as a bone-deep throb. His cock pulsed. He hadn't planned on finding his own release, had thought better of freeing his shaft when she was so close. He couldn't stop his fingers from pushing through the slit in his boxers and pulling out his erection.

Kristi's eyes opened, and a feline smile curved her lips. Fisting his cock, he imagined those plump pink lips opening to take him inside. . . .

Her tongue wrapped around his length, caressing with velvety strokes before dipping into the sensitive hole at the head. Precum oozed out, leaking onto her lush lips. She rimmed her mouth with her tongue, lapping at his essence, moaning so loudly it was as if she'd never tasted anything more satisfying.

Spencer returned from the fantasy of her mouth surrounding him with the sound of the sleeping bags brushing against the dewy grass. Kristi shifted on the bed, pushing her first finger knuckle-deep into her pussy, getting it good and wet, and then she brought it to her lips and lined them with her cream.

She turned that finger on him then, crooking it his way while a dirty-girl smile claimed her mouth. "C'mon, Spence. Be naughty. Let me suck your dick."

He shouldn't. For too damned many reasons, he shouldn't. He crawled over her anyway, straddling her breasts with his crotch so that his balls dragged heavily against her breasts, and guided his cock toward her mouth. The tip of her tongue flashed at him: pink, wet, anxious to lick his hard length. Her tongue retreated, her lips parting wide to receive him. He fed himself inside, inch by agonizing—

"We're here."

Spencer jerked from a light sleep with the tow truck driver's words. He straightened in the passenger's seat to find he had a stiff neck and a stiffer dick. His erection hadn't settled since crawling back into bed with Kristi last night. She'd been right about his inability to sleep with a hard-on, so he'd sneaked from the bed and set out on a predawn trek to find an area where his cell worked. Not even the walk had killed his rampant libido, and that only made concrete what he'd already known. If he had to spend one more day alone with her, he'd never be able to stop from giving in and fucking her.

Kristi climbed out of the small backseat of the tow truck. Spencer got out and, forcing a smile, looked at the clear blue sky. The nine-month rainy season was past and the temperature already in the upper sixties at ten in the morning. "Would've been a perfect day for camping."

Or romping around naked in the woods. She didn't have to say the words for him to know what was on her mind. More often than not, her face read like an open book. "You sure you don't want me to stick around and wait with you?"

"And make you waste a day like this? Not a chance."

She smiled in a way that looked more placating than happy. "Okay. I'll be home all day if you want me."

Spencer pretended to miss the double entendre. Pretended his dick didn't jump at the prospect. Pretended he wasn't aware she hoped for a good-bye kiss and that his tongue slid over his teeth with the same want. This was the end of the road for them. He'd rather deal with Cai's retribution when she learned that he failed her than lead Kristi into believing he wanted a relationship.

Kristi was obviously a terrible judge of character. She'd pinned Spencer as being the bad boy between him and Jack. He'd taunted her with words, had her blushing like a twit over the idea Cai wanted to sleep with her, but otherwise he'd barely touched her. This morning he'd been gone when she awoke, returning after a short while to tell her a tow truck was on the way. He could have climbed back inside the sleeping bags and used the time until the truck arrived to get closer with her on an intimate level—it was fast, but the crazy way she'd missed him when she'd woken to find him gone said letting him inside was the right thing to do. Instead he'd made them breakfast. She'd given him a second chance, suggesting they continue their getaway at her house. He'd turned her down with an excuse about needing to tie up some loose ends at his own place.

It was time to stop fantasizing about getting her pickle licked. To stop caring what or who Jack and Spencer were doing.

She had no claim on either man. No right to be jealous or hold out hope they would return to her.

Not both of them at once, of course.

She'd experienced one of the best orgasms of her life last night thanks to the Double Diamond. Getting off with a double-headed dildo was a very different thing than getting off with two men fillng her. One man was all she needed. Only, she didn't even need one. Solo sex suited her fine. And didn't leave her ass feeling like it had been visited by the Toaster Fairy the next morning.

Grabbing a soda, Kristi went into the office and connected to the Internet. She considered whining to the *G-Spot* ladies about her dud of a week, but then opted to check e-mail. A number of Web-site-originated orders filled her in-box, as well as a note from Cai. Spencer's claim that the woman wanted to fuck her stormed through her head. She told him she didn't want to sleep with another woman and she'd meant it. That didn't stop her cheeks from burning and her sex from growing moist.

Casting aside her stimulation, she opened the e-mail. The Ngos were back in Seattle and reported that the demo launch of the new line had been a huge success with the Wild Honey board. They wanted her to join them on the launch tour that would start at the headquarters location and extend to the overseas market. At this point there was no hope of having her name removed from her products, so she might as well accept the offer and help with publicity. Really, it wasn't like she had a man to spend her free time with or parents who would be talking to her much longer.

Oy. This month had been the dooziest of all doozies, and it was only half over.

Climax's yapping drove Kristi from the office sometime later. The knocking at her front door had her glancing through the peephole. Spencer stood there, in all his tall, dark, sexy wonder, and revived a spark in her she hadn't realized died.

Unable to contain her smile, she yanked the door open. "You came."

"Not yet, but hopefully before the night's over."

She laughed way too loud, thrilled by his attempt at amusement. "You have a bad sense of humor. It's perfect!" Like they were meant to be. And, of course, they were. He was her O-man. She just knew it.

He moved inside and closed the door, jerked her against him with a demanding tug that proved she wasn't entirely wrong about his character and that she wouldn't have to wait long for her climax. Thank God.

Bending his knees, he rocked his solid cock against her mound. His palms slid to her ass, squeezing her fleshy behind through her cotton shorts. "What's perfect is the way your ass is going to feel slapping against my balls when I take you from behind."

Kristi's pussy clenched, juice welling deep within her core. She raked her fingernails over his abdomen, loving the hard-packed muscle, or maybe it was the man she loved. It was far too soon—she barely even knew him, not to mention had been convinced he was gone forever less than five minutes ago. But then she'd always been overly emotional when it came to matters of the heart. It was just one of the reasons she hated to disappoint her parents so much by revealing the truth of her vocation.

Spencer rotated his hips, pumping into her with a sensual grind he probably used at Shenanigans on a daily basis. Her nipples still responded, leaping to hard, aching points that abraded his chest. "I missed you."

"I was only gone a few hours."

A few hours or a few years, it didn't matter. The moment she saw him again, she'd realized how much she'd missed the warmth his presence brought to her life. Only one other man had managed to bring about that warmth. Jack had no place in her thoughts now, or ever again on a sexual level. They would be friends. Somehow she'd explain moving on to Spencer so soon after sleeping with Jack. Somehow she'd forget how delectable he looked out of his clothes, his body long and lean and muscled to perfection. Somehow she had to get her mind back on the man who held her in his arms. The only man for her.

Kristi rubbed her breasts against Spencer's broad chest. The sensual friction on her peaked nipples thundered heat to her core and instantly had her back in the moment. "Want to see my bed? It missed you, too."

With a rough laugh, he moved against her in a quick and carnal rhythm, pushed his tongue into her mouth, and lifted her up his body. She locked her legs around his waist and met him stroke for ravenous stroke, licking at his tongue, over his smooth inner cheeks, letting his full-bodied masculine taste wash over her senses and strip her nerves raw. And when she felt the bed at her back moments later, he stripped the rest of her.

Kristi had him naked just as fast. His toned, tanned body bared to her touch, his monster member prodding against her damp inner thighs and teasing her with the ruby stud. And Climax humping his ass.

The terrier yipped with each pump. Kristi giggled through her bliss. "She really does have great taste." She used her foot to ease the dog away. "Scram, girl. He's all mine."

Hearing how possessive the words sounded, she looked at Spencer. She might care about him, might even love him, but she knew better than to think he was prepared to hear how she felt.

He frowned and she waited for his next move with held breath. "How can you be so worried about having your name connected with sex when you can't even call for your dog without leading the entire neighborhood to belief you're climaxing?"

The question eased her fears of scaring him off, but not her tension. "Climax is her private name. I just call her 'girl' in public. And I told you it isn't a big deal about my name getting out."

"Glad to hear it. If every woman responds to your toys the way you did last night, you're gonna be a household name." Kristi stiffened with the prediction. His frown returned. "That's something to be proud of, doll."

"I am." She just wished gaining the respect of thousands of others didn't come at the cost of losing that of her parents.

Spencer gave her a look that said he could read her mind. Before he could voice his thoughts, she climbed down the bed and licked the tip of his cock. Precum rushed out to coat her tongue. She lapped at the silky fluid, then opened her mouth to take him inside. He slid, hot, huge, and hard, between her lips, his piercing brushing over her tongue with naughty prospect. He gripped her sides, muscles she never even knew a person could have contracting beneath her with his moan.

"Don't think I'm letting you have all the fun again." His hands moved down her body with purpose, sliding over the rise of her ass to finger her sex from behind, extracting juicy wet slurping sounds. "There's one place this pussy belongs."

Tingles of anticipation shot from her nipples to her core. She sucked him with elation, her whole body quaking with each thrust of his dick. The hands at her sides gripped harder, lifting up and spinning her until she straddled his face with her thighs. Every concern Kristi ever had disappeared with the first stab of tongue into her cunt.

Fitting his mouth over her pussy lips, he suckled with vigor, stabbing his tongue deep, licking at her intimate flesh, using the bristly hair of his mustache to tickle her mad. He turned to her clit then. He devoured the bead, pulling it between his teeth, tugging with enough force to have her screaming around his cock. His shaft pulsed, throbbing between her lips, telling him how close he was to coming.

Spencer palmed her tits from above, squeezing the straining tips so hard it bordered on pain. Ecstasy barreled through her, mounting tension from her toes to her ears. Her heart hammered. Sweat trickled between her breasts and down her spine. She mouth-fucked him without relief, taking him swift and furious, deep and hard, until his fingers clamped down on her breasts and his cum slammed into the back of her throat.

His groan of fulfillment rippled over her pussy lips, tickling her clit with pleasure so intense it snapped her eyes closed. Her cunt thrummed with tiny explosions. Contracted with the building pressure.

Thrummed. Contracted. Thrummed and contracted. Thrummed and contracted. Just kept on thrumming and contracting with no relief, no release. No friggin' orgasm.

Kristi whimpered. This couldn't be happening, not again. He was the right guy for the job. The one who held the map to her G-spot. The one who could eat her pickle like no other. The one who wasn't giving up without a fight.

He just kept licking, sucking, tugging away. His hands as ceaseless as his mouth as they moved over her body, petting, fingering, fondling, but never sending her higher. Never pushing her over the edge.

Just when her tears of frustration and overstimulation were about to leak out, when it seemed things couldn't get any worse, they did.

A voice that was deep, male, and angry but that wasn't Spencer's boomed, "I guess this explains last week and your sudden decision to be 'just' friends."

Kristi jerked her mouth from Spencer's cock. She scrambled off him to the opposite side of the bed, her entire body on fire from being caught in the act by Jack. One-on-one sex typically didn't embarrass or unnerve her. It was unusual sex and that which involved more than two people that had the power to set her on edge.

How long had Jack been standing there, watching, witnessing Spencer going off in her mouth while he tongue-fucked her pussy?

She finally worked up the courage to look at Jack and discovered that his eyes held more than anger. They were dark with a hunger so keen it suggested he'd not only watched them from the beginning but had enjoyed it; even now he was hard and throbbing as a side effect. Even now he wanted to punish her by shoving his dick into her mouth and making her fuck him while Spencer watched, awaiting his own turn at revenge. Or maybe they would get revenge together, slamming into her from the front and the back in succession, fucking her raw with the intensity of their rage.

The explicit images the thought provoked danced around in her head and shot directly to her pussy. Ecstasy spiraled higher than it had ever before gone. Kristi's limbs went weak as a blistering inferno of pleasure scorched through her. Her pussy clenched tight. The air screeched from her lungs. She gripped the sheets white-knuckled and came so hard it was more than she could do to stop from crying out.

8

When he'd told Kristi they didn't need to have sex, that they could talk, Jack hadn't meant forever or that he wanted to be just friends. He'd meant there was no reason to rush things. What he sensed developing between them wasn't worth the risk of rash sex. He hadn't understood why she changed her mind so abruptly, and he had spent the last few days waiting for her to return from wherever she'd gone so he could ask that very thing and explain that friendship would never work for him.

As it turned out, asking was unnecessary. The answer was obvious. She'd been fucking Spencer behind his back, and when it came to Spence, she didn't have any problem coming.

She was still writhing on the bed, her face flushed and the breath panting from her mouth. She clawed her way to a sitting position that did nothing to hide every one of her curvy assets on full display. "It's not . . . what it . . . looks like."

"It looked like he had his dick in your mouth and your pussy in his." And it felt like he was more turned on than he'd ever been in his life. Jack never thought voyeurism was for him, but there was no disputing rock-solid evidence.

Spencer climbed from the bed to tug on his boxers. His cool smirk suggested he'd been lied to as well. "Sorry, doll, but I'd say that sums it up perfectly."

Kristi's breathing returned to normal, but her face remained red as she scooted off the bed and yanked on her short mint green robe with shaking hands. "Okay, so that is what was happening. But it isn't like you think. He tried to eat my pickle, but that didn't make me come. And it didn't make me come when you did either. So I thought maybe my memory wasn't a memory but wishful thinking. Only, now I know it wasn't wishful thinking. I just didn't see the other guy."

Jack dislodged his brain from the vicinity of his dick and thoughts of the last time she'd worn that short robe to focus on her ramblings. She wasn't making sense and looked jumpy as hell. She didn't deserve the sympathy that shot through him.

He refortified his fury with the knowledge she wasn't the sweet yet seductive woman he believed, but a bold-faced liar. "Just going to be friends with him, too?" he snapped.

Her throat worked visibly, her eyes dampening. "Oh, Jack . . . I'm sorry." She looked at Spencer. "So sorry. I didn't mean to hurt either of you. I like you both so much, but I can't come with either of you."

Pissed at himself for the resurgence of his sympathy, Jack thrust his hand toward the bed. "Then what the fuck was that?"

"You were watching. Both of you. I never would have gotten off otherwise." Kristi bit her lip, then admitted quietly, "My G-spot's broken. It only works when it's me or a toy doing the tickling, or when both of you are involved." She looked from Jack to Spencer and laughed humorlessly. "You guys look like I just asked you to fuck each other. I don't want that and, despite what happened the night we met, I'm not into threesomes. They aren't right. To some people, maybe. But I was raised on traditional values, and my parents would never respect me if they knew I slept with two guys at once and had an amazing time."

Spencer's smirk was replaced with a look of understanding. "Like they won't respect you if they find out what you do?"

Nearly all of Jack's fight drained away with the gloom in her admission. "I thought you didn't remember sleeping with us?"

"Yes. Like that," she said to Spencer; then to Jack she said, "I don't remember. But I know how I felt the next morning when I had to watch you guys walk away and that for me the night was incredible. But it obviously wasn't for you two, and I refuse to jerk either of you around a second longer. I'm sorry. So, so sorry."

Her eyes were damp now, and bright as if tears could be just around the corner. Jack let go of the remnants of his anger and fought the urge to go to her and offer his arms. So her body had the need for two men at once. That wasn't her fault. "Stop apologizing, Kristi."

"What he said, doll. Stop babbling and give us some space." Spencer looked at Jack. "We need to talk."

Kristi nodded. "Okay. I'll just . . . go for a walk."

Jack glanced at the short hem of her robe that covered only an inch or two of thigh, and the moment she squatted, all was revealed. "Wearing that?"

"Good point. I'll be on the couch, if you want me."

Spencer watched her go, her creamy white, pear-shaped ass peeking out from beneath her robe with each step. He should regret ever coming to her house. Ever taking Cai up on the offer that ultimately got him stranded in the woods with Kristi. Ever deciding a relationship with Kristi might not be so bad—it wasn't like they had to rush out and get hitched tomorrow. He didn't regret any of it. Not for one damned minute. All he could do was smile at her parting words. They were the same ones she'd used this morning. He'd wanted her then so bad it hurt. He wanted her now just as bad, if not more so.

First, there was Jack to deal with. "I like you, but I like her a helluva lot more. There's no way I'm walking away and letting you have her."

"The feeling's mutual."

"Then it looks like there's only one option. She's gonna be upset about it, but she hasn't exactly left us a choice."

Jack hesitated a few seconds, then nodded. "I can live with it if you can."

"She's worth letting go."

"Yeah, she is."

"You can come back in."

Kristi released three long breaths and then stood from the couch. She would never be ready to face the guys. Never be ready to let them and the warmth they brought to her go. But there wasn't any other alternative.

Hugging her arms around herself, she went into the bedroom but couldn't work up the nerve to move past the doorway or meet their eyes. "I'm sorry."

"Yeah, we got that," Spencer said dryly.

"There's only one thing to do here," Jack said. "We're ready to let go—"

"Please don't say the words." This was an extremely adult situation. Yet she never felt more like acting like a kid by covering her ears and wishing all the bad words away. "It's easier that way."

Jack's feet moved toward her, looking like they were already headed out the door. Her stomach cramped. "You'd rather we just did it?"

"Yes." Just leave. At least she would still have Climax. Or maybe the dog would take off after Spencer and offer him a consolation dry hump.

Jack's feet moved again, coming toward her. Which made sense, since she was in the doorway. Only, they didn't move past her and out the door but stopped inches from touching hers. Spencer's big bare feet appeared next to Jack's. Between the three of them, they formed a perfect triangle. What the hell?

"What are you doing?" Kristi looked up and gasped at the carnal hunger burning in both of their eyes. They looked like they planned to ravish her.

Jack took the last step toward her and cupped her face. His mouth came crashing down over hers, his tongue pushing between her lips. Spencer approached from the side. He reached for the sash of her robe, skimming her belly with his warm, rough hands as he made quick work of the loose knot. Parting the sides of the robe, he pushed it down her arms, letting it fall to the floor and reveal her nude body.

Kristi was naked in front of them less than a half hour ago. Had been naked with them individually on more than one occasion. Still, she couldn't stop her furious blushing as they both stepped back to look at her with an intensity she felt all the way to her core.

Her nipples stabbed to life. Her pussy grew instantly wet. Juices slid along her inner thighs, perfuming the air with the musk of her arousal.

Jack sent his gaze over her, his eyes dark green with lust. "Beautiful."

Spencer joined in, lingering on her pussy and exposing his tongue between his lips as if he couldn't wait to get it there. "Inside and out."

Her blood heated, burning as it shot through her body to pool in her sex. Her clit tingled with wicked want. The need to be possessed by two men. Not one. Two. Oh boy.

Jack returned to her, caressing her back with one big teasing hand while he nibbled damp kisses along her neck, speaking in between sucks and bites. "You can't decide between us, and neither of us is willing to give you up. Seems we don't have much choice but to let go of our inhibitions and share you."

"Share me?" The words squeaked out of Kristi's mouth.

She'd guessed their intentions, but hearing the words made them somehow more real. It made her remember she wasn't into threesomes. Not even with two stunningly gorgeous beefcakes who already held a place in her heart. Not to mention were already in her bedroom. One almost naked. The other fully aroused, judging by the press of Jack's cock against her side.

"Mmm-hmm," Spencer mumbled as he bent to close his lips over a nipple, drawing it sharply into the damp heat of his mouth.

Kristi arched forward, her hips pumping toward him without her approval, her nipple already throbbing for more. She forced herself to concentrate. To take deep breaths. To remember this went beyond her comfort level.

She definitely did not feel comfortable. Rather wicked, wanton, willing. Wet as all get out with the need to feel these two men seducing her together, driving her wild with need. Fucking her so deep and hard that it brought tears to her eyes.

Jack continued his descent until his lips were on her other nipple, his tongue licking the crest. Spencer twisted the one in his mouth, using the stinging nip of his teeth on it as he palmed the underside of her breast, massaging its heavy weight. Jack's hand slid along her spine, lower to cradle a butt cheek in his palm, knead the aching flesh and give it a tormenting squeeze. His fingers worked inward until they rimmed her crack and then slipped inside, fingering her puckered hole.

"Oh my . . ." Her head lolled to the side. She cried out with the deliciously sinful entry.

His mouth pulled free of her nipple with a sucking pop. He circled to squat behind her, use both of his hands on her sensitized bottom. "Have you seen this ass, Spence?" Jack's voice was tight with lust. "It's quivering for a good long licking."

His tongue pressed against her crack without hesitation,

sinking narrowly inside her hole and then pushing hard to its limit. He laved her taut passage with firm, commanding strokes, igniting a burning inferno of need that started in her belly and spread almost painfully to her cunt.

Moaning, Kristi closed her eyes against the awesome sensation.

Oh God. Could this really be happening? Could she possibly have her Jack and eat Spencer, too?

Spencer's mouth continued its sensual assault, twisting, teasing, tugging at her erect nipple. Massaging her aching tit with one hand while the other smoothed over her belly and down to pet her mound. She hadn't shaved today, and the Chia Pet look was starting to take effect. He didn't seem to mind but cupped her sex and pushed his thumb between her dripping folds. Jack added a second finger to her ass, thrusting them together, in and out, in and out. Spencer moved his thumb, finding her clit, pressing hard against the bundle of nerves. Her hips shot backward, her stomach clenching with a fit of erotic pleasure. Her knees threatened to give out. She grabbed hold of Spencer's shoulders, dug her fingernails into his muscled flesh and clung.

"We worked out a schedule." Jack's thready voice tickled her ear, causing her to writhe in their hands and find more pleasure still. "Three nights a week for each of us and Sunday we'll make it a threesome."

Kristi almost came from the words alone. "A threesome? Every Sunday?" Oh. My. God. Her parents were never going to talk to her again.

"That's what you need to come, right?" Spencer's voice was scratchy, his eyes midnight blue with his need. "Both of us fucking you. Sunday'll be your given. The rest of the week we'll have a helluva lot of fun trying."

With a feral grin that sprouted his dimple and made him look too wicked for words, he went down on his knees and spread her thighs, leaving her pussy lips open wide. Her clit edged from beneath its hood. He blew on the distended pearl, brushed it with his mustache, then rocked back on his heels. "Look at this delicious cunt, Jack, and tell me you don't want to lick it."

Keeping his fingers in her ass, Jack brought his head around to eye her sopping pussy. His mouth was inches from her sex, his tongue able to touch her clit with the tip if he only just extended it. Some part of her said she shouldn't want this so badly, one man spreading her, watching while another man ate her out. But she did want it, and Kristi couldn't stop herself from begging. "Please, Jack."

"Anything for this pretty pussy." He pressed his tongue against her sex, licking deep into her folds. He circled her clit with hard strokes, then slurped it between his lips, nearly bringing her to her knees.

She would have thought Spencer would feel the need to outdo Jack, but he didn't look in a challenging mood. Passion flared in his eyes as he watched the other man tongue her. Dark, intense, turning his eyes to near black with lust. Jack licked her pussy with another long stroke and then laved the juices rolling along her inner thighs. He moved his head back to smile up at her, his lips glistening with her cream.

Kristi laughed hysterically. It wasn't funny, not really. There was just so much sensation, emotion crashing through her. Her entire body was on fire. Her mind long since turned to mush. Her legs just as spongy.

"Time for bed, doll." Spencer nudged Jack aside. His biceps bunched as he lifted her up his hard body and wrapped her wobbly legs around his waist. Jack's fingers pulled free of her ass. She whimpered over the loss of contact.

Spencer carried her to the bed, sitting her down long enough to remove his boxers and leave his erection saluting her. His cock piercing winked at her with ruby-red promise. He held her gaze as he rolled a condom on, making it seem just another part of the seduction, then lay back on the bed, pulling her down with him. He gripped her butt cheeks with rough hands, parting them to reveal her juicy asshole.

Kristi's clit pulsed with the chafe of Spencer's pubic hair. Her pussy ached as her lips settled around the side of his cock. She could lift up and take him in easily. But something was missing. Someone. "What about Ja—"

"It's Sunday." Jack whispered the words hotly in her ear as his hands seemed to come out of nowhere to cup her breasts. The hard line of his cock cradled against her crack, his big body naked now aside from a latex wrapper.

Spencer kissed her openmouthed, holding her ass cheeks apart as Jack inched the fat head of his cock inside. Fingers of glorious ache gripped her stomach, fanned sizzling heat to her limbs and had her blood boiling.

She never believed they would share her. Thought both men too dominant to allow it. Maybe it came from the time they spent together on stage at Shenanigans, but they worked so incredibly together it was as if the joining was fated.

Spencer released her buttocks to turn his hands on her body. Rough to the touch but easy in their execution, his hands stroked, touched, and petted every inch of her burning flesh that Jack didn't already occupy.

He kissed her again, wet, long, and hard, pulling back to flash a licentious grin. "I'll eat your sweet pussy in a little while. Now I need to fuck you."

"Yes!" The moan erupted from Kristi's throat. Her fingers gripped Spencer's forearms. Jack's hands went wild on her breasts, pinching her nipples, twisting them into aching, throbbing, fiercely long points. "I need both of you. Fuck me now. Please."

Spencer opened her sex with his fingers. He rested his cock at the mouth of her pussy, spreading her juices over the condom before shoving inside. Jack pushed farther into her ass, thrusting his hips and knocking his heavy balls against the rear of her pussy. She cried out with the wicked thrill, the desperate need barreling through her body and soul.

The Double Diamond was no match for these two. They were longer, stronger, thicker, better. So good together. Everything she could have asked for and more.

They worked in unison, pumping into her, each sensual slide setting off new tremors of need in her pussy. Sweat coated her skin. Her heart beat a wild tattoo. Lust curled thick in her belly, licked hotly at her cunt. The tremors grew, shaking her to the core, spiraling her to a fast and furious completion.

This time, there was no teeter-tottering at the brink of ecstasy. No continuous thrumming and contracting that never went any farther. Kristi exploded with a scream, trapped between the men, thrashing up and down, back and forth, until they, too, found release, pounding into her from both sides, and leaving her floating in a hazy cloud of afterglow that told her this time the warmth wouldn't die. These guys were hers, and she wasn't letting them go at any cost.

Jack moved onto his side, pulling her against him, holding her back against his front as Spencer spooned her from the other side. Parts of their bodies touched, but neither man moved away. Spencer grinned that supersonic sexy grin that already was building fresh wetness, while Jack nuzzled her neck.

Kristi drank it all in, until her stomach growled. She'd been so determined to throw herself into business and forget about having her trip with Spencer cut short that she hadn't thought to eat lunch. "I'm starving."

"Then you'd better eat." Jack's hot breath whispered along her neck, sending delicious shivers down her spine. "I'm just getting started."

"Don't think you're having her all to yourself. That mouth is all mine," Spencer warned as Kristi slid from between them, her body already feeling the sweet ache of being loved by her twin toasters. Um, her two beefcakes.

She looked back at them, tall, dark, masculine beauties. Unlike the last time they occupied her bed, they weren't having a stare down. They were looking at each other, sharing hushed words that had both men grinning wickedly.

They were planning her next seduction, she realized. Trembling head to toe, she considered saying to hell with the food and diving back between them.

She forced herself toward the door. She needed sustenance if she was ever to keep up with the two of them. Two. Not one. Oh boy.

"Be right back." If she didn't pass out from the amazement of it all en route to the kitchen.

Kristi was almost to the kitchen when someone knocked on the door. The knob turned before she could move or make an attempt to cover herself. Her heart leapt into her throat at the sight of her mother standing in the entryway, eyeing her as if she'd just walked in on Kristi doing something immoral, like having her own personal orgy.

Kristi hurried to the couch, grabbed the throw blanket from its back, and wrapped it around her. "It's not what it looks like."

"Kristi?" Jack called from the bedroom.

"Don't leave us hanging, doll," Spencer put in. "Our Kristi burger just isn't the same without the meat."

Shut up! She wanted to scream the words, but what good would they do at this point? Her mother's eyebrows had shot so far up they were barely visible beneath her silvering blond bangs. She covered her mouth, undoubtedly hiding her mortification.

"It's your own fault for barging in," Kristi said defensively.

Her mom pulled her hand away to reveal a smile. Amusement shone in her eyes. Hysteria had to be setting in. If she drove her mother to the mental ward, she would never forgive herself.

"Sorry, but I was desperate," her mom said, sounding anything but hysterical.

"For what?"

"Do you have the blue bunny partner swing in stock?"

Oh. My. God. Kristi thought nothing else could shock her after today, but she'd been wrong. "You know?!"

"Aunt Karen made the discovery. A friend of hers is on the board at Wild Honey and couldn't stop talking about this great new line of products designed by Kristi Hill. She gave your aunt some samples."

"Aunt Karen's using my products?" With Uncle Larry. Ew. Not a pretty picture.

Her mom laughed. "We're older, honey, not dead. Now, about your inventory . . ."

Remembering her aroused body and the two men who had gotten it that way, Kristi nodded toward the bedroom. "You aren't even going to ask about them?"

"Some of the best years of my and your father's marriage were when we belonged to a swingers' group. Life's too short not to be happy in every way possible." She nodded toward the bedroom. "If they make you happy, I'm thrilled for you."

"But they're strippers!" And her parents were ultra-conservative tighty-whitey wearers. Kristi had folded their laundry on numerous occasions when she'd still lived at home. Unless they had a secret stash. For those days they had the urge to return to their swinging ways. Disbelief had her snorting a laugh.

"Strippers." Her mom waggled her eyebrows. "That's my girl."

Kristi gasped. "Mom!"

"Your father won't be happy if I keep him waiting. The swing?"

The swing. For her parents to use. To get each other off. In a way that was anything but traditional. She rushed to her office and grabbed a partner swing from the walk-in closet. She thrust it into her mom's hands. "Here. Free of charge. Just . . . don't tell Daddy about the guys. Or what I do for a living. He's so proud of my old job."

Her mom beamed at the swing, looking ready to lick her lips in anticipation. "I wouldn't dream of it. You'll be introducing your men yourself when you bring them to dinner next Sunday. You can tell your dad about your career move then, too. He won't be talking about it at the high school the way he did your old job, but he's going to be proud of you, honey. " Her mom started for the door with a little bounce in her step Kristi had never noticed before. She wondered now if it had always been there. She turned back when she reached the door. "I'll do my best not to check out their packages, but you really shouldn't have mentioned that stripper part. Curiosity might have killed the cat, but you can bet it had a good time burning up those nine lives first."

"Dancers! I meant to say they're dancers. And Jack is going to be quitting soon. And Spencer said he's going to quit eventually." And she still could not believe her parents were into kinky sex.

Her mom waved her hand in dismissal. "Whatever, honey. I'm sure they're nice guys. Have fun now. Don't do anything I wouldn't do."

Kristi stood staring at the door after her mom closed it. Her mind spun with the day's events. She'd had things sorted out so well. Her parents were purists and she was a borderline bad girl who liked to create sex toys but not use them beyond vanilla purposes. Only, her parents weren't purists and her love for toys and sex in general went way beyond vanilla.

"Kristi?" Jack called from the bedroom. "You okay out there?"

"Yeah. I'm coming."

Two husky male laughs followed her response, ensuring that while she wasn't coming yet, she would be, many, many times before the night was through. And she wouldn't feel embarrassed over indulging in the attention of two men for an instant. Not now that she knew the taste for a little more than the ordinary was in her blood.

DESPERATELY SEEKING SIMON

1

Most lawyers gave Jonah Meadowbrook fantasies of wrapping his hands around their necks and squeezing the money-grubbing, coldhearted life out of them. There was only one he wanted to fuck to death.

First, he'd have to separate Fiona De Luca from her fuck du jour. Or maybe tonight it was her vibrator buried between her legs. The granddaddy of all dildos, the first time she'd taken the thing out of its box and stroked it, he'd thought it a hoax gift, the kind of thing given at sex-toy parties to that one lucky attendant. Then she'd jammed that big black bad boy into her pussy. He'd been torn between coming in his sweatpants and rushing across the apartment common area to offer hands-on assistance.

Fuck du jour or vibrator?

Shouldn't make a damned bit of difference. But like the high ADHD kid he'd been twenty years ago, he had no impulse control. Not with Fiona. Not when all it took was a look out his bedroom window through his carefully angled telescope lens to see her stripped of her pretentious defense attorney gear to reveal one of the most appetizing birthday suits he'd ever seen.

He wasn't a pervert. This was research.

Fiona was the inspiration for Sorrina, the black-leather-wearing, whip-wielding, sexy-as-sin and twice-as-evil Italian villainess from *Hell Bent,* the latest in his erotic suspense comic series.

For research's sake, Jonah stood from his computer desk where a blank document, which should contain the text for the next issue of *Hell Bent,* filled his laptop screen. One orgasm from Fiona always got the creative juices flowing. Right out the end of his dick.

He grabbed the notepad and pen he kept on hand in the event a panel scene too spectacular to forget popped into his head. He didn't need to write down the carnal acts he witnessed in Fiona's bedroom to recall them. Every pump, thrust, and imagined moan—even with her windows open he couldn't hear her—stuck with him long afterward. Having the notepad helped to remind him that he wasn't a stalker in the making and that if he got off as a side effect of watching, it was merely a factor of taking advantage of chance and circumstance.

His apartment took up the top floor of the south wing of the East Lansing apartment complex. His bedroom window was the only one in the complex with a view across the quad and into Fiona's place. That was a view he'd discovered by accident, while stargazing one of many sleepless nights. The angle he had to put the telescope at to see into her bedroom ensured she wasn't aware anyone was witness to her naughty behavior.

She sure acted like she had an audience, though, Jonah thought twenty seconds later as he peered into the telescope and past her open bedroom curtains. No man tonight. Just the mammoth vibrator that had the power to harden his cock on sight and did so with throbbing urgency.

She held the black vibrator against the bed, angling it up into her pussy, riding it with deep, hard thrusts that had her ass pumping in the air and an openmouthed smile of ecstasy curving her lips that only Sorrina could pull off.

But this wasn't Sorrina, a one-dimensional serial killer created at his hands. This was Fiona, a three-dimensional serial killer that had him tossing aside the notepad and pen to stick his hand down his sweatpants, drag out his erection, and stroke.

She faced him, seemed to look right at him. Her smile turned from a full, ecstatic one to a thin, violent one that said she enjoyed making him suffer the same way she made the families and friends of countless victims suffer when she got yet another abusive or murdering scumbag out of a jail sentence and back on the streets to hurt, maim, or kill again. A serial killer by trade, if not with her own two hands.

She was for damned sure killing him now with her hedonistic acts.

Fiona slipped a finger between her thighs, running it the length of the vibrator before pressing it against her clit. She swirled her finger around the swollen bead, then pinched the highly sensitive flap of skin and nerves. Her eyes widened. Her ass shook to some pounding, driving beat. Cream dribbled down her inner thighs, lining the vibrator with each push.

Jonah's cock shoved forward, thrusting in time to the same pounding, driving, soundless beat. Precum emerged at the angry purple tip of his shaft, no tiny pearl but a full-steam-ahead burst of fluid.

The hand at her clit moved, talonlike fingernails digging into the tangle of lavender sheets beneath her. Her smile thinned further, her eyes slitting into a predator's glare. Perspiration shone on her forehead, slid as a thin drop between the jostling valley of her breasts. Black hair swept along her cheeks, the ends pressing against her lips, then sinking between them as those dangerous lips parted to mouth, "Fuck me."

He lost it on the spot. A hot rush of cum jettisoned from his dick to pound the curtains and the windowpane.

Jonah swore hotly. The man in him hated that he could find pleasure with the visual aid of the last woman on earth he should want. The Goth author in him loved the way only she could get to him, like some sick, twisted fantasy in the flesh. Naturally bronzed, glistening flesh attached to a long, graceful neck he'd never wanted to strangle more. Or kiss so damned bad.

A plot so disturbing and erotic that his fans would demand more of the same immediately filled his head. His fingertips tingled with the need to get it down fast. With a last look through the telescope to find Fiona lying in a postorgasm heap stroking the big black bad boy of a vibrator like it was her best friend, Jonah rushed back to the office and let the creative juices flow.

Fiona curled her fingers around the padded yellow envelope.

She had the case from hell to defend. An asshole of a man serving as the prosecutor and making no secret of his desire to serve her on the side. Her Benz had been T-boned by a college student running late for class, leaving the car she'd bought after winning her first solo case four years ago marred beyond repair and her temples throbbing. And now she had to deal with this.

What a delightful ending to an otherwise shitty day.

Her headache evaporated as lust curled thick in her belly, moistening her pussy with an excitement too long in the coming to curtail. Not that she had any longing to try.

Three long years of searching. Hundreds of men spent fucking, none of whom were able to give back the orgasm she gave to them. And, finally, Simon had arrived.

Simon King. The human version of King Simon—the best damned vibrator known to womankind. The big black beauty with its high-powered G-spot stimulator had been a gift from Kristi, a sex-toy designer and one of two women Fiona had connected with via the Internet. The three had a shared purpose, to find a man capable of locating their G-spot and bringing them to orgasm as no man before them had been able to accomplish. *Had* being the operative word. The other women had found their men, their G-spots, and were coming on a regular basis. Fiona wasn't a quitter and had little respect for those who were. But on this particular matter, she'd been ready to give up and accept that the only way she'd ever climax was around King Simon's massive, albeit plastic, shaft.

There would be no giving up. Not now. Not ever, if she had her way.

Elation humming through her and bringing her nipples stabbing to life against her silk blouse, Fiona tossed her briefcase onto the couch. She hugged the large yellow padded envelope addressed to Simon King and delivered to her apartment by mistake. Going by the label, Simon lived on the top floor of the apartment building across the courtyard. He'd been less than a hundred yards away all this time.

She sighed. All those meaningless men. All the missed opportunities.

She wasn't going to dwell on wasted time and missed orgasms. She was going to march over to Simon's apartment, hand him the package, and say the words she'd been dreaming of using on a man who could deliver her to ecstasy for years.

First, she would slip into something that made her look a little less like a woman set on kicking ass. And what better choice of attire than a raincoat over nothing at all?

It was fast. It was naughty. It was cliché as hell. Perfect.

Fiona stripped quickly, her heart throbbing with anticipation as clothes fell to the living room floor she normally kept spotless. She grabbed the beige, calf-length raincoat from the hook by the door, and slipped into it. The cool brush of nylon over her aroused nipples spiked delectable tremors from the aching points to her slick sex. Darting to the closet, she grabbed her black spiked heels reserved for special occasions and slipped them on. If tonight wasn't special, nothing was.

A quick application of the sunfire-red lipstick she wouldn't be caught dead wearing in court, a dab of lavender perfume at her pulse points, and a few bobby pins to secure her bangs and the sides of her hair away from her face and she was grabbing the envelope and hurrying out the door.

Doubts settled in halfway across the courtyard and slowed her pace. What if Simon wasn't single? What if he was her grandfather's age? What if he was bald? Or short? At five nine, she couldn't do a short man. Leaving the heels off would have been the wise option.

Too late now. She wasn't going back. She'd been searching for the human version of Simon too long. He could be an old, bald troll without any teeth and she was still going to screw him until they were both shouting their release.

Fiona's stomach twisted with apprehension as the elevator cruised to the fourth floor. She stepped out, impressed to find that only two doorways occupied the hallway. One led to the stairwell, the other to the man of her dreams.

She dealt with touchy situations on a daily basis. Had her life threatened at least twice a year by the family and friends of a victim whose supposed killer she helped walk free. Her knees had never knocked together with panic until now.

With a trembling hand, she pushed the doorbell and waited.

Ten seconds passed. Twenty. Thirty. He wasn't home. Good. No, not good. She didn't get intimidated, time to remember that. Just in case Simon was hard of hearing, on top of old, bald, and short, she pressed the doorbell again. Another ten seconds. Twenty. Thirty.

Screw this. She had better things to do than lean on his doorbell.

She started toward the elevator, disappointment churning her insides. A husky masculine voice stopped her dead. "Did you need something?"

A shiver snaked through her with the sexy timbre. She slowly turned—if the body matched the voice . . . It didn't.

Simon leaned out of his doorway, revealing himself from the neck up. He wasn't her grandfather's age or bald, but closer to her own thirty-one. But he was short, in an average way that matched his looks. Damn, she was such a narrow-minded bitch. If he was any guy but Simon, she wouldn't even look his way twice. But this was Simon, and she was going to move past her pettiness. Kicking off the heels couldn't hurt.

Ah, much better. He had a good inch on her now. Not tall by any means, but at least he wouldn't be eyes to breasts with her when standing.

Frowning, he emerged from the doorway to reveal baggy gray sweatpants and a white T-shirt that had seen better days. "Did you need something?" he repeated.

What Fiona needed was to remember her mission and stop judging the man by his appearance. She was catching him off guard. If he'd expected her, he would have dressed differently, shaved the scruff off his face, and done something with his unruly brown hair, like comb it for what looked like might be the first time in a week.

Taking comfort in the thought, she moved back to his door, grabbed the sides of her raincoat, and parted them. Simon's breath dragged in on a hiss. His gaze raked over her naked body, his pupils dilating in an instant. The front of his sweatpants tented.

Fiona purred her relief. The rest of him might be average, but that tent suggested he was packing King Simon's twin brother. Her entire body quivered as she gave voice to her fantasies with two little words. "Fuck me."

2

Jonah closed his eyes. Opened them again and blinked. Either he was having the most lifelike wet dream of his life, or Fiona was standing naked in his doorway asking him to screw her. "Excuse me?"

"Fuck me," she repeated, her voice breathy, her nipples so hard that if he bent down, they were liable to gouge out his eyes. Might be a good thing. If he couldn't see, he wouldn't know she was built like the proverbial brick shithouse.

He'd thought he'd done a good job with Sorrina's proportions, but it appeared he would be adjusting the curviness of her hips and narrowing out her waist a bit. His gaze slid lower, and a megadose of lust punched him in the gut. Neatly trimmed black pubic hair curled in a triangle over her mound, glistening with wetness he only had to inhale to deduce were the juices of arousal dripping from her sex.

Jonah forced his attention to her eyes. He'd thought they were green through the telescope. They were closer to hazel. Another change needed. Shit, before he was through, he'd be lucky if his fans recognized Sorrina. At least he'd gotten her breasts right. Generous C cups topped with long brown nipples.

Accepting this wasn't a wet dream, that she really was standing nude in his hallway, he looked away. Fantasizing about her from afar was bad enough. If he laid a hand on her, he would never forgive himself. Lisa would never forgive him.

Thoughts of his late fiancée knotted his gut. Anger that he could want to sleep with Fiona so badly, knowing she was the enemy, pushed through him.

"You obviously have me confused with someone else." He snapped the words out and turned to go back inside.

"No confusion. I want you, Simon."

He swiveled back. "How do you know my name?"

Smiling in a dangerously carnal way that made him think her daddy might just be Gotti, or at least a relative of the dead Mafia boss, she held out a padded yellow envelope he'd managed to miss during the bodily perusal—something about her lush tits and damp pussy giving him tunnel vision. "This came to my apartment by mistake."

Jonah grabbed the envelope and glanced at the label, saw it was from his editor. He turned the package over, surprised to find it sealed. "You didn't open it?"

Her smile disappeared. She thrust her hands to her hips, pushing her breasts out in the process. "Mail is a very private thing."

What a prude. He smiled at how contradictory the thought was from the woman he regularly watched masturbate. He caught himself then, and glared. "So are your tits and pussy, but you don't seem to have a problem flashing them at a stranger." He moved into his apartment and started to close the door.

Fiona stuck her foot in the way, eyeing him through the three-inch space that remained. "Is that a no to the fuck?"

He shouldn't have looked down. Up until that point, he

hadn't realized she was barefoot. Hadn't noticed that each of her toenails was painted a different color. Odd-as-hell quirk that would never fit Sorrina's character. Or the cutthroat lawyer image he had of Fiona. It made her seem human, like she didn't belong in a mold. It made him want to jerk her inside and suck on each one of her sexy toes. Hell.

The sound of the elevator pinging as it reached the top floor made the decision for him. Jonah jerked her inside and slammed the door closed. The doorbell rang a handful of seconds later, followed by his mother asking if he was home. He'd asked her to stop by with her carpet cleaner. Last week's wad shot had managed to hit the floor, as well as the curtains and window-pane. He wanted the stain gone. Every time he looked at it, he thought of Fiona riding that big black vibrator and got hard.

"Honey? It's Mom."

The door jiggled and he swore. He'd given his mother a key so that she could check in on the place when he'd been on a signing tour last year, and she obviously still had it. Urging Fiona toward his bedroom, he pushed her inside. A siren's smile curved her mouth as she glanced at his bed. She raised a black eyebrow suggestively.

Jonah groaned. He'd forgotten about the blatantly hard state of his cock. At her hot look, it reminded him with a pulsing throb. "Not a word," he hissed. "I'll be right back."

He darted into the bathroom and stripped. After wetting the annoyingly thick and curly hair he'd never been able to comb into submission, he shrugged into his robe, then opened the bathroom door and made his way back out to the main room. His mom sat on the couch, jotting a note on a pad of paper on the coffee table. "Hey, Ma."

She stopped writing to look up at him. Her dark blond hair had long since gone gray, but her eyes were still the same warm shade of ash as his own, and few wrinkles appeared when she smiled. "There you are. I left the cleaner by the door." She tsked. "I wish you could remember what the stain's from. I couldn't fit all the cleaning solutions into the car with the size of the unit, so I grabbed the ones I thought might work the best."

Cum stain, Ma, from blowing it while watching my neighbor fuck herself. By the way, she's probably naked in my bed right now. Jonah smirked. He could imagine her first stunned and then elated expression to that admission. "Just got out of the shower."

"Did I see a girl come in?" She glanced toward the hallway that led to the master bedroom, two other bedrooms, and two full baths. More rooms than he'd ever need, but then he'd bought the place with Lisa and the kids they would have in mind.

His amusement died with the reminder of his late fiancée. She'd been killed by a drunk driver almost four years ago. It was time to move on. His mother had been telling him so for months, illustrated now by her hopeful look.

Jonah shrugged. "If you did, she must be hiding somewhere in the apartment. Like I said, I was in the shower when you got here. Alone."

She let out an elongated sigh meant to make him feel guilty enough to start dating again. "It was probably wishful thinking, but I thought I heard a female voice coming from the bedroom."

He dismissed the words with a wave of his hand. "Thanks for dropping the cleaner by. I'll walk you to the door."

She eyed him down hard. "Are you trying to get rid of me, Jonah?"

"No. Okay, yeah. The next issue of *Hell Bent* is overdue." That much wasn't a lie. After whipping out two-thirds of the text following last week's telescope session, he'd gone to bed. He hadn't been able to form a damned sentence since. It was

Fiona's fault. She was on a cold snap. Hadn't had a guy at her place in a couple weeks, and, unless she did it in the early morning hours, she hadn't even paid her mac daddy of a vibrator a visit in days.

Maybe she'd broken it, and now she was horny but without time to go window-shopping for her fuck du jour. It would explain why she was here. Waiting in his bedroom. If her actions so far were a sign, she was probably on his bed, with her thighs spread and her fingers jammed in her pussy. His shaft twitched and he just managed to stop his moan.

He tuned back in to his mother to hear her saying, "What a shame."

She'd never made a secret of not loving his work—it was too extreme for her taste. At the same time, she was proud of his success, so he took her words as the teasing she meant. "Use that tone of voice around my fans and you're liable to get horse whipped."

"I believe that bunch would have the whips to do it." She laughed.

Jonah joined her in sound but not feeling. All he could think of was the woman in his room with a whip in her hand. Sorrina owned one, used it to kill more than a few of her victims. She used it for sensual acts just as often, turning it on her lovers until they were mindless with their need. He'd spent many a night waiting for Fiona to pull out one of her own.

His cock throbbed savagely with the imagined thwack of a whip across his ass. Despite what he wrote, he'd never been into hard-core sex. Fiona might be able to convince him to give it a try. Not that he'd ever let her get that close. After tonight and one speedy screw to get his creative juices flowing again, he wouldn't even be watching her through his telescope.

His body taut with anticipation, he walked his mother to the door. She opened it, then turned back to kiss his cheek. She pulled back, eyes shining with something akin to amusement. "If that girl who's not in your bedroom decides to stay the night, you might want to remind her that her shoes are in the hall."

Fiona had considered displaying herself in a number of poses: naked on Simon's bed, draped over his dresser with the raincoat concealing strategic parts, cuddled up beneath his sheets just in case he was into that sort of thing. She'd settled on leaving the raincoat on and standing right where he'd left her.

If this guy was her Simon—with a name like Simon King, how could he not be?—she wouldn't need to convince him to sleep with her. He would want to be the one calling the shots, to do the dominating. And she would let him, at least until they were both naked; a woman could only pretend to be submissive for so long.

The bedroom door opened a couple minutes later, and there stood Simon. And he wasn't average anymore.

Fiona's mouth watered at the sight of his bare, leanly muscled torso. Dark brown hair curled along his chest, tapering into a treasure trail that arrowed to more dark brown hair and some mighty impressive family jewels. Atop those jewels and sprouting from the nest of hair was the most luscious cock she'd ever laid eyes on. The head dark purple and pearling with precum, she didn't need to ask to know he was ready to accept her offer. She also didn't bother to curb her elated smile. "Like to play fair, I see."

"Too bad I can't say the same about everyone."

The coolness of his voice had her taking a step back. "I can still leave."

"I wasn't talking about your choice of seduction."

Then what was he talking about?

She didn't get the question out before his hands were on her, gripping her forearms hard, moving her backward until her legs hit the bed. They fell onto the mattress together with him on top. He didn't waste time with kisses or strokes but stripped the raincoat from her body and grabbed a condom from the top drawer of the nightstand. Rolling it on, he settled between her thighs, nudging the plump head of his cock into her opening and then pushing deep without any thought to foreplay.

Fiona cried out with the entry, not from pain but dizzying pleasure. She'd already been so wet for him, had been building up the wetness for years. She noticed the way he'd scented her out in the hallway, the lingering glance at her damp crotch. He'd known she was ready for immediate impact.

Simon scooped her thighs up, gripping her legs and bending them back so that her feet circled his head. Sucking a big toe between his lips, he pulled his hips back and thrust hard inside of her. Her pussy clenched with the commanding way he entered her, gushed with moisture when he rimmed her toe with his tongue. He lapped at the pad, applying pressure in just the right spot to have her blood simmering. His hips rolled back again, giving another hard thrust. This time he didn't stop at one, but set a fast, urgent tempo that matched the suddenly mad sucking of his mouth.

She curled her fingers into the sheets, gaining leverage so that she could give as good as she got. Panting with the heat blistering through her and the crazy beat of her heart, she arched up, meeting him halfway, glorying in the feel of his balls slapping against her ass and the constant suckling of her big toe.

Dear God. She'd always balked at the idea of having her toes sucked, thought it sounded comparable to having a dog stick its cold, wet nose up her ass. Simon made the act feel so heady she couldn't stop from squealing.

He'd called her a stranger out in the hall. He didn't fuck like they were strangers but a man who knew her more intimately than she knew herself. In a way only her Simon would. She tested him: "Don't be afraid to use a little force. I can take it."

His eyes met hers. They were the color of smoke. And the man knew exactly how to make her go up in flames. He opened his mouth, her toe slipping out. "I know what you like, Fiona. I know everything about you."

Her creepiness alarm should have gone off with the words, the fact that he knew her name. But Simon chose that moment to give her the added force she craved. Pulling from her sex, he moved off the side of the bed, hauling her with him. He turned her to face the bed, not bothering to give her the time to brace herself before he rammed into her dripping sex from behind, shoving himself deep while his hands roughly gripped her breasts and pinched her nipples.

Her pussy pulsated with each fierce tug at her nipples, clenching tight and releasing with each demanding plunge of his dick. With King Simon, climax always came fast and hard. With Simon King, it was no different.

Tension spiked through her body and had her fingernails clawing into the bedsheets. Delicious pressure balled in her belly, working its way fast to her throbbing core. Her heart gripped tight in her chest. Breathing became a thing of fiction. At the cost of dying from lack of air, she managed to scream out her triumph as her cunt exploded with cream. "I'm coming, Simon! I'm really coming!"

He didn't announce his orgasm, but he came seconds after her. The rush of his climax filled the condom and further warmed her insides through the latex. He stood against her a few seconds, retaining his hold on her breasts while he slowed his breathing with long, steadying inhales. Then with a grunt, he pulled out of her and turned her around so that she faced him.

His expression neutral, Simon grabbed her raincoat from the

floor and held it out. "Thanks for bringing the package by and for the fuck. I have to work now."

Maybe Fiona should feel put out by his quick dismissal, but at the moment she couldn't do anything more than grin. "Anytime. King Simon."

3

Fiona: O. O. O. O. O.

Liz: Have an orgasm by any chance, Fi?

Fiona: Not an orgasm. *The* orgasm.

Kristi: King Simon's outdone himself again?

Fiona: No, but his human twin has.

Liz: No way! You found Simon?

Kristi: Oh, Fiona, honey, that is so awesome.

Fiona: He lives next door. Well, not right next door. But in my apartment complex.

Kristi: So, is he a beefcake?

Liz: Or a stripper? Some of us go for the stripper types, but only if they come in packages of two.

Kristi: Hey, I'm the bad-humor girl here. And be nice to the guys. Sunday's coming, you know.

Liz: Trust me, I know. You tell us all about the weekly ménage session every Sunday shortly after it happens. I end up horny and having to make a trip to Dusty's bar to get some action.

Fiona: Order. Order in the court! I started the chat; that gives me the floor.

Kristi: Sorry, Fi. Didn't mean to interrupt. So, what's this guy like? Does he have a name?

Fiona: It really is Simon. Simon King. Ironic, eh? And he's . . . Well, honestly he's not that tall or good-looking. Not that he's bad-looking. He's pretty average from the neck up.

Liz: But hung like an elephant from the waist down?

Fiona: With a Capital H.

Kristi: Ooh . . . no teeny weenies, gotta love that. Tell me you're seeing him again.

Fiona: I don't know. I was convinced I would when I left his apartment, but now something he said is bothering me. He called me by my name without my telling it to him and said he knows all about me.

Liz: Duh. They ran that exposé on you in the "People" section of the Lansing State Journal a few months ago, remember?

Fiona: Actually, I hadn't. Phew. For a minute there I thought he was a stalker. Worried me a little.

Kristi: Well, don't let it. Learn from my and Liz's mistakes and go with the flow and enjoy yourself. And when you're at it, don't forget to party like it's 19 . . . 69.

Fiona: *groan* You and your 69 jokes. Just to be nice, I'll listen this time. But it's going to be a huge hardship sucking that lovely cock. And I do mean huge.

Saturday at Seven. Il Giardino, Suite 803. Blow Job.

Jonah fisted the note in his hand, struggling to ignore the sweet scent of lavender that clung to it. The message had been tucked in an envelope and taped to his door. It wasn't signed, but the sender was obvious. He'd had a number of fans—both women and men who believed he practiced every one of the sordid acts he wrote about—offer him sex through the years, but never at his home, since he kept the address and his real name private. And never in a way that left their scent behind and had him thinking about the last time they'd been together in cock-hardening detail.

If Fiona thought she could convince him to go another round by offering a blow job, she was mistaken.

He'd finished the next issue of *Hell Bent* thanks to her unexpected offer and their ensuing fuck. He felt Sorrina read more alive and wickeder than ever. Hands-on research wasn't worth the cost of selling his soul. Fiona might have incredibly sensitive toes charmingly decked out in every color of the rainbow and a full-bodied cry of surrender that haunted his sleep, but she was still the enemy.

All the proof he needed of her ability to screw with his life was the call he'd gotten from his mother this morning. She'd reiterated that she knew he'd been stowing a girl in his bedroom last night and hoped he would bring her to Sunday dinner. He'd denied said girl's existence, but it didn't matter. His mom would already be planning the wedding.

Jonah snorted. *Girl* hardly described Fiona. She was 100 percent woman. Passionate as hell and verbal to boot. He'd thwarted the moans and dirty talk that attempted to spill out of his mouth. Something told him if he'd expressed his pleasure aloud, she would have been that much louder herself. It had been consuming enough just feeling her pussy sucking him inside after months of daydreaming about it. Of feeling her heavy tits filling his hands. Her lips . . .

Damn. He hadn't gotten a kiss.

The way Sorrina kissed was as important to bringing her to

life as the knowledge that her hair felt like black silk gliding through a man's fingertips.

Fine. For the sake of pleasing his fans, he would make the meeting at the hotel. And, meanwhile, be damned glad it wasn't the real Sorrina who left the note.

The real Sorrina would use the blow-job front as a way to lure him to death's door. Fiona wouldn't kill him. She would just dredge up more memories of his late fiancée, whose death had never been avenged thanks to the serial killers who disguised themselves behind power suits and luxury cars and called themselves lawyers.

Fiona pulled into Il Giardino's unloading zone and swore. She was a half hour late for Simon's seduction. If he'd showed to begin with, the odds that he was still here were slim.

With a thank-you to the valet, Fiona tossed the man the keys to her rental sedan. She waved away the baggage handler and, hefting her overnight bag, hurried inside the hotel.

Her heart pounded as she grabbed a key card from the front desk and rode the elevator to the eighth floor. She stepped out of the car and hustled to suite 803. LA SALA DI LAVANDA—the Lavender Lounge—was engraved on a gold nameplate next to the key-card apparatus. Each room in the Italian hotel was themed with a different European flower; this suite was her favorite and far too pricey to waste. But no other man seemed worthy of the extravagance. If Simon wasn't here, there would be only one alternative. Drive back to her apartment, pick up his battery-operated fraternal twin, and bring the black beauty back here for a long, hard night of loving.

Fiona sighed. Every other time she'd imagined the vibrator slamming into her, she'd felt damp and empty in a way only it could reconcile. She felt damp and empty this time, too, but not for King Simon. After the day she had, only one dick would do and it was attached to Simon King.

God, she hoped Liz was right and he wasn't a stalker but knew about her through the newspaper feature. And that he didn't run for cover when she stepped into the suite wearing a stiff black pantsuit that gave no hint of curves and, when combined with the tight hair twist and chunky black shoes, shouted "back off or die." She'd wanted to send that message to Barrett Stanley, the prosecuting attorney who'd not only managed to get his slimy hands on evidence that suggested her client's testimony was fabricated and that the woman was guilty of murder, but also had cornered Fiona after court yesterday and attempted to place those slimy hands on her ass.

Frustration sizzled through her, tensing her shoulders. She wasn't going to think about Stanley and how, just when it seemed she was making headway for the defense, he would magically have another new witness ready to come forward and put a client she was convinced was innocent behind bars. She was going to think about Simon King and the way he could make her come like no other.

Drawing a calming breath, Fiona slid the key card through the lock apparatus and pushed the suite door in. Her gaze fell on Simon instantly. At least, she assumed it was Simon. A man with thick, curly brown hair sat at the dining area table with his back to her. She stepped into the suite, closed the door, and set her overnight bag down. The man at the table stood and rounded. She sucked in a breath. How she'd ever thought Simon average was a mystery.

Her belly gave a delighted rumble as her gaze slid the length of him. No baggy sweatpants and wrinkled T-shirt today, but tan chinos and a pressed white dress shirt with its sleeves rolled up to just above his elbows, giving him the appeal of a man hard at work. Crisp brown hair spilled from the partially unbuttoned neckline of his shirt. Her pussy throbbed as she remembered where that hair led. To a magical cock that could deliver her orgasm in short order; thinking about sucking it had gotten her through the day.

Needing to wrap her arms around him and forget the last ten hours, she smiled and started for him. "Thank God. You're still here."

"Not for long."

The edge to his voice had Fiona stopping in her tracks to meet his eyes. Cool gray stared back at her, killing her smile. "I wanted to be here."

He moved past her to grab a small black suitcase and continued to the door. He reached for the knob. "Then you would have been."

Typically, Fiona prided herself on her composure. Right about now she wasn't feeling composed but desperate. She'd searched too damned long and hard to find Simon to lose him over something as inane as tardiness. She dragged in a breath and let out a scream.

Simon's hand slipped from the knob, and he looked back at her like she'd lost her mind. "Feel better?"

"A little. But not as good as I'd feel if you put that bag down. I wanted to be here, Simon. Instead I was stuck in judge's chambers, arguing with a prick of a prosecuting attorney who's convinced that I want his hands on my ass."

The coolness of his eyes slowly warmed until a sympathetic smile curved his lips. He set the suitcase down and walked back to her, dragging out the dining room chair he'd previously occupied. "Sit." She did as he asked, and he pulled out another chair. Slipping her chunky shoes off, he sat in the chair and rested her feet between his thighs. "Close your eyes and relax."

Another time, when she wasn't worried he would leave with the slightest negative remark, she would let him know she wasn't into being told what to do. The moment she closed her eyes and his hands began to knead her aching arches, Fiona was ecstatic to have kept her mouth shut. She was not, however, relaxed.

Between his killer toe-sucking ability and now this, the man was going to give her a serious foot fetish.

Each press of his thumbs into her arches had shards of heat dancing up her legs to come to rest between her thighs as a restless ache. He massaged from the balls of her feet to the pads of her toes. He peeled her socks off then. Her pussy fluttered, and she shrieked with the feel of his warm fingers circling her big toes, pulling the length of them like it was his lips and tongue issuing a silent assault.

"Not a good relaxing move?"

Simon sounded amused, and she could easily imagine his smile, which was odd considering she'd never actually seen him smile. Maybe it was a sign of fate, that he truly was her Simon. Fiona opened her eyes to find her vision almost accurate. His mouth was curved in a teasing smile that showed a glimpse of even teeth, but it was far sexier than she ever would have guessed. Damn good thing she'd cast her pettiness aside and given him a try.

Returning to digging the pads of his thumbs into her arches, he sent his gaze the length of her. He gave a wolf whistle. "Very sexy outfit."

She laughed, enjoying the humor after a long, tiring day almost as much as she would enjoy the sex they were about to have. "I wore it for Stanley's sake."

"The prick of a prosecuting attorney with grab-ass issues?"

"That would be the one." She looked up at him from under her lashes, concentrated on keeping her voice low, throaty. Making his cock harden with words if not her appearance. "I had other plans for you."

His eyes lit with interest. "Share."

Fiona closed her eyes again, falling into the hypnotic press of his thumbs. "I was going to meet you at the door wearing a red, crotchless, peekaboo teddy and before you could get a word out push you up against the wall and give you the best blow job of your life. Then, just when you thought I was done, I'd turn my hands on myself, fingering my nipples and petting my pussy until you were hard again, and then I'd take you with my body, ride you fast and hard, slick and deep, until we were both shaking with the urgent need to come."

The rhythm of Simon's hands changed, concentrating on an area of her feet he clearly hadn't touched yet. An area that was directly connected to her sex, judging by the sudden furious lick of heat and resulting wetness.

"You have this teddy along?" She nodded, and he let go of her feet. "Put it on."

The gruff command pushed through her, enlivening a need to be possessed she never realized existed. Opening her eyes, Fiona stood and went to her overnight bag; she pulled out the scrap of cotton and lace that fit into her fist when balled up yet had cost her almost as much as her first car and started for the bathroom.

"Going somewhere?" he asked when she passed by.

She frowned. "To the bathroom to put it on."

"No, you aren't. You're changing right there, where I can see every inch of you."

4

Fiona gave Jonah a look that said he was nuts to suggest she change into her racy teddy while standing in front of him. "Won't that kill the effect?"

He angled his chair to get the best view possible. Despite the hesitant question, her face was flushed. He could easily envision her nipples beneath her funeral garb, puckered and long, ready for his mouth.

Mouths were the reason they were here. Learning how she kissed so he could write Sorrina true to life. He should get that kiss and get the hell out of here. Fiona's scream had stopped him from leaving earlier—she'd sounded so human, so in need of a shoulder after an exhausting day. It was a combination of that and her multicolored toenails stopping him now.

Christ, he was such a liar. It wasn't just her humanizing scream and her zany toenails that kept him from walking out the door. And it sure as hell wasn't research. It was the ache of his groin and the desperate way his dick jumped at the thought of seeing her naked again. It was the mad need to fuck her senseless.

Jonah reclined back in his chair and grabbed the glass of brandy he'd poured earlier but hadn't taken the time to drink. He brought it to his lips, enjoying the warm slide of liquor down his throat. If he had a brain, he would down the entire bottle and pass out before he could make another move. He lifted the glass from his lips and confirmed he was, in fact, brainless. "Only one way to find out. Undress, Fiona. Show me those luscious tits."

She blinked at him, but then did his bidding, peeling the dowdy black jacket off, followed by a puritan-white blouse. One flick of the clasp of her plain white cotton bra and she no longer looked like a hard-ass lawyer but a fully aroused woman his hands itched to touch.

He lingered his gaze over her nipples, flicking his tongue out as if he could reach the hard brown points from where he sat. On a breathy cry, she arched back, her eyes falling to half-masts. "Simon," she mouthed. "Please."

His shaft pulsed with her pleading. She wasn't nearly stimulated enough for him to give in, but he wanted to do so damned bad. "Not yet. First, you finish undressing."

Catching her lip between her teeth, she gave a small nod of her head. She unbuttoned her pants and started them down her legs, not using the brazenly slow technique meant to drive a guy crazy with lust he'd seen her use on men through his telescope; rather, she used a quick, jerking move that made it seem she was too eager to go slow. Panties that matched her spartan bra came off with the same haste, and she stood before him, naked as she'd been two nights ago.

Then he hadn't taken the time to peruse. Now he drank in every inch of her, from the tips of her vividly colored toes to the dimples in her knees to the cream that rolled from her sex. . . .

Jonah kept going, his body hardening a little more with each passing second. He reached her hair, still up in lawyer fashion, and shook his head. "Let it down. I want something to run my hands through when I'm fucking you."

"Yes." Fiona's hand trembled as she pulled the clip from her hair. It fell in silky black layers almost to her chin. He wanted to take those layers between his fingers and tug her to him, savor the kiss that had brought them to this moment.

To raise both of their needs a little higher, he continued to look at her, edging his gaze back down her body, pausing at the small scar near her belly button. It was the only flaw on her golden skin and somehow managed to make her that much more appealing.

She was beautiful in a way he could never bring to life with Sorrina, and if she wasn't a lawyer, he could well fall in love with her. If. And even then he could never feel for her what he had for Lisa.

The regret that had always come when he thought of his late fiancée while wanting Fiona failed to surface. But that didn't change anything. Lisa was still with him, always would be. Reminding him why he and Fiona could never work out.

Without his needing to ask, she picked up the teddy and pulled it on. This time she moved with grace, easing the lace up her body slowly, skimming it along her thighs until her pussy plumped out through the hole in the crotch. She slid the straps along her shoulders, and her nipples stabbed through the holes cut out over her breasts.

Her eyes met his then, filled with a soul-deep trust as she moved her hand down her body and between her legs. She stroked her slit where her lips puffed out, whimpering with each pet. The urge to slide to his knees and bury his tongue in her body clamored through Jonah. He was ready to push off the chair when a knock sounded on the suite door.

"Room service."

Regret filled Fiona's eyes. "I ordered it when I got the room, before I knew how late I'd be. Or how badly I'd be aching to fuck you."

His cock throbbed with the admission. He stood and went to the door anyway. "Have you eaten dinner?"

"I only had time for breakfast today."

"You're going to need more than breakfast to get through this night. Have a seat."

When she was situated on a chair, he opened the door. A kid in his late teens waited with a cartful of steaming food. Jonah had planned to take the cart from him at the door. His own teenage years came to him then—what he would have done to get an eyeful of a woman as stacked as Fiona—and he waved his hand to usher the kid inside.

The teen didn't look around the suite but lifted one of several lids to reveal the rich aromas of parmesan and garlic. He started his spiel, and Jonah waved a hand to stop him.

At the kid's questioning look, he smiled and glanced at Fiona. "She's too hungry to care about the details."

The teen followed his gaze, his eyes widening. He gulped loudly. "Uh, yeah, man. I'd say so." He seemed frozen in place, so Jonah slapped a tip in his hand and guided him to the door. "Thanks."

"Nah, man. Thank you."

Fiona laughed huskily the moment the door was closed. "Why do I have the feeling I'm going to be his masturbation material tonight?"

"Be the best sex of his life." He should know. Masturbating to Fiona's naked body from afar had been the best sex of his life until he'd gotten to sleep with her for real. As much as he'd loved Lisa, she hadn't been big into the physical. It was one of the only things they'd differed on.

"Maybe he's a virgin."

He pushed aside thoughts of Lisa to laugh. "He's at least seventeen."

"And you lost your virginity long before that."

He narrowed his eyes, surprised at the words. "You didn't?"

Fiona shook her head. "I was twenty, and I'd been dating the guy for almost two years."

"One good fuck and you never looked back." Or what the hell had happened to turn her into a woman who lured a different guy into her bed at least three nights a week?

She shrugged. "Something like that."

Her eyes said differently. Was her string of lovers a new thing, started shortly before he'd discovered the sensual treat of her open curtains? And if so, what had brought it about?

As much as he was curious for an answer, Jonah didn't ask the question. If she chose to share on her own, that was fine. Otherwise he was here for the sex and research.

Pulling the cart to the side of the table, he sat down and lifted the lids off the dishes. Fiona's desperate-for-release look was gone, and while he was anxious to have her again, the kid's interruption had calmed his own need enough to eat first. "I'd guess you're the expert when it comes to Italian food. Tell me what's best."

Minutes ago Fiona had been sure she'd never make it another second without Simon's hands on her body, his tongue buried in her mouth. The arrival of the food had faded her lust a little. Just enough that she could enjoy introducing Simon to the taste-bud-tantalizing delights of her heritage. After describing each dish in detail, she loaded their plates with a little of everything while he opened the wine she'd ordered to go with the meal and poured them each a glass.

She took several bites of food, moaning over the way each separate ingredient exploded on her tongue. Washing the food down with a drink of wine, she watched Simon attack his food with gusto, emitting moans of his own. Had hers sounded as provocative? Every sound out of his mouth sent a new shiver of need coursing through her, until her blood was back to its earlier boil and her pussy so damp it was liable to leave a permanent stain on the seat.

Thinking he needed a bit of his own medicine, Fiona had a few more bites of the main entrees and then turned to dessert. She pulled the goblet of tiramisu toward her. "You know everything about me, from what you said the other night. Tell me about you."

The words had the desired effect; they lifted his attention from his food to her face. She skimmed her finger along the top of the tiramisu, coating the digit with chocolate as light as air and kissed with the rich flavor of mocha underlain with sweet liquor. She pulled her finger into her mouth, suckling it long after the heavenly dessert was gone.

Some of the heat had died from Simon's eyes as he ate; it returned now, igniting them to that mesmerizing shade of smoke. "I lead a very boring existence."

She laughed. "Somehow I can't see that. What about your parents? Do you have them, or were you hatched on a rock?"

"I have them."

"And?"

"And they're alive and well. How's the tiramisu?"

"Succulent." She sank her finger into the dish again, savoring it just as slowly as the last time, moaning her bliss aloud. "Closes up at the mention of family," she said as she went back for more of the delectable dessert. "Interesting."

"You a shrink now, too?"

His expression was teasing, but something in his tone didn't sound amused. "It's part of my job to read people, know whether they're lying or not."

"I'm not too shabby at it myself." His mouth curved in a naughty smile. "Right now you're wishing I'd stop eating food and start eating your pussy."

Fiona's cunt gave a throb. She shifted on the chair, rubbing her tingling thighs together. "Wow. You are good at that."

Simon pushed his plate back and stood, extending his hand. She took it, assuming he would lead her to the bedroom. Instead he guided her to the door. "It's almost seven. I'm going to be here any second. You'd better be ready." He opened the door and slipped out into the hallway.

Realizing the game he played, she laughed anxiously. It was ridiculous to feel so excited at the prospect of him opening the door to find her half-dressed and wet with need when he'd not only watched her put the teddy on but she'd worn it all through dinner. Fiona shook with excitement all the same.

She jumped with his rap on the door. Remembering she was supposed to be the one in control, she took a quick calming breath, then asked, "Who is it?"

"Simon. I hope I'm not late. I ran into traffic on the way over."

She opened the door a couple inches, peering out at him. "Just checking to make sure it's you." Amusement lit his eyes, and she almost laughed again. Holding on to the humor, she opened the door the rest of the way and grabbed for him. Fisting his shirt in her hand, she yanked him inside the suite, closing the door with her foot. His breath rushed out on a gasp as she placed her hands on his chest and pushed him up against the wall.

They both knew what was about to happen, but he seemed as excited by her actions as she was. His pupils dilated; his eyelids drooped. "What are you doing?" he asked innocently.

"Fucking you. Stand still and let me."

With a hiss of his zipper, she had her hand in his pants. His cock leapt into her fingers, huge and hard, and her mouth watered in a way that put her response to the heavenly tiramisu to shame. Going to her knees, she withdrew his erection from his pants and ran her tongue over the weeping tip, greedily licking at the precum.

He groaned and she looked up at him. "Do you like to be sucked, Simon?"

"No."

Fiona lost character with the word. "No?"

Humor shone in his eyes. "It disgusts me when a woman puts my dick in her mouth."

Oh. The answer had been part of the game. For a second there she thought he was the only man alive who didn't love getting head. She fell back into character, narrowing her eyes at him in a punishing glare. "Then you shouldn't have been so bad, because that's exactly where yours is going. Put up a fight and I'll draw it out all night."

Simon fell out of character to give her an elated look. "Really?"

She laughed and shook her head. "Only if you want me to implode on the carpet."

Clearly he didn't, as he gripped the base of his shaft and guided it back to her lips. She took him in gladly, thrilling in his rich masculine scent as she licked the length of his dick. He pushed his pants and briefs down his hips, and his balls sprang free, brushing against her chin. She used her hands on them, petting their heavy weight while she sucked his cock with skills honed by wasting her time screwing too many men who didn't mean a thing to her, in the hopes that one of them would be her Simon. But, of course, one never was. Not until two nights ago.

Fiona couldn't change the past, so she saw that Simon derived the most pleasure possible in the present. Cradling his ball sac in her hand, she licked over the rough pink flesh and then pulled a nut into her mouth, suckling it with a force meant to bring him to the brink fast.

He groaned. His hands clamped down on her shoulders, his fingers pressing painfully into her skin. "Unless you want your hair full of cum, I suggest you quit."

"I'd like it in my mouth, thanks."

Taking his cock back into her mouth, she milked him with the force of her lips, clamping down a little more with each thrust, until the slick slide of his shaft turned to an uneven pump and grind. Using one hand at the base of his cock, she moved the other between her legs, driving two fingers into her pussy through the hole in the crotch of the teddy. She murmured a cry of pleasure with the entry. Simon's fingers once more dug into her skin, his cock jumping between her lips. Seconds later, his shout of release shook through her as a delectable quiver that had her fingers driving upward in a hard thrust that summoned her own orgasm. Riding on the wave of climax, she swallowed his cum to the last drop, then licked the tip of his cock clean.

His eyes dark with passion and his breathing shallow, he pulled her to her feet. "You weren't kidding about that blow job being the best ever."

Thankful for his arms since her legs weren't feeling any too stable, Fiona laughed. "And just think, we still have the parts to act out where you watch me finger myself and you tackle me into bed and fuck me until neither of us can remember our names."

5

Fiona curled into Simon's body, not wanting to open her eyes and acknowledge morning had arrived. Last night had been incredible. Anything but average.

She took pride in her ability to stand on her own two feet financially. She'd never cared if she had a man in her life on a permanent basis. Cuddling had never been her thing, and while small talk was nice, she could do it with girlfriends or relatives. Or so she'd always believed all that stuff. After another helping of tiramisu, more of which ended up on their bodies than in their mouths, and two more amazing rounds of sex, both of which ended with her climaxing like she'd been doing it her whole life, she'd eagerly curled into Simon's arms and they'd talked until she'd fallen asleep. If he'd been secretive about his family at first, it had to have been merely because he'd had his mind on sex, because the second time she'd asked, he'd offered the information freely. They'd discussed most everything but his job and that only because it hadn't come up. Whenever he woke, she would ask about it.

Or maybe he was already awake, Fiona thought an instant later when Simon brushed his mouth along the back of her shoulder, stubble tickling her nerves to awareness. The hand that had held her through the night moved from her waist to slip between her legs. Two fingers pushed into her intimate folds and caressed her clit. Pleasure built slowly, sweetly, cascading warmth through Fiona until orgasm washed over her in a blissful wave of release far gentler than anything she'd experienced last night. In some ways it was much more enjoyable.

Returning his hand to her waist, he nuzzled her ear. "Good morning."

Shivering as delightful sensations rippled through her, she grinned. "It most certainly is. If I woke up that way every day, I'd have to quit my job. Somehow I don't think a smiling-like-a-loon defense attorney would go over well."

Simon quit nuzzling to roll her onto her back. In a serious voice, he asked, "Would you really quit your job?"

"Of course not. I love being a lawyer. There's not a lot of laughs in it, but there's nothing quite like the high of winning a case."

For a second she thought she saw anger pass through his eyes, but obviously it was only her imagination as he gave her a suggestive smile and tweaked her nipple. "Nothing at all?"

Laughing, Fiona squirmed under his touch, new heat building in her sex. "Nothing other than that."

He tweaked her other nipple and then lifted his hand away to pull her back up against him and lazily stroke her hip. Disappointment reared its head, but she tried not to be too upset. He'd given her more orgasms in the last fifteen hours than all her other lovers had managed combined. Then there was the fact that it was still early. They had the room for three more hours, and after that their apartments were only a quick walk away from each other.

They had the rest of their lives for pleasure. Except for the fifty to sixty hours she had to dedicate to the law firm each week. What about his job? "What do you do?"

"I thought you knew." Simon sounded more pleased than surprised that she knew nothing about his career. He hesitated before saying, "I write and illustrate comic books."

"You work for kids. How refreshing." She hadn't lied about loving her job or the thrill of winning a case for a client she believed was innocent. Winning cases for those clients she felt were guilty and who she worried about walking free on the streets left her cold. Then there were those cases she had to take on as part of her responsibility with the law firm. She'd much rather bring joy to a child than deal with a reluctant and often belligerent client.

The soothing slide of Simon's hand along her hip stopped. He released her and rolled out of bed, quickly tugging on the clothes he'd worn yesterday. Then he'd looked handsome. Now he looked rumpled, but surprisingly not in a bad way. Rather sexy. She didn't want him going out for coffee looking like that.

Was that jealousy talking? She never would have believed herself the type.

He started for the bedroom door without a word, grabbing his small suitcase before disappearing into the suite's main room.

Fiona's thoughts of jealousy died while her stomach clamped down on an immediate sense of dread. Coffee didn't require a suitcase. She tossed back the covers and jumped out of bed, hurrying into the main room. He was already at the door. "Where are you going?"

Without looking back, he reached for the doorknob. "Home to work." The chill in his voice sent a shiver through her. "The kids are anxious for the next issue of *Small-Minded*."

Was that supposed to be some kind of cut? She would be the first to admit she could be small-minded, but she hadn't been with him. Had she? "Simon?" He turned back, malice clear in his eyes. She resisted taking a step back by reminding herself she didn't get intimidated. Though, with that glare, he would have made a formidable attorney. "Did I say something wrong?"

"Not at all, Fiona. You fulfilled my expectations perfectly."

Liz: You around, Fi?

Fiona stared at the Instant Messenger box. She'd logged on to her computer to conduct research for a case. The ache in her belly that surfaced the moment the chat window popped up told her to ignore Liz. Her need to share what happened with Simon wouldn't allow it. Even if the night had meant nothing more than sex to him, her Simon wouldn't have left the way he had unless something serious was wrong. If she hadn't been naked, she would have chased after him and demanded an answer. Or maybe she wouldn't have, since he only lived across the courtyard and she'd been dressed the majority of the three days since he'd walked out on her and she'd yet to run over there and demand an answer.

Ignoring her bellyache and the sense of foreboding that accompanied it, she started typing.

Fiona: I'm here. What's up?

Liz: Do you know what your guy does?

Fiona: He's not my guy and yes. He makes comics.

Liz: X-rated suspense comics about a female serial killer who gets her kicks by fucking men and then snuffing them out. I thought his name sounded familiar when you mentioned it. The latest issue of *Hell Bent* came in the mail yesterday, and it clicked where I knew him from. You need to check the series out, Fi.

Fiona: You read porn?

Liz: It isn't porn; it's erotic suspense and I'm telling you, you need to check *Hell Bent* out. Pay attention to the villainess.

Fiona: Fine. I'll check it out. I'm sure Wild Honey carries it. I have to get some research for a case wrapped up now, but I promise to pick up a copy first thing in the morning.

Liz: Don't forget. And don't see Simon again until you do.

"How's your girlfriend? I was hoping we'd get to meet her today."

Jonah groaned at his mother's question. He'd managed to forestall sharing Sunday dinner with his parents, but when they'd showed up at his place with dinner in tow tonight, he could hardly tell them no. "I don't have a girlfriend, Ma. I told you that."

His dad gave him a disapproving look. "You best not be sleeping with women off the street. All the diseases floating around these days, you just can't risk it for a few seconds of pleasure."

"Jonah!" his mother shrieked. "You better not be sleeping with some trashy hooker. She finds out how much you make in a year and she'll be winding up pregnant and expecting you to marry her."

And this was exactly why he hadn't wanted to spend time with his parents. He'd always looked forward to their visits, but then Fiona had come along and screwed things up just the way he knew she would. Guilt slammed him in the gut with the thought and had him barking out, "For Christ's sake, I'm not sleeping with a hooker."

His dad looked heavenward. "Thank the Lord."

"She's a lawyer." Jonah clamped his mouth shut around the word. Why had he said that? It had to be the guilt.

The hurt look Fiona had given him just before he walked out on her had haunted him for days. She deserved it for the way she responded to learning what he did for a living. Of course he hadn't told her exactly what he did—he wasn't about to risk her picking up an issue of *Hell Bent* and recognizing herself. But he might as well have told her that he cleaned shit pits for a living, the tone of her voice had been so amused.

With her insane toenails and her throaty laughs, he'd allowed her to get to him. And that had been an asinine thing to do. She was a money-grubbing, blood-sucking lawyer, not someone who gave a damn about the rest of humanity, let alone some guy she'd randomly made her playmate for a few days. It wouldn't be any more than that. He'd already taken too big a chunk out of his self-respect by wanting her so damned bad and giving in with hardly any fight.

"Does she know about what happened with Lisa?" his mom asked, looking like she was torn between being thrilled and being stunned with his admission.

"No, and she won't. It's just about sex and it's over anyway."

She frowned. "This isn't like you."

"I doubt many kids talk to their parents about their sex lives." Jonah purposefully misunderstood her. Fiona had given his mom hope by leaving her shoes outside his door. He refused to fan that hope any higher.

"That's not what I meant," she continued, unfazed. "You like this girl. I can tell."

"She's a woman, and no." He'd been roped in by her quirks, stuck with fantasies about her from all the times he'd witnessed her masturbating and having sex, but he didn't like her.

He shot his dad a "help me" look. His father didn't look any more interested in changing the subject than his mother, but he stayed true to the man code and gave in. "You been keeping up with the Tigers, Jonah? Pudge is on another homer streak."

Perfect. Sports talk. A guaranteed way to drive his mother out of the kitchen and away from talk of Fiona. The enemy, who deserved everything she'd gotten thrown her way, and he wasn't going to feel guilty about it a second longer.

Leather felt like shit riding up the crack of her ass, Fiona decided as she stalked across the apartment common area. More than one person stopped to do a double-take over her getup. She sneered back at them, cracking her whip and laughing maniacally over their reaction.

Oh, but she was saving a few laughs for Simon. The asshole.

The elevator to the fourth floor seemed to crawl today, and she spent the entire trip letting her temper build. She still couldn't believe the size of his balls. When they'd been in her mouth, they hadn't seemed that ungodly huge. Thanks to Liz, she knew they were, though.

The elevator pinged, announcing her arrival on the fourth floor. Fiona stepped off, grinning over the thought that Simon's balls were about to get a whole lot smaller. When she reached his door, she didn't bother with the doorbell or the old-fashioned approach of knocking but turned the knob and let herself in. She didn't see him immediately, so she shouted for him. "If you still want your balls attached when I leave, get your sorry ass out here now!"

She'd never tried the screaming approach in court, but she might have to soon. It worked really well. Simon appeared less than five seconds later wearing his old faithfuls of sweatpants and a ratty T-shirt. Somehow he still managed to look too damned appealing for his own good, even with the exasperated expression.

His look went from annoyed to worried the moment he saw her costume. "I'm sorry."

"You bet you are, you prick. How dare you walk out on me like a complete ass and not even call to apologize."

He blinked, shook his head, and blinked again. "What?"

Fiona almost laughed; having him confused felt so good. Only, it wasn't time for laughter just yet. "Don't 'what' me. I gave you my trust. My first goddamn man-induced orgasm. And what did you do but make me feel like some cheap slut who didn't even deserve a good-bye."

"Your first orgasm? More like your millionth and first."

The unexpected words had her momentarily forgetting about revenge. "What are you talking about?"

"What are *you* talking about?"

The childish urge to say "I asked you first" crept up, but she managed to refrain from speaking it. Keeping the ball in her court was the only way to see this played out right. "I want an apology, and you're going to give it to me, and then we're going to have makeup sex."

"You're nuts."

"For a guy who makes kids' comics, you really suck at being nice."

"Fine. I'm sorry, but I'm not sleeping with you."

"Yes, you are." She cracked the whip at him; a stab of longing piercing her pussy with the angry way it licked the air. "Get naked now!"

"Look, it's obvious you're on a power trip, probably won some case to let some homicidal maniac back on the streets to kill again, but I'm not into the hard core."

She cracked the whip again. The end came inches from hitting Simon's thigh, and he jumped back with a squeak. She gave in to her laughter. What a humbling experience for the prick. "I said get naked. Unless you want to feel this whip on your ass."

For a fleeting instant, Fiona thought he was actually considering the idea. Then he mumbled something about checking her into the mental hospital and started stripping. The moment the last of his clothing was gone, she was on him, knocking him to the ground with her unexpected tackle. She kissed him open-mouthed, sliding her tongue against his and suckling until he responded in kind, all the while hating herself for enjoying it so much. She moved her hands over his body, scraping her nails—make that talons—over every inch of his flesh with enough pressure to tease him into a full arousal but not offer anything in the way of release.

Simon started to thrash beneath her. She sat back to straddle him, eyeing him through a predator's glare. "Lie still and keep your mouth shut, or I swear I'll live up to your expectations for real this time and whip you."

His eyes flashed with fear, but the way his dick bobbed beneath her told her it was the kind of fear that was only a step away from passion. Fiona's lust rose with the idea she was turning him on so completely. She didn't want to enjoy fucking him one last time, but she'd known before coming over she could never take him inside her body without feeling ecstasy. For the sake of revenge, she would suffer through one last man-induced orgasm.

Wanting out of this apartment and Simon's life as soon as possible, she raised his hands above his head and looped her whip around his wrists, securing it with a knot.

He kept his wrists still but tried to argue his way out of it. "You don't want to do this. Think about what will happen to your career when this gets out."

"Like you give a care." She raised her hand, palm side toward his face. "Now shut up. The whip might be in use, but I still have plenty of other weapons."

Shooting to her feet, she stripped off the leather thigh-high boots and the tiny little leather thong that had absolutely no ass coverage. Pulling the condom from between her breasts—the ridiculous Sorrina costume had no room for breathing space let alone pockets—she tore the package open with her teeth and quickly sheathed his erection.

He groaned as she sank onto him in one quick move. "Do you really think this is going to make you feel better?"

Fiona snapped her eyes shut against the flood of pleasure. She'd never been this wet before. How twisted. "Yes. And I told you to shut up."

"You won't hurt me, Fiona. You don't have it in you to be evil."

Grabbing hold of his chest, she tossed her head back with ironic laughter and rode him hard. Emotion consumed her with each downward pump, with each sigh that left her lips against her will, with each moan out of Simon's mouth. Refusing to let those emotions out, she picked up the pace, fucking him with a vengeance that went way beyond his using her as a model for some make-believe serial killer.

If he hadn't treated her so coldly, she wouldn't even have cared about the comic. She'd actually found the two-dimensional likeness of her rather flattering. But he had treated her coldly, hadn't even told her good-bye before he called her small-minded and walked out on her.

The emotions she'd done her best to contain bubbled up, tears slipping out of her eyes before she could stop them. Orgasm followed on the heels of those tears, pushing through her body to an extreme she'd never before known. The stupid part of her brain that had allowed her to care for Simon had the audacity to open her mouth and shout his name in a voice too laden with lust for him to even consider she meant it to be another warning for him to keep silent.

As if he'd been waiting for that very thing, Simon chose that moment to come. Fiona waited for the hot rush of fluid to leave his body and her own heart to stop beating so hard it felt like it might burst. Then she pulled off of him, swiped the tears from her cheeks, and rushed out the door.

6

Jonah had never known the feeling of someone hating him so much they would rather bare their entire lower half to the world than spend another second with him. Fiona probably hadn't even realized she was half-naked when she'd bolted out his door two weeks ago. But he had, and if he hadn't been whip-tied and naked himself, he would have chased after her and told her so. He hadn't liked the thought of countless men viewing what should be for his eyes alone. And that was foolish thinking for a number of reasons.

Not only had he covered the pages of *Hell Bent* with her nude body for months now, but he also didn't have any right to be jealous. He'd had her to himself, had had her heart in his hands, if the tears she'd shed before running away were a sign, and he had thrown it all away. And not because he thought of her as a money-hungry, coldhearted lawyer either. But because he'd been scared to death of caring about someone again.

It had taken his remark to Fiona, that she wouldn't hurt him because she didn't have it in her to be evil and her ensuing disbelieving laughter to make him see the light. From her charmingly mismatched toenails to the way she screamed to let off steam, she was not a serial killer of any kind. She was simply a woman passionate about her job, who at the end of the day had her fair share of complaints about the people she worked with and for, just like everybody else. She was also the woman he liked, probably even loved.

It had been so long since Jonah had experienced the emotion, he was no longer sure where the lines were drawn. He just knew he was sick and tired of watching Fiona sit in her bedroom alone at night and not even find a worthy companion in her big black bad boy of a vibrator.

He wanted his Fiona back, and he would get her, in the only way he knew how.

Liz and Kristi said she had to take him back, that he'd jeopardized his best-selling author status in order to seek her forgiveness. Fiona wasn't so sure.

When she'd been in Wild Honey buying the latest issue of *Hell Bent,* there were two other people purchasing the comic book. They'd heard about a shocking twist that had all the fans going wild and had rushed right out to buy their own copy and find out what the big twist was. Liz had already told her, but Fiona had had to see for herself. And she had, and she still didn't think Simon had jeopardized his best-selling status but maybe hiked it up a few notches.

Who would think to soften a serial killer by having her fall in love with one of her intended targets and not want to fuck him to death? It was such twisted logic, the kind of logic it seemed Simon regularly partook of. And maybe that was why she'd fallen for him so fast.

She spent the better part of her week surrounded by strait-laced lawyers and judges. Yeah, she ran into her fair share of nutcases in the form of clients, but it wasn't the same. She didn't like most of those nutcases. She didn't love any of them. She probably still loved Simon if her reluctance to even turn King Simon on once in the last three weeks was a sign. And she could maybe forgive him since he'd dedicated the latest issue of *Hell Bent* to her, complete with an apology for being such a prick—apparently it was okay to use those kinds of words in comic books that weren't intended for kids. Apparently an author could even get away with telling a woman he loved her in an adult comic book.

Fiona sniffed as she read the words for the hundredth time. Her sterling composure was totally shot to hell because of Simon, and she should hate him for that. But she didn't, and she wasn't going to sit here, hugging the dedication page of a comic book a second longer. She was going to find her man and have some really great makeup sex—this time dressed as herself. The run back from Simon's place might have been fast, but even two steps would have seemed to take forever when she'd been bare-assed and still dripping with arousal.

Jonah wasn't in the mood for company. Hadn't been for weeks. Three, to be exact.

The only reason he went to the door was because whoever the idiot was pounding away like he didn't own a doorbell wouldn't stop. He yanked the door open, primed to shout the unwanted visitor's head off with a snarled "What?" The moment he saw the owner of the offending pound, he changed his mind.

Heart in his throat, he forced out words. "Fiona? What are you doing here?" He noticed her raincoat and his groin tightened. The last time she'd had that thing on she'd been naked beneath. It had been the best and worst day of his life. Could she be naked again?

Her expression was neutral. "I can leave if you want."

"God, no. I don't want that. I want you."

"Then you're in luck." She opened the raincoat, and his

mouth watered at the sight of his favorite fantasy come to life. He inhaled her lavender perfume tinged with the scent of arousal. Then she spoke those beautiful words. "Fuck me."

"Excuse me?" He had to be hearing things.

A siren's smile curved her vivid red lips. "Fuck me. Please."

Jonah shook his head. This was too good to be true. Still, he fell into the conversation, repeating the words he'd spoken a month ago, back when he'd been living in fear of falling in love again. "You obviously have me confused with someone else."

"No confusion. I want you, Simon."

Even if he hadn't been able to smell her stimulation, Fiona's eyes gleamed with the truth of her desire. And dare he hope her love? "How do you know my name?"

"I saw it on the cover of this really awesome comic book. The best part is the heroine. Oh, I get that most people think she's the bad girl, but anyone that sexy and tough has to be a heroine."

He gave in to laughter for a few seconds, then sobered to ask, "Did you really come here just to sleep with me?"

"Maybe." She looked past him, into his home. "Can I come in? Not that everyone within a ten-block radius hasn't seen me naked, but I'd rather not be standing here if your parents decide to drop by."

"Actually, they'd be elated to see you."

She raised a black eyebrow. "Naked?"

"Naked, clothed. It wouldn't matter, so long as you're here for the right reason."

"And that would be?"

Jonah pulled in a breath. Groveling time had arrived, and he would be damned if he didn't get it right. "To accept my apology, realize I'm a terrible person who doesn't deserve anyone as wonderful as you and then let me atone for my imperfections by giving you lots of really great makeup sex."

A smile twitched at her lips, finally blossoming into a grin that warmed him through. "I think I'll come in." She moved past him. "But you aren't getting sex."

He closed the door. "Good. I don't want it."

She whirled back on him, stunned. "You don't?"

Though he already knew his body would pay for it, he gave in to his urge to send his gaze the length of her. His cock responded as expected, giving a painful throb of need. "Well, yeah, of course I do, but not until I have a chance to explain myself."

Fiona sat down on the couch. "I'm listening."

He considered sitting next to her but knew he would never be able to get all the words out if he was that close to the temptation of her naked body. He'd returned a short while ago from a trip to the grocery store and hadn't yet taken the time to change into his writing gear of sweatpants and a T-shirt. Taking advantage of his jeans, he jammed his hands in the back pockets. "I hate lawyers."

"That bodes well for our relationship."

He laughed. "I should have said I hated lawyers. Or I thought I did anyway. My fiancée was killed by a drunk driver four—"

"Oh God, Simon! That's horrible."

"It wasn't easy to take, and it took me a long time to move past it." He added grimly, "The defense attorney was able to get the driver off with little more than a hand slap and a couple months of house arrest."

Fiona nodded. "The attorney probably didn't have a choice but to do everything in their power to see the driver free. Most of the cases I take on are ones I hand select, but I have to handle a certain number of clients that I don't want to represent, too. It's part of being involved in a law firm with lifetime clients." Revulsion took over her features. "The first time I won a murder trial, I went home and threw up. Then I didn't sleep for days. I just kept seeing the faces of the victim's family. They hated me."

Jonah felt like punching himself. He'd called her small-minded, but he was the one who'd been such. Until she'd made him see the light, he'd never even considered that a lawyer might not be happy about winning a case. "Then you can understand why I felt the way I did."

"Yes. Completely." Her face brightened a little. "That you were able to move past your hatred for lawyers is amazing."

"No, it's this wonderful woman named Fiona, who, by the way, my mother is demanding to meet immediately or she'll disown me."

An overjoyed smile curved her lips. "I'd love to meet her, Simon. I'd love to meet both your parents."

"Anything else you love?" Or anyone?

She nodded. "The way my ass looks smaller in print than it does in real life."

Laughing, he grabbed her hands and pulled her to her feet. Unable to go any longer without touching her, he pulled her into his arms. "I might have gotten the proportions wrong."

"Don't you even *think* about changing my ass! If you feel the need to change anything, then give me a boob job. I've always wanted a D cup." Fiona rubbed her breasts against him to emphasize the point.

Jonah felt the press of the soft mounds all the way to his groin. He brushed a kiss over her mouth. "You're perfect the way you are."

"Men in love are so blind."

"What about women in love?"

"We need lots of great sex."

He was only too happy to oblige, sweeping her into his arms and carrying her into the bedroom. He laid her back on his bed and stripped the raincoat away. When he would have moved his hands down to ready her for penetration, Fiona stopped him. "You don't need to bother with foreplay. Just thinking about finally having you back in my body has me wet enough to turn this mattress into a waterbed."

Taking her at her word with a huge grin, Jonah grabbed a condom from the nightstand and rolled it on. He returned to the sensual cradle of her thighs. Driving into her sweet pussy, he kissed her long and deep and hard, showing her with his hands and mouth and body how much he loved just in case she ever decided to doubt his words. Orgasm rocked through them as a unifying force that left both shaken and breathing hard.

When he regained his bearings, he held her to him, rolling them so that he was still embedded within her, but she was on top. Fiona looked at him, her chin digging into his chest, her smile positively feline. It warmed him in places he'd forgotten he'd possessed.

Stroking her back, he kissed her temple. "What are you thinking about?"

"How relieved I am to have finally found my Simon."

"Your Simon? I've become a possession?"

"Yep. But that wasn't what I meant exactly."

"What exactly did you mean?"

She rose up on her elbows, her smile fading just a little. "I have a confession. I didn't randomly pick you to flash and then beg for a fuck. I've been stalking you for almost three years."

"You have?" By God, he'd never seen that one coming.

"Yes. I was desperate to find a Simon."

Jonah frowned, not quite understanding. "Just any Simon?"

"You, Simon. I was desperate to find you. King Simon only helped me to see that."

"You're close with a king named Simon?" Now this was getting really weird.

The naughtiness returned to her smile. "Very close. He's my vibrator."

He laughed. "King Simon wouldn't happen to be black and about twelve inches long and three around, by any chance."

"How do you know that?"

"I have a confession of my own." One he hoped she wouldn't get too pissed about. "That window right there"—he nodded toward the pane, where a telescope was positioned—"gives an excellent view of the apartments across the quad. And if you angle that telescope in just the right direction, it gives a mouth-watering view of what's happening in a certain sexy lawyer's bedroom."

"How long have you been watching me?" He breathed a sigh of relief. Fiona didn't sound upset, just intrigued.

"Long enough to be jealous of several dozen men whose faces I never saw."

Jonah's very real jealousy came through in his voice, and she took his face between her hands and leaned down for a lingering kiss. "Lose the jealousy, because you're the only man who's ever been able to make me come."

He inhaled a sharp breath. "You're serious?"

"That's the rest of my confession. I knew from the second a friend of mine sent me King Simon and he was able to make me climax—something that had never happened before—that only a human Simon would be able to accomplish the same. Just in case I was wrong, I did sleep with some other guys. But none of them mattered because you're the only one for me. My Simon. My love. My sexy, naked stud of a bed warmer."

"I think you might be pushing it just a little, but what the hell, I'm not about to complain." Fiona laughed, and Simon joined in with his own laughter, though his was for an entirely different reason. The happy sounds turned to sighs of bliss as he slid his tongue between the warm, sweetness of her lips. Still, he smiled to himself.

Eventually he would have to tell her that his real name was

Jonah Meadowbrook; Simon King was simply the one he'd chosen to publish under. And he would, after he'd given her another ten or twenty dozen orgasms and she had no doubt that his ability as her lover and the man who loved her were anything but 100 percent authentic.

From Vivi Anna, author of HELL KAT,
comes a trip into INFERNO,
coming this month from Aphrodisia!

1

Not again. Oh, please, God, not again.

That was all Hades could think of when he stepped into the dank, dark chamber of his dreams and smelled the familiar metallic tang of blood.

She was there, hanging by her wrists, shackled to the ceiling of the cold, empty, cemented room. Blood pooled beneath her feet. Hades knew there would be long raised welts across her slender but muscular back. He'd seen them before in his dreams.

With slow, hesitant steps, he neared her swinging body. Praying under his breath that she still had a pulse, he reached toward her and stroked her leg. Her waxy skin was cold to the touch.

Swallowing the bile rising in his throat, Hades swung her around and glanced up into her face. With a heavy sigh, he closed his eyes.

It wasn't her. It wasn't Kat.

He didn't recognize the dead woman. Her anonymous face

would, hopefully, not haunt him in the future. But if he was here again, in this nightmare, Kat was here somewhere, too.

He never came alone.

Cautiously he strode through the lofty chain room to an open metal door. Stepping over the threshold into a dimly lit hall, Hades had the distinct sensation of being led. As if some phantom chain had been attached to his neck, and he was being tugged forward into the unknown.

With each step, the overhead fluorescent lights flickered. When Hades reached a T intersection in the hall, each thin bulb blacked out one by one, and he was once again thrust into darkness.

There were only two ways for him to go. And he suspected that horror lay in wait in either direction.

Turning to his right, Hades reached out blindly for the door. He grasped the metal handle and pushed down. The door unlocked with an audible click and creaked open of its own accord.

At first, the room seemed just as dark as in the hallway. But then Hades could see a glow emanating from the middle of the room. Compelled, he stepped into the room and walked toward the faint yellow light. It grew brighter as he advanced.

Eventually he came to a four-poster bed. A red candle burned brightly in a glass holder on a small table next to the bed.

The bed was empty. But Hades could hear movement near him, a soft swishing sound, like flesh rubbing against fabric. Undeniable aromas of sweat, musk, and arousal floated to his nostrils. The overpowering scent of sex.

Scrutinizing the mattress, he could see the bedcovers ripple and bunch as if one or two people were moving over top of them. Clear indentations of a hand, a knee, and other body parts pressed into the mattress.

A low whimper reverberated from the bed. He recognized

that low, husky sound. He'd heard it moan deliciously into his ears.

Kat.

She was there. Somehow she was on the bed in front of him, although he couldn't see her.

A light breeze blew over his arms as if someone was moving in front of him, moving toward him. Within seconds he felt a hand on his forearm. Her hand. Unable to pull away, he allowed the phantom fingers to stroke him, trailing up and down his skin. He sucked in a raspy breath when that hand brushed his crotch with a knuckle or two. It didn't take much for his cock to respond to her touch.

Iron hard and aching with desire, Hades allowed the apparition to pull him onto the bed. Reaching out, he found her body, all hard planes and slopes but soft and pliant where a woman should be. He molded his hands over her breasts, teasing her rigid nipples with his thumbs.

Again she moaned. This time it was in his ear. He could feel her lips so close to him, so warm and inviting. Turning his head, he captured her mouth with his. She tasted as he remembered, like rain, cool and refreshing. She swept her tongue over his and then nipped at his bottom lip.

Before he could respond, he could feel her pulling away. Blindly he reached out but couldn't find her again. He knew she was still there, could feel her heat and smell her scent. Why couldn't he touch her?

He motioned as though to sit up but was forced back down onto the mattress. A heavy weight settled on his legs, as if someone had straddled him. Hades reached forward and touched warm, inviting flesh. He moved his hands up over the smooth skin of Kat's muscular thighs. When he could reach no farther while lying down, he felt her take his hands in hers and raise them up.

Sighing, he closed his eyes when a pair of soft, full lips

touched his skin. A tongue traced a wet path over his wrist, suckling every now and then. His eyes sprang open when he felt the scrape of pointed fangs on his flesh.

Pain, immediate and sharp, sang up his arm. He scrambled away, pulling back his arm. Hades jumped off the bed and cradled his hand to his chest.

Shocked, his stomach roiling in revulsion, Hades watched as two forms materialized on the bed.

With smiles, blood dripping down their chins, Kat and Baruch reached out to him and spoke in unison. "You can't escape, Hades. You're ours."

Heart hammering in his chest, Hades bolted up in his bed. Cold sweat dripped down his forehead and into his face. The salty liquid stung his eyes. Lifting a shaky hand, he wiped at his eyes.

It had been more than seven months since he'd had a nightmare like this—one his mom would have called a premonition. When he was a child, she had called him a Dream Seer because of the constant images in his head that had come true. Like so many times before, he hoped this was just a dream and nothing else.

Swinging his legs off the bed, he set his feet on the cold wood floor and peered around his small bedroom. It was still dark, and the air felt crisp. He had heard that there might be a frost in the night. Frost. Cold. These things were still so new and surprising to him he welcomed the ice on the ground and the bitter chill in the air.

He'd spent his whole life on the outer rims, where the scorched earth tried to resurrect itself from the devastation caused by nuclear war. Snow, cold, and ice were foreign occurrences, ones he had read about only in books and heard about through rumors of the Promised Land in the north. A land he had finally found.

With practiced ease, he found his fur-trimmed leather slippers with his toes without the aid of light. Sliding his feet into them, he stood, wrapped his deerskin robe around his bulky form, and shuffled to the small window. Cracking open one wooden shutter, he peeked outside. The sky was still dark, but the promise of the sun had started to trim the edges with a dull pink. Dawn was close by.

It being a little earlier than he wanted to be rising, Hades resigned himself to starting his day. He still had wood to cut and a fence to mend before winter settled in for the year. Rubbing a hand over his bald head, he sighed and shuffled into the kitchen to make tea and start his breakfast. Maybe a shot of whiskey would help erase the bloody images of his dreams.

Even in the dark, Hades made his way around his cabin with proficient effortlessness. When he neared the stove, he opened the little iron door, tossed in a few logs, and grabbed the box of matches sitting on the counter. Before he could strike the flint, the hairs on his arm stirred to attention.

Someone was in his cabin.

Dropping the match, Hades reached for his knife lying on the counter near the sink. Even now, his weapons were not far from him. When he spun around, knife poised to strike, a soft light emanated from the kitchen table. The lantern sitting on the wooden surface sparked to life, and the person, sitting in one of the chairs behind it, took form.

A pale luminance played over Kat's sharp, angular face. "You've lost your edge, Hades. Country living and clean air have made you slow."

The sound of her voice instantly tightened things inside him. She had that effect on him. Her laugh alone could spur a raging hard-on. He must be getting lax if he hadn't noticed the moment she had stepped into his cabin.

He took in a ragged breath, inhaling her scent. She still smelled of spice and musk. His cock twitched at the memory of her.

He eyed her, taking in everything. Some things had stayed the same. The way her full lips lifted at the corners in a sexy sneer. The sharp cut of her cheekbones and chin. In addition, the look in her eyes—that devilish, dark look that sent shivers down his back.

Other things *had* changed.

She no longer possessed the tumbling mass of ebony hair. Instead, shocks of dark hair stuck up in random order over her head. Short and spiky, her hair was a carefree mess. Somehow it suited her and only helped to accentuate her piercing facial features. Hades also noticed the absence of her eye patch and the fact that her eye no longer looked opaque and useless but seemed to be changing back to its original emerald green even as it tracked him from across the table.

Obviously the Dark Dweller virus was still hard at work inside her, healing past wounds.

Turning, Hades set the knife back on the counter and reached for the banged-up teapot. "Do you want some tea?"

There was a long pause while Hades lit the stove and set the teapot on the burner.

"Yeah, sure," she finally said.

Taking two cups from the cupboard above, Hades set them on the counter and added some peppermint and sage herbs from his tin canisters. He grew his own herbs in a small boxed garden in the den. Kat, he was sure, would laugh at that—Hades having a garden. But he would not feel ashamed of it. He had earned this little thing. Had bled for this place in utopia where he had found relative peace and sanctuary. A haven he had hoped to, one day, share with her.

"Nice place. Very cozy."

Hades turned back around. Leaning against the counter, he crossed his arms over his chest to cover his hands. He hoped she didn't notice the slight quiver in them. They ached to reach across the table and touch her. To fill his palms with her hard, hot flesh. It had been only in the past three months that he had stopped aching for her in the middle of the night, stopped having sweaty, erotic, wet dreams in which he could find no release.

"Built it myself."

"Huh." She nodded. "Who knew you had skills?"

He chuckled. "You know I do, babe."

His heart skipped a beat when the smile finally lifted the corners of her delicious mouth. The woman didn't smile often, but when she did, it squeezed him in low erotic places like his cock.

He sighed. "Damn, woman, where have you been?"

"All over the fucking place." She spread her hand over the table and leaned back in the chair. "Ended up in Atlantis for a month."

"You're kidding? That's the last place I'd expect you to go back to."

"I guess I needed a place to heal and think. I even did their weird cleansing ceremony." She rubbed her hand through her cropped hair as evidence of her words.

"Hmmm, I was wondering about that." He smiled, lifting his brow. "So is it growing back in other places, too?"

He remembered watching one of the Nerieds' cleansing ceremonies during which the young woman had had all her hair removed. Even over her pubic mound.

"Maybe."

When she cocked her brow with that sexy grin, Hades realized how much he had truly missed her. And how much she had hurt him when she had left. Seeing her now made him realize that he could go on without her, maybe even find some happiness, but he damn well didn't want to.